YEAR vuoo

YEAR 0033

J. M. Evans

DERNIER PUBLISHING

London

Copyright © J. M. Evans
Published by Dernier Publishing
P.O. Box 793,
Orpington,
BR6 1FA,
England

www.dernierpublishing.com

ISBN: 978-1-912457-44-1

All characters appearing in this work are fictitious. Any resemblance
to real persons, living or dead, is purely coincidental.

For my husband, Andrew, who spent many evenings alone
while I wrote this book.

Contents

ONE

Strange Night

Chella shivered as a cold draught seeped down her neck. She pulled her cloak closer round her shoulders, tucked in her hair, and tried to get comfortable on the hard floor.

At least she wasn't alone. Amma was curled up a short distance away, her African hair bound up tightly in her nightcap. Mikiah, Amma's grandson, was asleep in his pramcot. And Chella only had to turn her head slightly to see Jedan, fast asleep and snoring gently.

Jedan! Chella's heart beat faster as she caressed her fiancé's sleeping form with her eyes. Even in sleep, stretched out on the floor, Jedan looked serene. He should be the worried one, having just escaped from prison, but that was Jedan all over – nothing seemed to faze him.

Chella shifted again. Her arm throbbed where the Correctioner had twisted and pinched it so hard, and her legs ached from walking. She was desperately tired, but it was all too strange, dark and cold to truly relax. She stared at the black windows, wondering who had last looked out of them.

This house must have been the height of fashion and luxury when it had been built, Chella decided. This one room was almost as big as her whole apartment! Earlier, when they arrived, she had walked around the empty rooms in the darkness and marvelled at the size of the house, and its fading grandeur. The peeling paper on the walls and the ragged drapes at the windows were a sad shadow of what they had once been, but the quality still shone through.

As she lay there, Chella wondered what it must have been like to live there in the times of the Old Order. She knew about the lifestyle of people who lived in houses like these from history books, of course, but now, being here and seeing it for herself, brought it all to life. Things were so different now.

Chella's heart lurched as she remembered the apartment she had so recently left, filled with so many precious memories, and a lump came to her throat at the thought of everything and everyone she had left behind. She forced her mind back to the familiar evening prayer.

"Shine your light into our darkness, Lord," Chella prayed silently in the empty, deep silence, *"and by your grace protect and deliver us from all evil this night; in the name of your Son, our Saviour Jesus Christ, we pray."*

She had already prayed it once that evening, with Amma and Jedan, but felt reassured as she prayed it again. She needed to be strong. She remembered the people she had left back in the Area had promised to pray for them, and as she thought of them, was reminded of a chorus the church sometimes whispered together:

Although we often stumble,
He will not let us fall,
For underneath His mighty arms
Are there for those who call.
He lifts those who are bowed down,
Gives grace to all in need;
The darkness may seem close right now,
But God is here indeed.

Chella let the words and the tune go over in her mind, trying to forget where she was, but remember God was with her, until she fell asleep.

The moon was lower in the western sky and the first light of dawn was breaking when Chella was woken by the screech of an owl. She sat up quickly. Through the murky glass, she saw the bird's ghostly outline fly away, its wings gliding smoothly in the crisp, clear air.

Chella lay back down. Mice pattered overhead and behind the walls – she was used to mice, they were just a part of life, but when she turned round and something larger appeared, staring at her with big moon eyes, she gasped in shock.

"It's only a cat," said Jedan softly. The cat turned to look at Jedan, then with a swish of its long black tail, jumped noiselessly out through the open window.

Chella nodded. "Gave me a fright!" she whispered. "Must be a descendant of a pet from round here. I didn't know you were awake," she added, glancing at Amma to make sure she wasn't disturbing her or the baby.

"I wasn't, but I am now – it's cold."

"It is," agreed Chella. Amma stirred and opened her eyes, then closed them again. Mikiah snored gently in his pramcot.

In a louder voice, Jedan suggested that they prepare to set off. "The sun is rising. We can get warm by walking."

Amma sat slowly up, yawned and smiled. "Whatever you say, dear," she agreed with a nod. She took off her nightcap and ran her fingers through her tight black curls, flecked with silver. Chella nodded too, and then smiled, in spite of the tiredness and the strangeness. For the first day ever in her life, she wasn't going to hear a loudspeaker.

TWO

The Prayer Meeting

Little did Chella know yesterday as the loudspeaker boomed twice outside her apartment at six o'clock in the morning, that she would be doing the unthinkable; leaving Area IF208. Living here was all Chella had known in her twenty years and never, ever did she think she would leave it. Nobody did, except for the Elite who visited other Areas from time to time to trade goods, and a few Workers whose job it was to cut wood or quarry stone outside.

This Monday, however, was not a usual day for Chella.

The six o'clock loudspeaker call warned people on Shift Two that they needed to rise, but for the church in Chella's apartment block there was extra hurry. A secret prayer meeting had been arranged, due to Jedan's arrest and imprisonment the previous day.

With heavy heart and dark circles under her eyes, Chella had quickly run a brush through her hair, then padded quietly in her felt slippers along the dingy corridor and up the concrete stairs. Someone, somewhere, was toasting bread for breakfast – the smell mingled in the stairwell with the usual odour of damp, stale air.

"Welcome!" Amma mouthed with a smile, as Chella, the last to arrive, entered Amma's apartment with the tiny code tap they all used. Amma's apartment faced east, so the morning light was already lighting up the living room and the kitchen area. Lavitah, who had recently moved into Chella's apartment, was there; she had managed to get away early from Shift One in the Wash Room. It was Lavitah who had heard of Jedan's arrest, through a friend who worked in the Correction Unit.

Old Erimah and Emine sat together on Nidala's old bedsettee, squeezed up with another older couple, Garem and Jott, plus of course Amma was there, and little Mikiah, who was still asleep in his pramcot. Chella couldn't resist going over to peep at the baby; her best friend's first-born. His little body lay outstretched and peaceful in his tiny blue vest, his innocent little mouth, chubby legs, dark skin and curly hair the perfection of a loving Father's design.

Tears came to Chella's eyes. She quickly wiped them away – she and Jedan had talked of having a child, but now Jedan was gone. The tears were not just for herself, but for her friend, Nidala, too, who, if still alive, must sorely miss her son.

So much loss. So much heartache.

"Have faith in God," whispered Lavitah, as the girls took their places. Sometimes it was a bit of a squeeze for them all to meet together in such a small place, but it was always good to be together in fellowship. Today, with Jedan missing, and others who hadn't been able to get away from

6

work or family at such short notice, there was room for Amma and Lavitah on the dining chairs, so Chella sat alone on a cushion on the worn wooden floor.

Chella swallowed and smiled, not daring to reply; she trusted in God, but she also knew that Christians disappeared. Regularly. Forever. Yes, she should pray. But what should she pray? She had to pray that Jedan would return. Since she had heard the terrible news of his arrest she had prayed for his release, again and again, desperately, with every fibre of her being. But how could she have faith that he would return when so many never did? Chella's mum had been arrested fifteen years ago and had not been seen since; she was only one of many believers who had been lost to them over the years. The last to disappear were Nidala and Hamani, Amma's daughter and son-in-law. Amma had gone for a walk with Mikiah three months ago; she had come back to find her apartment empty. A rough sketch of Jesus healing a man born blind lay in pieces on the floor. A sheet of paper with the story neatly copied out on it, was crumpled in the waste bin. Amma had gone to the Correction Facility to ask what had happened, but nobody would tell her anything. The church had prayed, but Nidala and Hamani had never returned.

Old Erimah led the silent, sombre group in an opening prayer and Bible reading in hushed tones, then each brought a scripture in turn.

Chella brought hers first, which she had been reminded of after she had gone to bed the night before with an aching heart. *"Draw near to God and he will draw near to you"*. The words had been a comfort to her. She kept her words short

7

for fear of breaking down and as the others shared, she tried to concentrate on their words of trust and encouragement, instead of thinking about Jedan, missing.

Then it was time to pray. They all knelt quietly on the floor in a circle. "Let us..." began Erimah, but Amma interrupted quietly, "I have another request for prayer, while we are here. Mikiah is nearing the age when he will have to be cared for in the Nursery. I have only two more weeks with him. It will soon be dangerous for me to bring him to meetings, in case he gives us away. Please pray. The thought breaks my heart."

Amma's simple request brought silent nods and sighs to the faithful group. They understood Amma's dilemma. It was the same for all believers. If a child repeated the name of Jesus in public, or mentioned gatherings, the whole family could suffer. And if Amma was arrested, what would happen to Mikiah?

No murmuring was allowed in meetings, in case it was overheard by neighbours, but this time the silence was complete. As Old Erimah bowed his head, the sun rose over the easterly apartment blocks and brought a sudden strange, warm glow on to those assembled.

"Dear Sister, we will intercede for you. May the Lord hear the cry of our hearts and answer according to his mercy. Remember that our loving Father is Almighty God. He loves to answer our requests, and nothing is too difficult for Him."

With that they prayed, quietly, earnestly, one at a time, in their ring of fellowship. They prayed for Jedan's release, then for all their loved ones in places unknown. They prayed for Amma's difficulty with the child, for safe keeping for them all, and, as they always did, that Jesus would come back soon. Then while Old Erimah was pronouncing the blessing, there was a tap at the door.

Everyone stopped and listened as it came again.

"It is the given signal, but we are all here," whispered Amma, a sudden fear in her eyes as she glanced at her sleeping grandchild.

"Places, brothers and sisters!" mouthed Old Erimah. Everyone got up silently from their knees and in a short time all were in hiding, except Erimah and Emine, who sat on the dining chairs as if they were visiting for breakfast.

From under Amma's bedsettee, Chella felt the chill of the hard floor against her cheek. She stared unseeingly at the tassels hanging from the faded quilt and waited with thudding heart for Amma to open the door. Had Jedan been forced to give them away?

THREE

The Miracle

Chella screwed her eyes shut as she heard the door opening. Then came Amma's stifled cry of joy. "Jedan!"

For one long second Chella stayed where she was, then scrambled out, along with everyone else. Jedan ran straight over to Chella and helped her to her feet. After several incredible minutes of nearly silent hugs and tears, when Chella thought her heart would burst from surprise and happiness, Old Erimah called everyone to order.

"It seems that the Lord has performed a miracle," he said quietly, his eyes gleaming with joy. "Jedan has been released, by the grace of God! We await your testimony, dear brother. Places, please, everyone."

Everyone quickly and quietly took their usual seats. "Are you well?" Chella asked Jedan, her heart flooding with joy and amazement. "Did they treat you..."

"I have never been better!" replied Jedan, kneeling on the floor next to Chella, and taking her hand in his. "Sorry if I smell!" he added with a smile. "I missed the morning wash!"

Laughing out loud wasn't possible, but they all grinned at Jedan and at each other. To have a prisoner released to them was unknown, but oh, so wonderful! The grey correction suit hung loose on him, and it did smell bad, but that hardly mattered, Chella decided, as he hugged her again. His face held an aura of joy and victory, which was reflected in the eagerly expectant faces of the little group, transformed in a moment from sadness to joy.

"Oh Jedan, it's so lovely to see you!" whispered Lavitah, to a chorus of almost silent Hallelujahs.

"Did you see Nidala in the Correction Unit?" Amma asked. "Or Hamani?"

"I didn't see anyone I know, but my release was for a purpose, of that I am certain."

"Go on," urged Old Erimah, as Jedan paused.

Jedan stood up as if he could no longer remain seated, and pulled himself to full height. Chella's soul tingled as she heard the confidence in his voice. "I know this is going to sound crazy, but an angel came to me last night, in a vision. I was in my bunk, but I was in heaven, too, at the same time, I can't explain it. There was this light, brighter than anything you can imagine. It was, it was... more terrible and more joyful than anything I have ever experienced."

Everyone exchanged silent looks of puzzlement and wonder.

"No words were spoken," Jedan continued, "but I felt in my spirit the assurance that I would be released today. When it was time for us to go to the prison washhouse this morning, the cell doors opened and they called each prisoner

11

out by name. But they didn't call mine! So after everyone else had left, I walked out the back door."

Despite the quiet rule for assemblies, there was a murmur. Old Erimah frowned. "So you haven't been released, exactly?"

Garem leaned forward. "Were there no Correctioners on guard at the entrance?"

Jedan shook his head. "No. I escaped, I suppose. And I don't think I was followed. I checked behind me several times. I guess they must have forgotten to add my name to the register. But don't you see, it's of the Lord! I went to Chella's apartment first, but as there was no answer I thought I would try here. And here you all are!"

"Praying for your release!" said Lavitah, with a smile.

"It is truly a miracle," breathed Emine, Old Erimah's wife.

"Delivered from prison!" added Amma, raising her hands to heaven. "To God be the glory! He sent an angel, as he did for Peter in prison, and I believe in our own days there have been such miracles."

There was another silent nod of approval, then Jedan indicated for them to gather closer. As they leaned towards him, he whispered, "After the light had gone, in the night, I fell asleep, but in a dream I saw the Old Church, praising God in beautiful song, more glorious than I have words to describe."

"What a wonderful dream," sighed Jott. "A vision of heaven maybe?"

"There's more," said Jedan. "The Old Church does exist, outside!" There was silence. Some of those present

12

looked hopeful, others unsure. "They are living in an ancient village, called Anderley, and I have to go there." More silence as everyone looked at each other in surprise. This was unexpected news indeed, if it were true.

"It's not a name I remember," Jott said eventually, and all the older people shook their heads.

"Wherever it is, I have to find it and go there," stated Jedan firmly. Chella's heart began to beat faster.

"Who told you this news?" asked Old Erimah quietly. "How do you know all this?"

"It was while I was on the treadmill in the Powerhouse yesterday, after my arrest," said Jedan. "Two of the guards were talking near me. I overheard one tell the other that they had found evidence of people living outside the Area, in a place called Anderley."

"So it's true – people are living outside," whispered Lavitah. "We always wondered!"

Old Erimah raised his eyebrows. "But how do we know they are believers in Christ?"

Jedan replied, "These people were heard singing *hymns* in an ancient church building! They were seen going in and coming out. The guards were scoffing, but you see, it must be the Old Church!"

There was a general intake of breath. Old Erimah raised his eyebrows. "They must be people who stayed when we came to the Areas," he said. "Or their descendants. But they are in danger, if they have been discovered meeting to worship God!"

Jedan nodded. "Yes! The Area Council is going to meet in a few days to decide their fate, if what I heard is correct.

But the people were watched in secret — they do not know of this threat."

There was stunned silence from the group, but Jedan's soul and spirit shone from his eyes. "My arrest was for a purpose, so I could hear this news of the Old Church, I'm sure of it. I have to go and find our brothers and sisters, and warn them. I feel it in my spirit. Somehow I think I've always known. I need to leave now, before I'm missed."

Everyone looked at each other as they tried to take in this news. Chella's heart began to beat faster. The Old Church existed — that was wonderful news, but Jedan was going to find it — he was going to *leave*?

"Anderley," repeated Lavitah. "Don't you have a book of maps, Amma?"

"Yes, well remembered, Lavitah!" said Amma, getting up from the dining chair. "All villages and towns had names when we were children, before the Areas. If it exists, it will be in there." She went to a chest under the window and after rummaging for a minute, drew out a large, crumpled book. It bore the legend *Road Atlas*.

"Ancient maps with dwellings and roads!" breathed Jedan as Amma wiped dust off the cover, took the book to the table, turned to the index and slid her finger down the alphabetical list of places.

FOUR

Anderley

Everyone crowded round Amma as she searched through the index of place names in the atlas. "I didn't know such a book still existed!" Garem said, stroking the pages.

"I have nearly thrown it away a few times but something always stopped me," muttered Amma, concentrating on her job. "It must have been the Lord! Anderley, did you say, Jedan? A-n-d-e-r-l-y or -l-e-y?"

"Could be either, I guess," he replied.

There was a low murmur of excited voices as Amma's finger went down the column of strange names beginning with the letter A.

While Old Erimah reminded everyone of the assembly quiet rule, Chella stood on the outskirts of the buzz in a daze. A few minutes ago her beloved was in the Correction Unit – that was terrible. Now he was back, but talking about going away again – leaving, running away, after seeing a vision! And he hadn't been released, he had *escaped*.

She frowned to herself. This couldn't be happening! What about their forthcoming marriage?

Amma's voice cut through her tangled thoughts. "Here it is, it *does* exist," she said, finding the page and pointing to Anderley on the map. "It's a village on a river, look, right out in the country. See this X, added with a pen?" she continued, turning the page. "That's our Area. It's maybe two or three days' walk away, I'm guessing, looking at the scale of the map." Everyone leaned forward as Amma pointed to Anderley, then flipped the page to the X, and back again.

"The X, that's our Area?" asked Jedan in surprise.

Amma nodded. "That's right. My father marked it when we left our old home."

"So we can not doubt what Jedan heard!" nodded Old Erimah, his voice catching with emotion. "Praise the Lord! A remnant of the Old Church, singing hymns in praise to God in freedom, not so very many miles away – that is truly a miracle, a miracle indeed, if it is so. And Jedan's release is also a miracle."

Garem had tears in his eyes. "Unheard of, impossible but for the grace of God! He has sent Jedan deliverance from prison for a purpose, that much is clear. Now my boy, you must obey the word of the Lord!"

"Of course," nodded Jedan, lifting his head.

"How long did you say, until the Council are due to meet to decide what to do?" asked Old Erimah.

"They said next week. As it's Monday today, I should have a week to get there."

There was a general chorus of *"Amen"*, then, *"Sh!"* and while Chella looked on, her heart beating loudly, feeling

16

alone and confused, Jedan stepped towards her and took her hand.

"I have another announcement," he whispered to the gathered congregation. "Chella will come with me. If she wants to," he added quickly, bending down to look into her eyes, with such tender hope that Chella couldn't speak. Her thoughts were spinning so fast she found it impossible to reply. How could they walk for two or three days through unknown territory to a place that was no more than a name on an ancient map? Where would they sleep? How would they know the way? And how *could* they leave? Nobody left!

Chella stared at the expectant faces of her dear church family, evidently all waiting for her answer. Not long ago she had promised Jedan that wherever he went, she would go with him. But now, like this, with no time to plan? And they weren't even married yet!

Everything in her screamed that she must stay and Jedan must stay and everything must go back to how it was before, but as she looked up into Jedan's face, his eyes alight with a new fire, she knew that nothing would ever be the same again. Jedan had escaped from prison, seen a vision and received a call from God, or at least he thought he had.

Jedan's eyes searched hers, changing from expectation to seeking the reason for her hesitation. "Chella, you do want to come?" he murmured, loosening his grip on her fingers. She struggled with her feelings.

"I want to be with you, wherever you go," she affirmed eventually. At least that much was true, she told herself, as Jedan drew her close and kissed her forehead.

People were whispering in excitement and dread, then

17

Amma declared, "I wish to go, too." There was a shocked silence. "I will take the child with me," she added. Another murmuring was stifled.

"But Nidala and Hamani?" objected Jott. "What if they come out of Correction to find you have gone away with their son?"

"We do not know if they are still alive," said Amma, her voice catching, stating the words they all avoided saying, but acknowledged in their hearts. "I need to take the child to safety, while there is still time. There could be no better place to take the child than to the Old Church. If it is the Lord's will, Hamani and Nidala will be able to join us in his time."

"But it won't be safe," objected Lavitah. "How will you manage on such a journey with the child? We have all heard the dogs howling at night. And what about the pramcot? If it rains and the basketwork gets wet, what will you do?" She shook her head at Amma. "Pramcots are made for strolling round the Parkland and the gardens, not for journeying through the forest!"

"It will be a treacherous journey you have to make," agreed Garem, looking again at the distance on the map and shaking his head. "It's different for the young ones, but you have nearly reached your half century."

Amma smiled. "Dear brothers and sisters," she said quietly, looking round at the gathered church, "we have been praying this very hour for wisdom that I should know what to do. I feel this is right for me, and for Mikiah. The Lord will protect us from danger, and I'm not so old I can't walk! Remember the Israelites in the desert, that the soles of their shoes didn't wear out? If Erimah is in agreement?" She looked towards Old Erimah, who nodded slowly. Amma's eyes welled with tears as she turned to Jedan and Chella and hardly managed to ask, "Just as I am, will you take me?"

"Gladly, Amma," Jedan assured her. "Your love and wisdom will help us hold to the right path."

"I'll try not to hold you back."

Jedan smiled. "You won't hold us back!"

Chella hugged Amma, unspeakably glad that she would be going with them. "Oh, Amma," was all she managed to say, but her heart flipped with relief. If Amma wanted to go with Mikiah, leaving couldn't be as crazy as it sounded.

"Will you leave at nightfall?" asked Emine.

Jedan shook his head. "I think we should leave at once, before I am missed. Every minute we delay, we risk my discovery, and the Old Church's destruction."

There was another silence as the church took in this new development. This was serious. Not only was Jedan going to leave them, but Chella was going to leave, too, and Amma and the baby, with no time to think or plan.

"What about your family?" asked Old Erimah quietly. "Will you say goodbye?"

Jedan sighed, and for the first time his shoulders dropped. "I think it best not to."

Old Erimah put his hand on his shoulder. "We will pray."

"I will lend you clothes, brother," Garem said to Jedan, wiping his eyes and heading for the door. "You can not leave in that correction suit, neither must you go back to your apartment, in case a search has begun."

"While Garem is fetching clothing, let's put all these things in the Lord's hands," said Old Erimah, getting back down on his knees. "All this has happened quickly and we need to be careful not to get swept away. We need to spend some time before the throne of grace. Come, saints of God, let's unite in prayer. We need to be certain of His will. We must beware of running ahead, as Saint John warns us in his second letter, and of deception, of which we are warned over and over again in these end times. We must be sure that this is truly the will of God."

FIVE

Sudden Change

At first, Chella hardly heard the quiet prayers; she was just glad of this reprieve. Even now she was hoping that Old Erimah would say that Jedan had made a mistake, that it wasn't a vision, that the Old Church couldn't possibly still exist, that for now at least they must stay, perhaps until they had more information. But as she attuned her ears to the earnest prayers of the people who loved her most, heard Scriptures being quoted and little words of encouragement, it seemed that the confidence of the church began to grow until there was a gentle swelling of praise to God for visiting them in their affliction.

As the minutes passed, Chella couldn't help noticing an increasing note of victory and triumph in the prayers, of thanks to the Lord for preserving the Old Church, and for Jedan's deliverance from prison. The chorus of almost imperceptible voices was swelling up to God in peaceful, true and beautiful praise, but her own heart was still full of doubt and fear. What would they do in the forest

21

at night? What about wild beasts? What if they were caught by Correctioners? What would they do for food and water? But they had to go – how could Jedan stay? An escaped prisoner?

And then, as Chella's thoughts raced, she felt a gentle touch on her shoulder. Emine was praying for her, for assurance and courage, until finally Chella felt herself letting go into the loving presence of her Lord, uniting with the others. Gradually she felt her panic subside, and her heart and soul began to join the others in praise to her faithful Father who loved her, to her closest friend Jesus, who by His Holy Spirit would never leave her or forsake her.

When the praying had ceased, Old Erimah stood up and spoke quietly, so as not to disturb the still, gentle presence of God. "I think we must all agree that this event is of the Lord, and that this whole situation is indeed part of his perfect will and plan. Imagine, brothers and sisters, the Old Church exists outside, as we have for so long hoped! But it is facing danger, and we need to send our brother to warn them."

There was a general nodding. "Amen," whispered Lavitah.

"It seems that Jedan has had direction given him from God," continued Old Erimah, "and we must not grieve the Holy Spirit, however hard it will be for us to see our dear ones go, with an uncertain journey before them. It seems that Chella, Amma and Mikiah must also go. It is an understatement to say that we will miss them all, but we must trust our Sovereign God, that he has a plan. Perhaps one day we will all join them, but now, dearly

22

beloved brothers and sisters, we must entrust our precious ones to the Lord, and to His grace. We must pronounce the blessing before we go our separate ways. Time is now of the essence."

Chella heard Erimah's words as if in a dream. During the blessing, most of those gathered began to weep silent tears. As she looked round, Chella realised that she might never see these people and this room ever again. In the space of a few minutes, her life had changed. She was about to do the unthinkable.

She was going to leave.

The next few minutes passed in a whirl as the church left silently one by one after many hugs and whispered encouragements and promises of prayer, and kisses for the sleeping baby.

"Well, we'd better plan the route," said Jedan when everyone else had left, "and then you'd better go and pack, Chella. We'd better avoid the road the Elite use," he added, picking up the road atlas. "We'll need to go through the forest until we can pick up a different old road. This one, I think," he said, tracing one of the lines with his finger. "Then we can take this road, then this wider one. There may still be traces — we'll have to pray for direction."

Amma glanced over and nodded, before picking up a pile of Mikiah's clothes. "That seems like a sensible route. I'm sure there will be some traces of the roads left. Andan had a compass, I'm sure he did. I'll see if I can find it, it might be useful. Where shall we meet and at what time?"

Chella felt the panic beginning to return — everything

was happening so quickly, and Amma was talking like they were going to the Parkland for a picnic!

Jedan thought for a moment. "Could you pretend to be taking Mikiah for a walk in his pramcot, then go over the border somehow? I think it would be good to leave separately."

"Yes, we could follow the old track through the forest to the clearing where we had our Easter celebration, if you think that would be a good idea? It is in the direction we will need to take. The track might even be an ancient footpath. It might keep going as far as the road."

Jedan looked at the map again and nodded approvingly. "Amma, you are going to be a great help to us! Let us all meet there as quickly as we can. Under the big oak tree."

"Whoever arrives first will wait for the others," agreed Amma.

"The map is providential — can you not just see the hand of the Lord in all this? I will leave as soon as Garem returns with clothes. Chella, could you pretend you are going to work at the usual time, then when you get to Walkway Five, turn off and make your way to the border? Do you remember the way?"

Chella struggled to reply. "Yes, I know the way, but first I . . . I will need to pack a few things," she stammered.

"Of course!" said Jedan, heading to the sink for a wash. "We'll see you soon, under the oak tree. Don't worry about what to take. Bring some food if you've got some. It'll all be fine."

Chella couldn't help smiling back. That was just like

Jedan – they were about to leave everything behind and it didn't matter what they took!

Amma smiled, too, as she went over to the pramcot to pick up the sleeping baby. "Come, my dears, or we risk losing our advantage of time."

SIX

Packing

Chella let herself quietly into her apartment, which she shared with Lavitah, and stood on the threshold, hardly able to close the door. Lavitah rushed to give her a silent hug. Chella couldn't speak, so deep was her emotion.

"I've made breakfast," said Lavitah after a pause, as Chella finally pushed the door closed behind her, "and put all the eggs on to boil, for you to take with you. I bought an extra half dozen yesterday, and cheese, and an extra loaf of bread – you can take it all – you might need it."

Chella looked round at the familiar room. Tears sprang to her eyes as the reality of leaving it all behind began to sink in.

Lavitah put a plate of bread and jam on the table, then started to pack food into a bag. "I'll start packing while you eat."

"Amma leaves her Scripture portions with you," Chella told her friend quickly, handing her a key as she sat down at the table in a daze. "She said please to make sure everyone has a turn to read them. She said to take all the books and anything else you want, and share the rest with any in need."

Lavitah nodded as she took the key, then poured two cups of tea from a teapot. "I will do my best."

Chella nibbled the bread. "Lavitah, I've got to pretend to be leaving for work, then meet Amma and Jedan outside the border where we met at Easter."

"Don't tell me any more," Lavitah said quickly. "It's better if I don't know."

Chella's hand flew to her mouth and she looked towards the door. "Oh, I didn't think! What will you do if Correctioners come looking for us?"

"I'll think of something."

"Thank you. For everything." Chella shook her head and looked around. "Oh, Lavitah, this is all so sudden! It hasn't sunk in yet. What we are going to do is against the law – and I might never see anyone here ever again!"

Lavitah sighed as she cut the cheese into slices and wrapped them deftly in a cloth. "I know. I will miss you. We all will. So much! But you are following the will of God, so all will be well. Isn't it amazing, what happened to Jedan?"

"Yes, and I did feel the Lord's assurance, after Emine prayed for me," admitted Chella, finishing her bread and going over to her cupboard. She opened the door and began to pull out clothes. "And I guess at the back of my mind I knew it might come to this." She sighed and gave a wry smile. "But not yet! And I'll have to leave almost everything behind..."

The words choked in her throat as she looked at all her belongings around her, which held so many memories. The curtains her mum had embroidered with birds and flowers – faded now, but still precious. The rugs and blankets and quilts, the familiar pictures on the walls, the checkers game she and her dad had spent so many evenings playing, her birthday clock, even the well-worn plates and bowls on the dresser... she might never see any of it ever again.

"You must trust that all will be well. I will take care of everything for you. And you know you will have better and lasting possessions."

Chella nodded, her heart and soul too full to speak, knowing the scripture Lavitah was referring to, from the letter to the Hebrews. She wiped away a stray tear as it ran down her cheek. "Yes, I know. It's just that it's all so sudden. And people don't leave!"

Lavitah smiled gently as she filled a bottle with water. "Now they do!" She looked thoughtfully at Chella. "Perhaps you will be blazing a trail. Perhaps this is the beginning of a new thing the Lord is doing – a deliverance for the people of God. Just think, the Old Church does exist, and you are going there! To perform a vital task, to let them know they are in danger."

"Oh, Lavitah, why don't you come too?"

Lavitah sighed as she checked the egg timer. "I wish I could! But I was spared for a reason. I am called to stay. I have a job to do here..." She paused for a moment, and Chella wondered if she was thinking about all the believers in her previous Block who had disappeared. Lavitah had left for work in the Wash Room one day, just before Christmas, and none of them had ever been seen again.

"I'll need to help Amma with Mikiah," reflected Chella,

adding her hairbrush to the growing pile of clothes on the bedsettee.

Lavitah nodded and smiled as she drained the eggs and plunged them into cold water. "Yes, you will. Maybe one day we'll all come and join you! Wouldn't that be amazing? In the meantime, I will pray for you. We all will, you know that. Now look at the time! Are you going to take your usual work bag, if you're pretending to go to the Studio?"

"Yes, good idea." Chella stroked her bed quilt. Was she really going to leave all this behind? There was one particular person who might cause trouble, if he found out. She jumped as someone walked past in the corridor.

"It's OK!" soothed Lavitah, with a smile.

"It might not be."

Lavitah looked Chella in the eye. "You're thinking about Solod."

Chella bit her lip. "What might he do if he finds me gone?"

"Do you think he still cares?"

"Cares is maybe the wrong word. Cares for me? No. I'm sure he will have found someone else by now. But I think he will still care that I left him. And if he finds out that I have left the Area with another man who is a believer in Christ and an escaped prisoner and we are to be married. . . yes, I think he'll care about that. He told me one day he'd get me back, remember? What if he tries to follow us?"

Lavitah breathed in deeply. "You still haven't told Jedan about Solod?"

Chella sighed. "You know I've tried! I just can't bring myself to tell him. He's so trusting and. . . I don't think he'd understand. Every time I try and talk about the past, he changes the subject."

"Jedan loves you just the way you are – you must trust that love."

Chella smiled. "You're right."

"I am! And remember, you are stepping out in faith, as Sarah did with Abraham when he was called to leave Ur of the Chaldees. Abraham was made a promise, like Jedan has been. God will guide you and lead you – and think about it – you're going to a sort of promised land too. You are going to find the Old Church. Just think, it really does exist! You'll be able to worship in freedom and pray and sing openly without fear – how wonderful will that be?"

Chella laughed out loud. "I've been thinking so much about leaving, I'd almost forgotten that I'm going to be joining the Old Church! Lavitah, how awesome does that sound?"

"Amazing! I'm so jealous! And just think, in just a couple of days you'll be there!"

"Yes!"

Lavitah grinned at her. "Imagine that!" Her face suddenly dropped. "I am a bit concerned about Amma and Mikiah. You will look after them, won't you?"

Chella hugged her. "Yes, of course I will. I'm sure it will be wonderful, but oh, Lavitah, I'll miss you, and everyone. . ."

Lavitah nodded. "Just keep your thoughts on the good things. I'm so glad I made a new batch of sweet biscuits yesterday. Mikiah loves them. You can take them with you. You should wear your warmer shawl. I'll fold your thinner one in your bag with your cloak – you might need them both for the night."

The night, Chella thought, as she swallowed the last mouthful of tea, then stopped herself thinking. Never, ever, had she been away from her apartment for a night.

SEVEN

Setting Out

Lavitah offered to walk with Chella as far as the Wash Room. "I'll pretend I left something at work," she had suggested. "Then I'll just say, *see you later*, when I turn off. It will help to keep things looking normal, in case anyone is looking. But at least I can share the first part of your journey with you."

Chella was grateful to have Lavitah walking with her — closing the door on her apartment for the last time would have been almost impossible alone.

In the final few minutes, she and Lavitah had packed her work bag as best they could with food, water, clothes and a few essential toiletries, along with a pack of purifying tablets, just in case, and the wooden cross Chella's father had carved for her baptism, wrapped in her cloak, as a keepsake.

Chella and Lavitah hardly spoke as they walked, arm in arm, along the stony path towards the Central Zone, then parted near the Wash Room in the end with no words, just a silent hug.

Chella concentrated on breathing normally as she walked on alone. Everything looked strangely normal, considering the momentous thing she was about to do. Despite the sunshine and blue sky, the morning was still holding on to its early freshness. The acrid smell of smoke from the smithy wafted on the breeze. Children chattered and laughed on their way to school, and adults on Shift Two headed towards the Central Zone for work.

People were praying for Chella – she knew it, she could feel it. Although her pulse was racing and her legs shook, she felt a strange confidence that she was doing the right thing, and as she walked on she nodded and smiled at people she recognised on the walkway.

To keep her thoughts on good things, following Lavitah's advice, Chella pictured herself singing in the Old Church with Jedan. From the description of his vision, and what he had said, it sounded wonderful. Perhaps all churches had been like that before the Dwelling Areas existed. People were allowed to worship as they wished, then, in this land at least, and sing and pray as loud as they wanted. Everyone had had a lot more freedom then; they even voted for the government.

There had been so many changes since the last Great War, the Plague and the Famine. Before then, you could do whatever job you wanted, worship however you wanted, go wherever you wanted, live in whatever dwelling you chose, anywhere you liked, as long as you could afford it. There were pictures of different dwellings in history books: estates where every house had its own little garden, pretty cottages in the country with gardens full of flowers, big mansions for the Elite of their day. People even lived in castles and windmills and boats.

33

Now the Areas were the same the world over, built in concentric circles leading out from a Central Zone, which housed all the public buildings. Workers' apartment blocks surrounded the Central Zone on three sides: the final quarter was reserved for the larger, Elite dwellings, separated by a high wall and a thick hedge. The apartment blocks were surrounded in their turn by a communal fenced garden zone, then beyond the gardens the Parkland stretched out: Elite and Workers separately, of course. Farmland surrounded the Parkland, right up to the perimeter fence, where animals grazed and crops were grown for food.

Walkways criss-crossed the gardens and the Parkland in the Workers' area in Area IF208, but there was no official path through the fields to the perimeter fence. Courting couples and groups of teenagers sometimes made their way to the edge for a bit of privacy, but leaving the Area was not permitted; only one road reached the Area, and that was in the middle of the Elite Zone.

Chella rehearsed the route she would need to take in her mind. Through the gardens. Across the Parkland. Three fields to the border. Under the fence at the Scots pine.

First, she passed the apartment blocks. They were the same everywhere; six stories high with six apartments on each floor. Areas had been carefully designed for energy efficiency, unity and fairness by the World Council and were held up to be one of the greatest feats of mankind, according to the loudspeakers. Not that everyone agreed with that assessment. Her grandad certainly hadn't. Chella only vaguely remembered him, as he had died not long after her mum had disappeared, but she hadn't forgotten

34

his stories of the Old Days, or the far-away look in his eyes when he used to talk about the happy times when he lived with his family in a real house with its own garden, in a real old town.

Grandad loved to tell stories of the Old Order. He would tell anyone who would listen about the holidays he used to have when he was a lad; the treats, picnics, and trips to beautiful places. They attended special church buildings in their town; places built for Christians to meet in. Then came the War, the Plague and the Famine, all three of which had swept through the world, causing untold suffering.

The Christians had helped as many people as they could during those terrible years, so Grandad said. Despite the lack of food, clean water, and medical treatment, they had done their best to feed the hungry and care for the sick, the orphans and widows, but when the World Council was set up and the New Order established, laws were passed to outlaw religious observance, supposedly for the sake of world unity. Religion had caused the war, the Council reasoned; now there would be no religion. Church buildings, mosques, temples and synagogues all over the world were razed to the ground and religious writings banned.

It was at that time that the World Council set up the new date system, and the rebuilding programme. The new Areas were designed to rehouse the remnant of the population in the most efficient way possible – the few who had survived those terrible times.

Apartment blocks, farms, windmills, schools, medical units, and correction facilities were set up in new Areas the world over. It was hailed as a time of great optimism for

35

world peace, but it wasn't true peace, as Grandad had been fond of saying; absence of war was only a kind of peace. For those who wanted to worship God, there was no peace.

The church went underground.

In the early years, some Christians had refused to move into the new dwelling areas, preferring not to live under the eye of the new Area Councils. In the end most had complied – but not all, it seemed.

Grandad and his family had been almost the last people to leave his almost deserted dwelling place. Only two elderly Christian women remained in his neighbourhood when he had left, so he had said, determined to live out their lives where they felt they belonged. Chella had seen a photograph of them. No doubt they had died alone, long ago.

Rumours did circulate from time to time of groups of people living outside the Areas. Not many believed the rumours, but now it seemed that perhaps they were true. The Elite, of course, knew more than the Workers, but the Elite kept themselves to themselves and no word ever came over the loudspeakers about the matter.

As Chella approached Walkway Five, she turned to look at her apartment block for the last time, wondering with a beating heart if she would ever see it again. It might not be perfect, but it was all she had ever known. *I'm frightened*, she admitted to herself.

The thumping of her heart intensified as she turned and saw two Correctioners walking towards her on the path. It was unusual to see Correctioners on the walkways. She remembered something Solod had said. *We know everything.* They didn't, of course, but they did have a file on each of the Workers, she knew that. What if they were looking for Jedan?

She stopped to tie her shoelace so she didn't have to look at them as they drew close, but as they reached her, the taller of the two put his hand on her shoulder.

"Come with us, please," he said.

EIGHT

Questioned

The Correctioner who had spoken was a tall young man with a grave expression. The shorter Correctioner was bald and looked bored.

"What have I done?" Chella's eyes were round with fear as she straightened up. They would only have to look in her bag to know that something wasn't right. Who walked around the Area carrying provisions, a winter cloak and a woollen shawl in their bag at the height of summer? And there was the wooden cross.

"It's OK, dearie, nothing sinister," replied the short Correctioner, finishing his sentence with a yawn. "I assume you know your fiancé was arrested yesterday?" Chella nodded, her heart banging in her chest. The Correctioner continued, "Did you know he has escaped? We need you to come with us, answer a few questions." Chella swallowed hard, deciding that the best thing to do was to stay silent. That was the general advice.

The Correction Facility was not far away, but it felt like the longest walk of her life as Chella was marched between the two uniformed men, her thoughts in a turmoil, her legs like jelly. People on their way to work looked quickly, to make sure the detainee was not one of their loved ones, then turned away their gaze just as fast.

Chella barely noticed the looks. Her thoughts raced on. The Correctioners had discovered that Jedan had escaped, then. Briefly she wondered about Amma. Had they stopped her, too? Maybe this was the end of everything; maybe she and Jedan and Amma were going to disappear, as so many had before them. Silently she spoke the name of Jesus. It helped, a bit.

She concentrated on breathing and gritted her teeth. She would never talk, never give Jedan away, or Amma, never, never, no matter what they did to her. *"Jesus, Lord, have mercy,"* she whispered under her breath.

Chella had been to the Correction facility many times, but not since she was little, and never to be questioned, only with her dad, who used to go every week to ask about her mum, until they told him not to go any more. As she walked through the double doors with her captors, she remembered the ache in her soul and her dad's sad eyes, better than she remembered the airy foyer and the smell of dusty wood.

She did remember the way words echoed in the high emptiness, the quiet rustle of papers on the main desk, the authoritative voice of an Elite somewhere in one of the small rooms that led off the reception area. A lump came to her throat as a stab of missing her dad touched her soul.

As they arrived at the reception desk, another Correctioner came out of one of the rooms, with more bands on his epaulettes: a higher official. "Thank you, gentlemen," he said curtly to the two Correctioners who had brought her in. "Bring her this way. I'm Sergeant Mahn," he said, turning his attention to Chella and holding out his hand for her to shake. "You must be Chella James?" Chella looked at his outstretched hand in amazement, before shaking it. His grip was firm and his eyes didn't smile, but his approach reassured her somewhat.

"Yes," she whispered. At least she hadn't been clapped in handcuffs. Not yet, anyway.

"We have informed your work you will be arriving late this morning," continued Sergeant Mahn, leading her towards the room he had just vacated, followed by her captors. "Forgive us this inconvenience, but we need to ask you a few questions."

As he led her towards the door, he pushed aside her shawl and caressed the top of her arm. She cringed, wishing she had worn a dress with sleeves, and tried to edge away, but he pushed her into a small, airless room furnished simply with two wooden chairs and a plain table in between.

The table was empty except for a black folder, a lamp and a metal box at the far side, which looked like it might hold jewellery, or an instrument of some sort. A high, barred window gave a dingy light and a fly buzzed somewhere near it.

Chella shivered in the sudden coolness of the dim room. The Sergeant indicated for her to sit on the nearest chair, so she did so, on the edge. She placed her bag at her feet, slightly under the table, so the men might not notice how full it looked.

Sergeant Mahn sat on the chair on the other side of

the table and the other two Correctioners stood behind her after closing the door. She couldn't see them, but she could feel their presence.

The Sergeant opened the folder and took several sheets of paper out of the file. He spent several minutes reading, with a frown on his face. The fly continued to buzz at the window.

While Chella sat there waiting, her thoughts came in anxious snatches. The Sergeant had told the Studio she would be late; did that mean they were going to let her go soon? Had Jedan made it to the oak tree, or had they arrested him, too? What was written on the papers the Sergeant was reading? Had they stopped Amma? If Amma and Jedan hadn't been caught, how long would they wait for her? Was it safe to be in this room with these men? Did the box hold a torture instrument? What might they do to her if she didn't tell them everything they wanted to know?

The thought of the Sergeant's hand on her arm made her skin crawl as she watched him turn the papers. He could do whatever he wanted with her, she knew that. The feeling of powerlessness made her legs shake, as she reached out to her bag with her feet for some assurance of normality.

"It's about Jedan Fran," said the Sergeant eventually, shuffling the papers and placing them in a neat stack on the table next to the file. Chella nodded and tried not to look at his hands. Her captor was looking at her, expecting a response.

"He was arrested," she managed after a long pause. That much at least was safe.

"Indeed he was. Does he mean anything to you?"

A dark, cold feeling crept into Chella's soul. What should she say? She closed her eyes, and when she opened them again, the Sergeant was staring at her, his eyes piercing her own, as if to draw something out of her. She decided to tell the truth. "We are to marry," she said simply. But they knew that.

"You are willing to wait for him?"

Chella was confused by this question. Wait for him where? Had they found him again, or not? What should she say? After a brief silence, she knew the answer to the question. "Yes," she declared, returning the gaze. "I am willing to wait for him."

The Sergeant gazed at her in mock compassion, as if she were a child. "Did you know he has escaped? We believe he may have left the Area."

Chella tried not to show that she knew. "Oh," she whispered, hardly daring to speak.

"I see that shocks you," said the Correctioner. "Perhaps it concerns you that the one you thought so loving has left you?"

Just the very thought that Jedan would leave without her made her heart flip. "He wouldn't do that," she replied, but even as she said it, she wasn't convinced he wouldn't, if he thought she wasn't coming.

The Correctioner leant over the table towards her. "Do you know where he has gone?"

"I, I..."

The Correctioner continued in a smooth tone. She could feel his warm breath on her face. "Perhaps he is planning to go to another Dwelling Area?"

42

"Another Dwelling Area?" Chella shook her head, and her voice rose. "No, no, I'm sure he would never do that!" Then suddenly she remembered the advice to say nothing. She looked down at her hands. "At least I don't think so," she finished lamely, looking back up. The Sergeant nodded slowly, keeping her gaze until she thought she would burst.

Then suddenly he stood up, scraping the chair legs on the floor. "Well, it's good of you to talk to us, thank you for coming in," he said. "You may go along to work now."

Chella was so surprised, she couldn't move. He was letting her go? He hadn't even asked if she had seen Jedan! Could she have given away something without intending to?

As the Sergeant indicated the door, and the short Correctioner went to open it, Chella picked up her bag and stood up, desperately wondering what she might have said that could have helped them. As she quickly turned towards the door, the tall Correctioner, who had followed her round the table, grabbed her right arm and twisted it so hard behind her back she cried out and dropped her bag, which fell to the floor with a thud. The Sergeant was close behind; Chella could feel his breath on her neck as her shawl slipped off her shoulders on to the floor. She struggled and cried out in shock. The tall Correctioner pinched the top of her arm so hard she thought she would faint.

"We *will* find him," the Sergeant said through gritted teeth, as he stroked her other arm, then suddenly the Correctioner let her go with a shove. "We'll let your work know you will be arriving shortly."

Chella struggled to regain her balance, then grabbed her bag and shawl and ran to the door, which the short

Correctioner opened for her. She fled out of the room, through the reception area and out into the sunshine.

On the walkway she paused, shaking with the shock, dazed from the pain in her arm. People were passing by as if nothing had happened. What should she do? Go left to the border or right to work? She turned and saw the Sergeant watching her from the open doorway. She turned right, to work.

NINE

Working for the Common Good

"At last!" chided the Studio boss, Odina, as Chella walked in through the front door. "Your assignments are on your desk. Hurry up, we haven't got all day! Correctioners this, Correctioners that. Why can't they just leave us all alone to get on with our jobs?" She bustled off, leaving Chella to hang her shawl on her peg and collapse at her desk in a daze. She sat there for a minute, taking deep breaths, trying to stop her whole body from shaking.

The scene was comfortingly familiar. A dozen people sat at two long wooden benches down the east side of the long room, working sewing machines. The smell of new cloth and carefully oiled machines hung in the air. The large shutters had been thrown back to welcome in the sunshine, and the workroom was light and airy.

At the central table, Mardinah and Spatch were cutting cloth carefully round a pattern. Hearing Chella arrive, they turned round to give her a quick nod and wave, before getting back to work. Nisrak was basting shirts in his usual corner and Odina was bustling about, checking that everyone was working.

Chella was one of two designers. Ena sat at the desk next to hers, frowning at her paper, chewing on the end of a pencil. As soon as Odina turned her back, she hissed at Chella. "You OK?"

Chella could barely reply, but managed to shake her head without catching her eye. "Sort of," she replied and looked quickly back down at her task list as Odina, with her usual intuition, turned round with a stare.

Chella looked at the task list. Her first job was to design twelve work suits to fit a consignment of cloth. Inwardly she groaned. Even eleven would be a struggle! She looked up. Odina had marched back and was looking at her. "It's a lot, I know, but do the best you can." With that she walked off.

Chella didn't mind Odina – some people did. She could be abrupt, but Chella knew she was only trying to do her best for the common good. Then a pang hit her and she put her face in her hands. She should be leaving, not sitting here looking at her daily assignments! Amma and Jedan must surely have already reached the oak tree by now, assuming they had both managed to get there without being arrested. What would they do when she didn't arrive? How long would they wait? But she couldn't go! Odina would notice straight away if she left. Odina noticed everything. And running away from work was impossible, ridiculous, crazy! Odina would send a message to the Correctioners, who would follow her, then they would *all* be caught – Jedan, Amma and Mikiah, too. The thought filled her with horror.

Then, as she glanced back down at her daily tasks, a different awful thought filled her heart. She couldn't let Odina down. She had taken Chella back after her three week break with no questions asked last year, because she needed her. Who else would help Ena design the garments to fit the cloth if she left?

Time seemed to stand still as the machines whirred on. The clip, clip of scissors cutting fabric, the smell of freshly spun cloth, and the familiar sight of everyone working quietly together seemed timeless, but every minute she delayed was a minute Jedan and Amma might not wait for her. As she sat there at her desk, her guilty bag sitting by her feet and her arm throbbing in pain, Chella was confused. She pretended to do calculations with her pencil on her workbook. *There was no good solution.* Staying was wrong; leaving was wrong. How could she leave when people were relying on her? Maybe she should let Jedan and Amma go in peace, and accept her fate here. *Show me what to do, Lord. You know all things*, she prayed silently in her heart.

Suddenly a clear thought came to her mind. The Correctioners hadn't looked in her bag. That had to be a miracle. And the church had prayed and sent her with their blessing. It seemed that God did have a plan. And how could she let Jedan, Amma and Mikiah leave without her? They needed her as much as she needed them. She prayed silently for a sign. *If Ena can do this assignment, I'll know I'm not abandoning the common good.*

"You having trouble with something?" Ena hissed.

Chella looked up with a start. Feeling slightly sick, she

took the assignment over to Ena's desk. "I wonder if you'd have a look over this? I'm not sure it can be done."

Ena looked at the sheet and frowned in concentration. Chella held on to the desk, trying not to show she was trembling.

"Well," said Ena, "I don't think there's a problem. If we make the sleeves a bit shorter, we can turn half of them lengthways across the fabric and fit them in like so..." she made a quick sketch, "...then it will leave..." she made a quick calculation and jotted down her result, "...around, let's say, 2.2 metres for the extra suit body – which might even leave a couple of centimetres!"

"Thanks, Ena, you're right, I think that would work," agreed Chella in surprise.

Ena smiled. "Who needs long sleeves anyway? We could always add something to the cuffs. I'll finish it off if you like – you look like you could use a break."

Odina missed nothing. She marched over. "You ill?" she asked Chella, in her usual sharp manner, frowning as if the cares of the world were overcoming her.

"Um..." Chella looked up. She didn't know what to say, but couldn't help tears filling her eyes.

"Actually, you don't look yourself. Go back to bed and don't come in tomorrow either if you've got a fever – the rest of us don't want to catch it." And with that Odina walked off again to check on the machinists.

Chella wiped her eyes and stood there for a moment in shock. Ena made a face at her. "Go, quick, before she changes her mind!" she whispered. Odina never sent anyone home, however ill they were. With a beating heart, Chella grabbed her bag and shawl, and ran outside. Then she ran back in.

"Say goodbye to everyone for me," she said to Ena, giving her a hug.

"Sure, enjoy your day in bed!" As she hugged her, Ena whispered in her ear. "Correctioners?" Chella gave an imperceptible nod. "Don't let them get you!" Chella didn't trust herself to reply.

She lurched back outside and began to run.

TEN

To the Border

To avoid passing the Correction Unit, Chella ran round the back way, past the Dining Hall, the Recycling Centre and the high walls of the Powerplant, wincing from the pain in her arm.

As she approached the school, she paused in an alley to catch her breath and wipe the tears from her eyes. She tried to stop her body shaking. She could hear little voices reciting spellings. The smell of the Laundry, the bees humming in the hedgerow and birds singing in the trees tried to assure her that everything was fine, but Chella knew that she couldn't go home and go back to bed as Odina had told her to. She had to leave. She had to get to the oak tree. The thought that she might never see the Studio again, or any of her friends who worked there, was something she pushed to the back of her mind. Only one thing mattered now: to get to Amma and Jedan. This was her destiny, and as she stood there she prayed silently. *Lord, help me to do my best. Be my strength.*

Only a few people were on the dusty walkways; most

people would now be at school or work, or in bed if they had been on Shift One. Chella looked round as she rejoined Walkway Five, half expecting a Correctioner to be looming, waiting to stop her, but there were only a few shoppers, a ginger cat, and an old man with a stick.

I can't run, she told herself. *It will look suspicious.* Anyway, her bag was heavy. So she walked towards the gardens, longing to look behind, but keeping her eyes ahead.

She walked tall as she walked on the familiar paths for what might be the last time, and nodded at people she passed. It didn't seem possible that she could be leaving. The dusty shrubs, the lake, the wooded areas, the sports field; each was like an old friend. The Playpark was getting old, and the fountain no longer worked, but she had so many memories of playing there; even a misty one of her mum laughing as she pushed her on a swing.

The scent of freshly mown grass reached her as she walked along the water's edge; workers were mowing the grass of the football field on the other side of the lake. Would either of them think it odd that she was carrying a bulging bag? Two young mums were out walking with their little ones in their pramcots, and a runner was doing the long circuit, but no one seemed to notice, or care, that she was there. A middle-aged man was feeding the ducks; he stopped and watched her approach, then smiled at her as she passed by. Her heart beat faster, wondering if he would follow her, but when she turned round to check, he had gone back to feeding the ducks.

Her thoughts turned to what would they find outside. Maybe she would see real houses, or gardens, or even the sea! Knowledge of living outside the Areas had now all but disappeared, apart from tales handed down in families. Still, she was about to leave. *If this is of you, Lord,* Chella prayed, *please keep us safe. Especially Mikiah.*

As she walked, Chella kept her eye on the tall Scots pine at the edge of the forest. It was rare to see a guard these days, although, apparently, they used to diligently patrol the perimeter fence. In Year 0013 there had been an uprising among the Workers led by a man called Dareve Bilton. His movement had been quickly crushed and all those who had supported him were arrested and never seen again. Chella thought about Dareve as she walked, changing her bag from one arm to the other. He had been full of courage where she was afraid, but maybe she would succeed where he had failed. Hope rose in her soul. Nothing was impossible with God.

Once over a dip in the land, where she could no longer be seen, Chella began to run with determination. *Three fields,* she told herself again. The wheat, still with a greenish tinge, rustled in the breeze. *It will make good bread,* thought Chella, *but I won't be here to eat it.*

The sun was getting warmer by the minute, and the skylarks sang praises high above. How fortunate the birds were to be able to sing in freedom, and fly wherever they wanted, Chella thought, as she walked and ran in turn. Her breath came in gasps. The skirt of her summer dress rustled against the undergrowth between the hedgerow and the wheat, and long grasses whipped her legs. Rabbits ran across the path as she approached, and a cloud of pigeons rose up from the field. Their beating wings made her jump.

Any other day she would have stopped to enjoy this glorious day: not today.

The shadow of the forest grew closer as Chella crossed the field of sheep and stumbled through the neat rows of apple trees. The perimeter fence rose up high and intimidating as she stepped out of the shelter of the orchard and pushed her way through the weeds and bushes to the Scots pine.

Would Correctioners be guarding the perimeter fence, knowing a prisoner had escaped? Topped with ancient barbed wire, the fence looked harsh and ugly, determined to keep her in. Beyond it the forest looked dark and frightening: judgment on all those who dared to abandon the common good.

Chella turned and stood at the edge of what had been her whole world up until that time, and listened. Had she been followed? Were there guards on patrol? It seemed not. She was alone, and could hear nothing but the bleating of sheep, the skylarks, the low buzz of insects, the rustling of wild grasses.

Beyond the apple trees, she could see the tips of the windmills and the apartment blocks rising up in relief against the sky. It was the only home she had ever known! Her heart lurched as she thought of all the dear people she was leaving behind. Part of her suddenly yearned to run back, but Jedan and Amma would be waiting for her – and her best friend's child needed her.

Nidala, she whispered towards the knot of familiar buildings, with tears in her eyes, *if you are still there, I will do my best to look after your mum and your son.*

Chella turned to do the unthinkable. She pushed her bag under the perimeter fence, crept under herself, and stepped into the dark forest.

ELEVEN

Into the Unknown

Stepping into the forest was like entering another world. It smelled of the earth, and vibrant, green living things. Birds and insects hummed and sang quietly, in harmony, as if they belonged, but she didn't. Even the light was green, and gentle. It was wildly beautiful, but it was forbidden territory, and it felt like it. Everything about it was strange, and against the law. Here there were no loudspeakers to remind you of your duty; no apartments, no work, no Correctioners. Never had Chella been here alone.

If Jedan and Amma aren't at the oak tree I'll go straight back home, Chella promised herself, her heart thumping in her chest. *I'll go back to bed, like Odina told me to, and go to work in the morning.*

She stood there for a few seconds, looking down the narrow, twisting animal track that was to take her into an unknown future. Then she saw the unmistakable print of pramcot wheels in the dust. Amma had made it through!

Relief quickly turned to panic as a sudden noise in the bushes made her jump. It was only a blackbird, but as it burst out from the brambles with a harsh cry, panic flooded Chella's soul, and she ran.

Living in Area IF208 was all Chella had ever known. A little over 12,000 people lived there, so the loudspeakers told them: mostly Workers and their children, with about 1,000 Elite to make sure everyone was working for the common good. Each block had its secret believers, most of whom had at least one hidden Bible, from which the believers copied out portions by hand. This was forbidden, but the fear of arrest was something they were accustomed to living with.

Two or three times a year, the churches from two or three different Blocks would meet together in a pre-arranged place outside the border. It was risky, but worth it for the freedom to be able to sing, pray and read Scripture out loud, with other believers. Chella anticipated those services with fear as well as joy because although it hadn't happened for a several years, meetings had been discovered in the past, and all the attendees imprisoned. Lookouts were therefore always in place, and church members crossed the border in twos and threes, with a few minutes' gap between each group. The meetings only lasted a short time, but the memory would last much longer. The only sad thing was that they couldn't take their children, until they had chosen to walk the Way for themselves.

Chella's dad had taken her to her first meeting when she was thirteen, a month after her baptism. It was Easter. He suggested they take a walk to see the lambs, but when they reached the field he told her to follow him in silence.

"Trust me," he had said, as he climbed over the gate into the field, and indicated for her to follow.

She remembered the panic rising up in her as she silently followed his footsteps to the perimeter fence, under the wire and into the forest, unable to ask questions.

Then, as he led her down a winding track through the forest, she heard the glorious sound of singing through the trees. *Light of the world, brighten our darkness. . .* She would never forget the pleasure on her Dad's face as he turned to look at her surprised face.

Chella had another reason for loving these meetings: six months ago she had met Jedan at the Christmas service. The breath of the faithful had made little clouds in the freezing air as they had sung ancient carols to celebrate the birth of their precious Saviour, in a clearing surrounded by pine trees. Most of the members of Chella's home church were there, including her best friend, Nidala, who had left her newborn son at home with her husband.

It was the first time Chella had met Jedan. His energy and passion amazed and fascinated her – she couldn't take her eyes off him as he sang and prayed. Their first meeting seemed a long time ago, now summer had come.

Chella ran along the narrow, overgrown path until her breath came in huge gasps, and she thought she must have missed the clearing. Then Jedan was there, running towards her.

"I thought you weren't coming!" he murmured, clutching her to himself and stroking her hair.

"I was detained," she told him, and for a second he

stood stock still. And there was Amma running to hug her, too, carrying Mikiah.

"Praise the Lord who has brought us all together!" said Amma, breathless but smiling.

Jedan squeezed Chella tight. "We'd better go. You must tell your story as we walk."

TWELVE

The Forest

They set off at a good pace, in single file because of the narrowness of the animal track they were following. Jedan led the way with Andan's compass. Amma followed with the pramcot. As she brought up the rear, Chella recounted most of what she could remember about her arrest, and how she had miraculously managed to get away. She left out the bit about the Correctioners hurting her, and of her suspicions as to who might be behind it all, but she went over everything she could remember of the Sergeant's questions and her answers, and assured them she didn't think she was followed.

"I wonder why they didn't they look in your bag?" wondered Amma.

"Or ask you if you'd seen me?" added Jedan. None of them could think of anything Chella could have said that would have allowed them to let her go so easily. In the end they put it down to the Lord answering the prayers of His people, and were encouraged.

Walking in the forest was strange, enclosed by trees on

all sides as far as they could see, but it wasn't frightening, Chella decided. Little by little her breathing returned to its normal rhythm. The silence was immense, apart from birdsong, the hum of insects and the gentle rustling of the tree tops way above them. The air was fresher than in the Area, and the coolness of being in the shade was pleasant. Shafts of sunlight broke through the leaf canopy here and there. Small birds chirped and flitted through the trees: larger birds soared silently above. They saw a group of deer once, in the distance, but they bounded away with a rustle into the bushes as the group approached.

Talking was difficult in single file, so the quietness gave Chella time to think. Everything had happened so suddenly! At first, she could only think of all the troubles they might face. What would they do for food, if they ran out before they found the Old Church? What about shelter – what where would they sleep that night? Would Mikiah be all right spending so much time in the pramcot? What about wild animals? What if one of them became sick? Would Amma's map still be right after all these years? What if they were followed when it was discovered they were missing? Solod would stop at nothing if he found out she had left, and the Sergeant had wanted to show her how much he could hurt her – twisting and pinching her arm was a warning, for sure. What if the Old Church didn't exist, and it was all a big mistake?

Then as Jedan turned and smiled at her, she knew she had to get a grip on her thoughts. The whole course of her life may have changed out of all recognition, but there could be no going back, and surely God was with them in this place. She had to trust Him to lead and guide them.

Amma was almost as quiet as Chella as they walked, but Jedan chatted cheerfully. From time to time he ran ahead to see if he could find evidence of the old road they needed to take, then called back to the others with encouragements such as, *"We'll find the road soon,"* or *"See how well we are doing!"* or *"This track is heading exactly the way we need to go – maybe it is an ancient footpath, heading to the road!"*

Chella recognised the Jedan she loved, with an extra layer of strength and certainty she hadn't seen before. It made her smile and lifted her spirits. He was delighted with her release from the Correctioners, and their getaway, and mentioned them both often – it seemed to give him an extra boost of faith.

As she walked, Chella mused over what Lavitah had said about Abraham and Sarah. Abraham had received the call from God to leave his father's country, not Sarah. But Sarah went with him because of the bond between them. It was what she was doing now, following Jedan. The whole thing seemed like a dream; something impossible. *Yet I should have known it would come to this,* she thought.

She had come to accept since her engagement to Jedan, that once her life was entwined with his, her life would never again have the quiet rhythm she was used to. The two of them were so different. She liked security and familiarity: he liked variety and surprise. She liked to plan in advance: he preferred spontaneity. Chella liked the comforting feeling of doing the same thing at the same time every day: he liked to make sudden alterations to plans as the mood took him. For Chella, routine was a good way to get everything done decently and in order, and a good way to forget things in the past she didn't want to remember. Jedan quickly got bored with routine.

There were other ways Jedan was different, too. He railed against what he called the straitjacket of the World Council. He hated having to be a Christian in secret. He said things against the Area Council, too, that none of the Christians in her Block had ever said. His passion for freedom, although understandable, concerned Chella. Had the Lord not given human governments for the common good? The World Council might not be perfect, but everyone had a home, food to eat and clothes to wear, and a Medical Facility if they were ill. Were these not great blessings?

Chella wanted to live a quiet life of worship, and work for the common good – she didn't want adventure. But Jedan had dreams. He didn't want to be a groom for the Elite for the rest of his life – he wanted to ride the horses himself, feel the wind in his hair, ride away and discover what lay beyond the perimeter fence. He wanted to explore the world, travel and be free; see ancient castles and cathedrals, rivers and hills, mountains and the sea.

The two of them had sometimes laughed about their differences, and agreed that they would make a good team.

How could I have laughed? Chella wondered now with a shake of her head and a wry smile, as they walked further and further into the unknown. But as she looked at Jedan, striding ahead, checking the map, cheerfully helping Amma with the pramcot and the bags, and blowing raspberries at Mikiah to make him laugh, her heart beat faster. She couldn't regret coming with him. Even if they walked until they died, they belonged together. Somewhere deep within she felt the ache in her soul that could only come from the bond that marriage would seal.

THIRTEEN

The Trick

Around noon, when the sun was overhead, Amma suggested a break for a rest and a snack. Jedan found them a secluded place, off the path, hidden by the trees and undergrowth.

As the three of them sat side by side on a fallen tree, Jedan surprised Chella and Amma by producing a folded, checked tea cloth out of his bag, with something inside. He laughed cheerfully at their open-mouthed wonder.

"What...?" asked Chella.

"Where did you..." began Amma at the same time.

"Guess!" teased Jedan, but they shook their heads, so he opened up the package to reveal a batch of Welsh pancakes! Jedan grinned widely. "Jott made them for us while Garem was sorting out clothes and things. The pancakes were going to be for their breakfast, but she said we must have them for our lunch and remember their love and prayers."

Amma spoke for them all. "What a wonderful surprise! How kind, and just like Jott," she said, with a weary smile and a sigh of gratitude.

Jedan gave thanks for the food out loud, which made

them all smile at each other, then he gave the first pancake to Mikiah to eat in his pramcot. Mikiah laughed, and they all laughed with him. There was something precious about praying together out loud, and sharing Jott's pancakes. It made eating lunch in the middle of the forest a bit less strange, and was a comfort, as if their brothers and sisters were somehow sharing in their journey.

After they had eaten, and Amma was watching Mikiah crawl in the soft leaf litter on the forest floor, Jedan took Chella's hand. "Did you pray for me, when I was in prison?" he murmured, kissing the top of her head.

She smiled at him. "Of course I did! I hardly stopped!"

"My escape was a miracle."

Chella stroked his arm. "I know. Tell me about your arrest, and prison. What was it like?"

"Well, you know I always wanted to go on holiday?" he said with a twinkle in his eye.

Chella laughed back. "It wasn't like going on a holiday! No, really, what was it like?"

"The cells were small and the bed was hard, but..." Jedan paused, suddenly serious. "Chella, I can't explain this, but it was like it was all meant to be. They arrested me at work. I always pray at work, if there's no one about. Used to work, I should say."

"So someone heard you praying?" asked Amma, following Mikiah as he crawled back to the others.

"That's the strange thing. I was about to say, I wasn't arrested for anything to do with my faith. I was arrested for riding a horse!" He grinned, but Chella frowned back.

"Riding a horse?" she asked. "What do you mean?"

65

"I was tricked, I'm sure of it. There's a young Elite lad there, Richan, whose horse I look after. *Looked* after, I should say. He'd never spoken to me before, but a few days ago he started to be friendly."

"An Elite lad talked to you?" asked Amma in surprise. "That *is* odd."

"Yes, it's never happened before in the yard. Normally they just tell you what to do. To start with we just talked about the horses, but he wanted to know about *me*." Jedan shook his head. "Looking back on it now... well, I'll get to that in a minute. At the time, I thought it might be an opportunity to share my faith, but it never got that far. I happened to mention that I would love to ride myself."

Chella shook her head. "Oh Jedan!"

He grinned back. "Richan looked surprised, as if he'd never considered the possibility that Workers might have ideas! But yesterday morning he came in and asked if I wanted to ride his horse. I said it wasn't allowed, but he insisted until I felt I couldn't refuse, and oh, for so long I had longed to sit on that mare! Elizabeth, her name is, after the queens of England. He helped me up, showed me how to sit in the saddle and hold the reins, then slapped the mare so she would walk."

Chella gasped. "You rode his horse?"

Jedan chuckled. "I know, I know, I shouldn't have. But I couldn't disobey him, so I couldn't win either way. So there I was on the horse... and two Correctioners came out from behind the stables and arrested me. It was obvious they had been waiting. I appealed to the lad, but he shrugged and

66

said nothing. He had a strange look on his face, which is why I think it was a trick."

Amma frowned. "A trick? Why would they do that, I wonder?" But Chella went cold inside. She knew why he had been tricked. This wasn't the usual arrest of a Christian who had been found breaking the rules. The whole thing had Solod written in huge letters all over it. He must have found out about her engagement, and bribed the boy into getting Jedan arrested, to cause her pain. Maybe that was also why she had been detained. To play with her, like a cat plays with a mouse – catch her, let her go, then catch her again.

Jedan shook his head. "I don't know what it was all about. I've been going over and over it in my mind. Had anyone found out I was a Christian? If so, I don't know how."

"Maybe someone heard you praying without you realising?" suggested Amma.

"It's possible, but I don't think anyone at work ever found out I am a believer. Even if Mum and Dad suspected it – and actually, I think they do – they wouldn't have given me away. It would mean too much trouble for them. They came to see me in the Correction Facility after my arrest, and Dad had a go at me for riding a horse. He didn't mention faith while I was there and neither did anyone else. I tried to explain that I was set up, but nobody wanted to know."

"That is all so strange," agreed Amma, shaking her head. "So you don't think your arrest was anything to do with being a Christian? We all assumed, of course, that it was."

"Well if it was, they didn't say so." Jedan grinned. "For just one minute, on that horse, I tell you, it was the most awesome feeling! The strength of the animal, the warmth, the power in her stride. . ."

Chella didn't smile back. A knot had formed in her gut, which had nothing to do with the pancakes. It was because of her that Jedan had been arrested – how was she going to tell him that? Amma knew about her relationship with Solod, but had never met him: she didn't know how spiteful he was. Solod couldn't get back at her officially, because he would never be able to admit he had allowed a Worker into the Elite Zone. Now, it seemed, even after all these months, he had found a way of causing her pain. He had to be behind it all.

Neither of them have any idea that this is all my fault, thought Chella, watching Jedan pack the bags, and Amma cheerily brush bits of leaf out of Mikiah's clothes.

"Well, whatever happened, we know all things work for the good of those who love the Lord," said Amma cheerfully.

"Absolutely," replied Jedan. "Now we'd better move as fast as we can. Find the Old Church, and warn them they've been discovered."

"It will be so good to join them," agreed Amma with a smile, settling Mikiah back in the pramcot. "Imagine that! I know this journey isn't going to be easy, but just think, in a couple of days or so, we'll be safe with our fellow believers! And free. This truly is an amazing turn of events."

"Yes!" agreed Jedan. "If I hadn't been arrested, I wouldn't have heard about the Old Church. And one day

I hope I will learn to ride properly. Do you think the Old Church will have horses?"

Amma nodded. "Almost certainly. Farmers had to have horses back in my day, not just for riding, but for pulling carts and working the fields, like they do here. I assume things must be the same now. I suppose we'll find out when we get there!"

"Shall we move on?" Chella said aloud, getting up and picking up her bags. As soon as she was on her own with Jedan, she would have to tell him everything. At least she had never told Solod she was a Christian. That was something. And it was true what Amma said, that everything worked for the good of those who loved God. Perhaps, in an amazing way, the Lord had worked everything out so Jedan could hear about the Old Church. Still, she needed to come clean. She had kept her secret way too long.

They carried on walking in single file through the forest after their lunch break. At first, Chella rehearsed over and over in her mind what she would say to Jedan once they were alone, each time slightly differently, but however much she worked on her speech, it never sounded right, and eventually she forced herself to give up and allowed herself to enjoy the forest instead.

None of them had ever walked so far. Mostly they walked in silence. Sometimes they walked uphill, sometimes down; sometimes they stayed on the level for a while. The forest was strange, like an enormous living thing, and it felt to Chella like it must go on for ever in space and time. Its beauty was captivating. The trees changed from mostly deciduous to mostly evergreen, then back to deciduous again. It was a whole new, wild world. Huge purple rhododendron blooms broke up the never-ending green. Squirrels raced around in the trees; rabbits bobbed away when they heard them approach; birds and insects sang and buzzed incessantly.

"I hope we're not going round in circles," Jedan said, as the afternoon wore on. Chella looked round at him with wide eyes.

Jedan grinned at her expression. "Don't worry, I was only joking! I've got this," he said, showing her the compass in his hand. "And we can see the sun, too."

"That is not funny," Chella retorted, but couldn't help smiling when he made faces back at her.

"At least it's not raining, or muddy," observed Amma, as Jedan helped her lift the pramcot over a fallen branch. "And there's something else I've been thinking," she continued, as they gently laid the pramcot back down with its sleeping occupant, "nobody could possibly be following us now."

"Do you think so, Amma?" asked Jedan, looking back the way they had come, almost as if he expected to see someone following.

"I don't see how they could, with horses," said Amma, removing a twig from her hair, "even if they did know which way we'd gone. And if they were following us on foot, surely they would have caught us up by now? We would be so much slower than them, with the pramcot."

"Plus we stopped for lunch," added Chella.

Amma nodded. "Exactly!"

They smiled at each other. Could it be true that they were safe here? Safe from the Correctioners? Chella shivered as she remembered her brush with Sergeant Mahn, not so long ago, and breathed out a long breath at the thought of being away from that fear, at least. And did that mean that Solod could no longer reach her? Surely it must! At that thought she breathed in deeply, stretched herself a little higher and let it all out again with a big sigh. That truly was a massive relief.

"Shall we sing?" suggested Amma with a smile, as they began to walk again with a lighter step. "Out loud?"

"Great idea!" said Jedan. "Don't know why we didn't think of it before!"

"We're so used to having to whisper," agreed Amma.

"But not any more!" called back Jedan. So they began to sing, quietly at first, as it seemed so strange, then bolder as they got into the swing of it:

We are walking with the Spirit
We are running the race
We are seated with our God in heavenly places!
We are fighting the good fight
We are taking our stand,
We are building up our treasure in heavenly places!

We are walking, we are running, we are standing,
we are building, we are praising, thanking God
in heavenly places!

We are caring, we are giving, we are meeting,
we are praying, we are singing praise to God
in heavenly places!

Mikiah woke and laughed and clapped as they sang, over and over, faster and faster, louder and louder, until they were all laughing so much they could no longer sing. Amma then started an old hymn of praise. Chella's spirits rose as her heart soared to the words of truth. It was such a relief to think they were safe now from Correctioners, and she was safe from Solod.

But while they were singing the last triumphant verse, a crashing and running behind them made them turn.

FOURTEEN

The Ancient Road

Chella cried out. Jedan grabbed a stick and let out a yell, as a pack of wild dogs ran up the track behind the little group, then encircled them. Chella instinctively huddled with the others around the pramcot, facing the dogs. Amma leaned over the pramcot to protect the baby as the dogs began to growl. There were about twenty dogs, maybe more; large dogs with shaggy coats, baring their teeth and slathering. "Lord have mercy," Amma prayed as Mikiah woke and started to wail.

The dogs crept closer, tightening the circle. As they did, Chella took a step towards Amma to help protect the baby, but as she did she tripped on a root and stumbled into the pramcot. The dogs nearest Chella moved towards her, but as she scrambled back to her feet Jedan let out an almighty roar and ran at the dogs with his stick. Amma cried out, "Lord, save us!" Then the dogs turned and were gone as quickly as they had come, bounding off back down the track.

Mikiah clung to Amma and wailed in shock and fear.

Chella and Jedan clung to each other in silence, recovering their breath and their composure, as the sound of the running dogs crashing into the undergrowth faded into the distance and Mikiah's cries turned to whimpers. Chella suddenly noticed tears running down her cheeks. "Sorry I screamed," she said, taking deep breaths to calm her racing heart.

Amma let out a massive sigh as Mikiah's cries faded. "That's nothing to apologise for, my dear. My goodness, that was frightening."

"Perhaps we disturbed their sleep," said Jedan grimly. "I'm glad that's over."

"Yes indeed," agreed Amma. "People used to have dogs like that, a long time ago, as pets, or guard dogs. I guess these are the descendants of those who survived."

"Maybe this is their track we're on," added Chella.

Amma sighed again, loudly. "At least it wasn't people," she admitted. "My first thought was that it was Correctioners, even after what I just said. But praise the Lord, we're all safe."

Jedan nodded. "Yes, at least they've run away. Are you all right, Chella?"

She nodded, but after they set off again, Chella could feel the tension in the air. Suddenly the forest didn't seem such a benevolent place. It was breathtakingly beautiful, but it was wild, too.

It wasn't long before another yell from Jedan, who had gone a little way ahead, made Chella jump once more, and fear rise in a wave through her body. But this time it was good news. "Here it is!" he called back to the others. "Now we can really move," he added with a sweep of his arm, as they ran up to join him. "Look at this!"

Chella stared. A scar in the forest lurched from east to west, as far as the eye could see, as if a giant had gouged out a walkway through the forest with his finger. Vegetation was claiming back the ground at the edges, and vibrant green patches had broken through the grey desert, but there was no doubt about it, this was an ancient road.

"You see this grey stuff? It's called tarmac," said Jedan, stamping his feet on the surface. "It's what they used to make their roads of. It's why we have to shoe the horses the Elite ride, to protect their hooves. One reason, anyway."

"Oh!" exclaimed Chella, eyes wide. "Not this road, though?"

"No. This is an old country lane, if we're where I think we are on the map. I don't suppose anyone's been down this road for years." Chella bent down and ran her hand over the surface. It was hard, and real. She looked up to see Jedan watching her. His eyes were sparkling. "The Lord is making the way for us," he said. "We're doing well!"

"Walking on this old road will certainly make pushing the pramcot easier," agreed Amma, with relief in her voice. She gave the pramcot a little push, which sent it running along the road on its own. "We'll have to go round the holes and cracks, but goodness, see how easily the wheels run on the good bits!"

"It's amazing," agreed Chella, giving Amma a hug before picking her bags back up.

"We need to go this way," said Jedan, indicating the left. The gap in the trees went up and down, then snaked out of sight into the distance. It looked as if it would go on for ever, but it would take them towards their destination.

A thrill of hope cheered the weary group, and they began to sing again as they walked on the road, side by side, with the warm sun on their backs. The smoothness of the tarmac felt luxuriously flat under the soles of their shoes, and although the trees no longer sheltered them from the sun, a pleasant breeze blew down the channel the road made. Things *were* going well, thought Chella. Hope rose in her soul.

"The last time I walked on a road like this," mused Amma, "was when we walked to the Area. I was about your age then."

"Not this road?" asked Jedan.

Amma shook her head. "No, no, we lived on the other side of the Area. I've never been this way. I was born not long before the War started, so pretty much all travelling had come to an end by then. Farmers would come in on market day, but apart from that only Messengers went more than a few miles."

"So you had Messengers?" asked Jedan. "To give you all the news?"

"Yes, when I was small they came on horseback from the government, as it was then, to the town square. You'd have loved the horses, Jedan. I remember the day the Messengers came to tell us the War had ended – the church bells rang and everyone celebrated, all over the town."

"That must have been a special day!" said Jedan.

Amma nodded. "It was – the whole town was one big party, and we had a wonderful thanksgiving service at

76

church. So much joy, I can't tell you! The little children started dancing to the songs, then by the end of the service, everyone was joining in. For those who'd lost loved ones, it was bitter-sweet, but at least most people felt they had died protecting our freedom. A few days later our dad came home – he'd been away for months, and we'd missed him so much. It was the best thing *ever* – I can't tell you how good it was to have him back. We all slept together in our living room that first night – we couldn't bear to let him out of our sight. Oh yes, that *was* wonderful. It didn't mean the end of our troubles, though, as you know."

"You mean the Plague?" asked Chella.

"Yes. Everyone thought once the War was over, we would be able to rebuild our lives and everything would go back to how it had been before, but it didn't happen, of course. Our family was back together – we were fortunate. But then the Plague struck, and people carried on dying, except they were dying at home instead of dying away in the War, and food was even harder to come by than before. And everyone lived with the constant fear that the Plague would strike their family next. So many of my aunties and uncles and cousins died. . ." Amma's voice petered away into sadness. "And the Famine was terrible. There just weren't enough healthy people to grow food, or harvest it. We were constantly hungry."

"I had no idea it was that bad," Jedan said. "I'm so sorry, Amma. I didn't know you lost so much – so many people."

Amma sighed. "They were difficult times, for sure. We did have freedom to do and think and say whatever we wanted, though, and go where we wanted, and pray and go to church. Before the World Council was set up, I mean. There was never the feeling of being watched. It all seems so long ago now – a lifetime ago, really. But walking on this road makes me feel – I don't know, how can I describe it – some of that feeling of freedom coming back. Like, bonds are loosening. You know, no longer being watched. Freedom is a very precious thing. It's difficult to explain."

"I've never heard you talk about the Old Days," said Chella. "Grandad used to, all the time."

"Most of us buried away our knowledge of the Old Order, once we reached the Area," admitted Amma. "I don't know anyone who hadn't lost loved ones over the years. The memories were too raw to share, too deep. And for those of us who were Christians, how could we talk about those days without talking about the church? We had to be careful. People from our old town knew we were Christians, and might not have minded informing the authorities if they heard us talking about the church in the Area."

"Wow," said Jedan. "I had no idea what you went through. Maybe this evening, Amma, when we have found somewhere safe to stay, you could give us a history lesson? Tell us a bit about what life was like back then? It would help us understand."

"I can talk now, as we walk, if you like," Amma replied. "I've been thinking about staying in a house again, since we set out. Shall I tell you about my old house? It would save me from thinking about walking!"

"It would help us to stop thinking about it, too!" said Jedan with a laugh, and Chella smiled in agreement, so after a pause for water, Chella took over the pramcot, and Amma began.

"We lived in a proper house, with stairs on the inside to go up to the bedrooms and bathroom. It was in the middle of a row of houses. You've seen pictures, I'm sure, of the sort of thing." Amma smiled as they nodded. "I loved our home! It had soft carpets on the floors, a little garden in the front and a larger one at the back. We had two main rooms downstairs, and a separate kitchen."

Jedan whistled. "It sounds spacious!"

"It wasn't a big house for those days, but it was certainly bigger than our apartments in the Area. All the houses were the same in our street, on both sides, with a road down the middle."

"Did your family have a car?" asked Jedan.

Amma smiled and shook her head. "No, cars were before my time. They had all been taken away for scrap before I was born, I think, or maybe soon afterwards. We had an old bicycle we shared with our next-door neighbours, but mostly we walked everywhere. Not that we ever needed to go far. We grew food in our gardens – in every bit of it. Between the rows of vegetables we'd grow herbs, to make the most of the space."

Jedan looked surprised. "Oh, I thought the gardens were for flowers, and lawns?"

"How old do you think I am?" replied Amma with a laugh. "No, we had to grow food. The Famine wasn't as terrible where we were, as I've heard it was in other places, but still, we had to work hard to grow enough food to live. In our little garden we grew potatoes mostly, and other

79

vegetables when we could get the seeds or plants. Things like beans and peas, carrots and leeks. . . and we had chickens in a little coup. Oh, and we grew tomatoes in the summer when we could get the plants. Mm, those tomatoes! It's strange, but even now the smell of fresh tomatoes takes me straight back to our garden. It was my job to weed the vegetables, and feed the chickens. And we had a pear tree at the bottom of the garden. Those pears were so fresh and sweet – makes my mouth water just thinking about them!"

"What did people do who didn't have gardens?" asked Chella. "Some people had apartments even then, didn't they?"

"Yes indeed. We all swapped things. Everyone did. Like, some people had chickens, some kept rabbits, some just grew vegetables. If you didn't have a garden you could do work for someone and get meat or whatever in kind, or people made clothes or quilts and exchanged them for food. That sort of thing. People with larger gardens kept animals, and our local park became a communal field to graze animals. Older children used to take the little ones out to play, but we used to have to watch out for sheep and goats! And there was the bee man, as we used to call him, who went round the streets selling honey from a big barrel in his wheelbarrow. Everyone ran with their pots and jars to get a ladle full, when they heard his trumpet! He was a funny little man. He had the most enormous eyebrows and was always a bit surly – I was afraid of him. But his honey was a treat."

"It sounds like a different world," said Chella.

"It was," agreed Amma. "It feels like a lifetime ago."

80

"So did you have proper bedrooms in your house?" asked Jedan.

"Yes, three, upstairs, and we had a bathroom, too, just for our family."

"Wow," said Jedan with a low whistle. "Maybe we'll find a house like that to stay in tonight! Imagine that!"

"That would be so strange, after all these years of nothing but apartments. Ours wasn't the poshest part of town, but we had proper beds upstairs, even for us children, and proper settees downstairs to sit on. Nobody had to sleep on bedsettees in the living room, or trundle beds. There was a lot more space."

"What did you like most about how things used to be?" asked Chella, thinking how strange it would be to live in a house with two floors.

"Hmm, that's a tough question," said Amma. "Apart from freedom, friends, I think. I had so many friends at school, at church and in the street. We were in and out of each others houses all the time. That was before the War took so many people, and the Plague and the Famine really hit, of course. Then people were dying every week. Schools and shops closed. Wagons stopped bringing food after the government collapsed. Anyone still alive had to concentrate on growing food for themselves, and look after the sick."

"Goodness," said Chella, shaking her head. "So much suffering. We knew lots of people died, of course, but hearing about it out here, makes it feel, I don't know, so much more real, somehow."

Amma nodded and sighed. "Being here is bringing it back to me, too. People were taking in orphans all the time.

81

We took in a little brother and sister from a Japanese family who used to live down the road – Sen and Daus they were called. As thin as pencils, they were. They died within a few hours of each other. My dad said they died of broken hearts. The day we buried them was the saddest day of my life, I think. Up until that time, anyway. People were dying all round us. It got so bad, we prayed Jesus would come back and take us. I remember a time when I cried every day. Day after day we buried people we loved. Family, friends, church family, neighbours. . . I didn't think misery like that could exist."

"Amma, I had no idea things were that bad," said Jedan, shaking his head.

"I didn't know it was like that, either," admitted Chella. "Grandad only talked about how wonderful everything was back in the Old Days!"

Amma sighed. "Perhaps things were easier where he lived. Maybe the Plague didn't hit as hard. And, to be honest, he was probably looking back to the time before the War. He was quite a bit older than me."

They paused for a minute, as Amma stopped to give Mikiah a different rattle to play with and Chella shared out some of Lavitah's biscuits: glad to have a moment's relief from the bags. She looked round at the silent road, and the unending trees, and tried to imagine cars full of families driving up and down the road, and people out walking, like them, but for fun. It almost didn't seem real, but it was. Now there was just the wind and the sky and the never-ending trees.

"When were the churches closed, Amma?" asked Jedan as they set off again. "Was it before the War, or after?"

"After the War, and after the Plague. During the Plague hardly anyone went to church, because you didn't want to spread anything, but you could still go if you wanted. The churches weren't properly shut until the World Council was set up in Year 0001, although there were precious few of us left by then, anyway."

"Didn't the Christians want to stay in your town?"

"Some did, some didn't. If we'd all stayed, we could perhaps have set up our own community – in fact, I've been thinking – that's probably how this Old Church in Anderley was set up. Maybe the remaining Christians from several towns and villages got together."

Jedan nodded. "That would explain everything. I can't wait to get there and find out!"

Amma smiled at them both. "Yes! Me too!"

Chella smiled as well. Suddenly the Old Church seemed a bit nearer. Perhaps Christians really had stayed in some of the towns and villages, and lived together in peace. When Jedan had talked about it in the Area, it had seemed impossible. Now it seemed so much more likely. The thought that they might have to go into hiding with the Church once they reached Anderley was too much to contemplate, so she brushed that thought right away. Today had enough problems of its own.

"Did your family go to the Area straight away?" Jedan asked Amma.

"No, we didn't go until the summer of Year 0003. We managed to eke out an existence after most people had left, but by then we were living pretty much as peasants, and there was only a handful of us left. We had to dig a well for water, and there was no medical help. Growing food and collecting firewood became all-consuming tasks. How long can you carry on like that? Almost everyone else from the church had died or left by then, anyway. Eventually we left because my brother and sister were sick – they needed to see a doctor."

"I didn't know you had a brother and sister!" exclaimed Chella.

Amma paused. "Sadly, it was too late to get help – they died on the way to the Area. Then Mum and Dad joined them, not so long after."

"Oh Amma," whispered Chella. There was a silence, punctuated only by the call of birds, the whisper of the trees, and the rumble of the pramcot wheels on the road.

"I'm so sorry," said Jedan after a while.

Amma sighed. "I missed them all so much, I can't tell you. The emptiness of them going, one after the other... Talking about it makes me feel the weight of loss all over again. And now I've lost Nidala and Hamani, as well as Andan." Her voice caught, and they walked in silence for a while – a silence too deep for words.

"I'm so glad the Lord spared you," Chella said, pausing to pick up yet another of Mikiah's toys from the road. "Honestly, I don't know what Dad and me would have done without you, after mum disappeared."

"Thank you my dear," said Amma, stopping to wipe her eyes and blow her nose. "Of all my family, I am the only one left now. And Nidala and Hamani, if they are still alive."

"And Mikiah," added Chella.

"Yes, Mikiah! In my heart I know this is right for him. I've been thinking about it as we've been walking. I'm doing the opposite of my parents. They brought me to the Area so I could live. I'm leaving so he can live, but it's so hard, knowing Nidala may still be there. Every step further away from the Area is another step away from her, and Hamani, too. It's perhaps the hardest thing I have ever had to do. On the one hand, I long to reach the Old Church, for Mikiah's sake, even if it means going into hiding with them. But leaving Nidala is such a huge wrench. Perhaps it's a good thing I didn't have too long to think about it. Even though many never see their loved ones again, all the while there is no news, there is hope. And maybe Nidala and Hamani are working in the Powerhouse, as Jedan did, waiting for their own miracle."

Chella sighed. "Oh, Amma," she said. "Why does there have to be so much sadness in this world?"

"You know why, Child," answered Amma, her voice thick with emotion. "But you know it won't be this way always."

FIFTEEN

Lengthening Shadows

As afternoon turned to evening the little group stopped under the trees for a proper rest, and for Mikiah to have a break from his pramcot. Jedan checked the compass and the map. Amma sat in the soft leaf litter with her back against a tree and closed her eyes while Chella supervised Mikiah. His eyes were wide as he looked up at the waving tree tops, then went crawling in the leaves. He found a pine cone, turned it over and over in his chubby hands, then tested it out with his mouth. He pulled himself up on a log and babbled cheerfully as he bounced up and down, then when he started to yawn, Chella sat him back in his pramcot and gave him a piece of bread roll, and some slices of apple and cheese.

While Mikiah was eating, Chella sat next to Jedan and rested her head on his shoulder. He didn't speak, but stroked her hair, and she felt his love through the gentle touch. Now, she thought – now I will tell him about Solod. Her heart banged in her chest as she carefully repeated the first phrase she had been rehearsing. "I need to talk to you about something that happened last year, before I met you," she whispered, touching his hand with hers.

"Maybe later?" he replied, passing her the map as he reached for a slice of cheese. "Would you mind holding this for a minute?"

Chella took the map out of his hand, her next sentence hanging in the air, unspoken. His words threw her off balance. He had never been very good at listening when he had something on his mind, and he never wanted to talk about the past, but still, she hadn't expected him to brush her off quite so completely. Before she could think how to carry on, he was already pointing out the ancient village of Tadworth.

"I don't think we can be far from this settlement now," he told her, indicating a little knot on the map. She wanted to stop him and try to get him to listen, but couldn't find the words, so in the end she just nodded. "We'll try to find shelter there," Jedan continued, seemingly oblivious to the reason for her silence. "I think we should walk as fast as we can, to get there before nightfall."

Amma opened her eyes and yawned. "It would be good to find a house to stay in," she said sleepily, "or any kind of shelter, really. The thought of those dogs worries me a bit. Although I'm not sure how fast I'll be able to walk."

Chella nodded, trying to take her thoughts off her dashed hopes of coming clean with Jedan. Spending the night in an ancient house would be strange, but it had to be an infinitely better prospect than trying to sleep in the forest in the dark. Who knew what other wild beasts roamed at night, along with the dogs?

"The Lord will help us," said Jedan, jumping to his feet and giving Amma a hand up.

"I'm sure he will," agreed Amma, stifling another yawn.

And so they walked on, their shadows lengthening in front of them on the old tarmac road. The cool smell of evening wafted on the breeze, and Chella was glad of her warmer shawl. Despite her weariness, she remembered her promise to Nidala, and helped as much as she could with Mikiah. She took turns to push the pramcot, and even when Amma was pushing, she picked up the toys Mikiah continually threw out, and tried to keep him amused with rhymes and songs.

Where were Nidala and Hamani? Chella wondered, as they trudged on. Were they in the Correction Facility, as Amma suspected? Did they work silently in the Powerhouse? Nobody knew where arrested people went after being detained – if someone went missing you just had to pray for them; there was nothing else you could do. But she also knew that sometimes they were "despatched". She had learnt that word much more recently, but kept the knowledge to herself, partly because she never talked about that part of her life, and partly because she feared to know the truth.

She knew more about the Elite than she cared to remember. The Elite of Area IF208, and, as far as Chella knew, in every Dwelling Area in the world, kept people informed of everything they wanted them to know, with their booming voices through loudspeakers on every floor of every apartment block. What they didn't want you to know, they kept to themselves.

One thing she knew for certain, was that when the

loudspeakers told them there was equality, they weren't speaking the truth.

Everyone knew that the War, the Plague, and the Famine had nearly wiped humankind from the earth, such was the devastation. And everyone knew that the new Areas were constructed following a master plan set up by the World Council. Poverty was then eradicated across the globe, so they were told. A new era had dawned. They were still informed of this fact, over the loudspeakers, at least once a week. No longer were there people who had nowhere to live and nothing to eat, the loudspeakers assured them. There were no refugees, no street children, no slavery. The "trinity of evils", religion, violence and ownership, were eradicated from this time forward. Now everyone lived in harmony for the sake of the common good. The Areas were held up to be the height of fairness, but Chella knew that wasn't true. She knew the Elite lived in luxury, with foreign servants to wait on them, while the Workers simply lived. She had seen it for herself.

The Elite had separate gardens, separate Parkland, separate shops, separate schools, separate everything. They worked separately, lived separately and kept themselves away from the Workers. The Area Council worked in a building not accessible to Workers. And the photographs of the Councillors, which took pride of place in all the public buildings, were ancient: surely those men and women must have been replaced by a new government, many years ago?

Something else that anyone could read from history books was that there was once a time when ordinary people had choices and freedom. No such thing existed any more.

Nobody said anything, though, about lack of choice and freedom, or wanting things to be different – not in Area IF208, anyway, since Dareve Bilton's movement had been crushed. Criticism of the World Council was not helpful if you wished to progress beyond cleaner, farm labourer, wood chopper or groom.

After a while, as the little group pressed on, Mikiah began to whimper. Even his favourite cuddly piglet didn't soothe him. "It's all so strange for him," Amma excused him. But there was nothing they could do about it, they had to go on.

Amma always smiled when Chella looked at her, even when she was too tired to speak, but as the evening wore on, her smiles grew more and more strained. Chella's thoughts often turned to Amma's sadness at losing so many of her family. What a terrible time she had lived through! Chella understood the emptiness and pain of grief, and felt humbled at Amma's faith and trust in God, even through so much suffering.

So they walked on. Although Chella's legs ached, she tried to concentrate instead on the beauty of the forest: the variety of the trees; the rhododendrons blazing with colour; honeysuckle releasing sweet fragrance into the warm air; the sun's rays streaming through the canopy; squirrels running and jumping; the never-ending birdsong. There was a harmony, and a sense of steadfastness about the forest that was solid and unshakeable. Still, since their encounter with the dogs, she was under no illusion that despite its glory, it was still part of fallen creation.

As they pressed on after Mikiah's usual bedtime, his

whimpers turned to proper cries. They all tried to cheer him up with toys and food and milk and songs and rhymes, but in the end they had to leave him crying, until at last he fell asleep.

Jedan stopped more and more often to look at the map. "Is everything OK?" Chella asked, as Jedan stopped once again at a bend in the road.

He frowned. "I hope we're on the right road. I would have thought we would have come across the village by now. I hope we haven't missed it. It's possible, I suppose, that it's been completely swallowed up by the forest."

Chella looked round at the never-ending trees in every direction, hoping to see something, anything, that might show they were near the village, but there was nothing. Her heart sank. Surely they wouldn't have to spend the night in the forest?

SIXTEEN

Darkness and Light

They knelt on that strange road, surrounded by tall trees, and prayed for the Lord's help, and then decided by mutual consent to keep walking until it was completely dark, hoping to have found shelter of some sort by then. There was no other plan.

The sun slowly dropped below the level of the trees behind them as they pressed on. Chella was so tired she thought she would drop. Her bag seemed a dead weight, and her arm throbbed, but the only thing that mattered was to keep walking – they had to find somewhere to rest.

Then Jedan pointed out something in the shadows in the distance. "Look! Chimneys, through the trees! That's got to be a house!" he yelled. They all put on a spurt of energy and ran to the house.

It was the first Old Order house Chella had ever seen. A stone wall, just visible through a creeping vine, separated the house from the road. A riot of bushes and trees surrounded the house itself, as if protecting it from harm.

"A real house!" breathed Jedan. "Made of those old

bricks! And it's *huge* – look at the size of it! This is so amazing! It is just one house, Amma, is that right?"

"Yes, it looks like it," said Amma, catching her breath. "I never thought I would see a house again!" she added, staring at the old building in the evening shadows, shaking her head. "A lovely one, too, this would have been. A proper country house. A cottage, really, I suppose."

Chella nodded. The house was a truly awesome sight, even in the twilight. A riot of fragrant pink roses almost smothered the front of the lower storey. There must have been a path to the front door a long time ago, but it was now invisible under a muddle of roses and brambles. The brick walls of the house rose up to dark rafters, with windows upstairs that seemed to smile at them. Part of the wall had crumbled and one of the windows was broken, but it held an aura of peace and tranquillity.

"Can we stay in this one, do you think?" asked Amma, hopefully. "I'm not sure I can walk much further!"

"It's beautiful," breathed Chella. She wondered about the family who used to live in that house before age and neglect had taken it; parents keeping an eye on children running and laughing in that garden, in sunshine and freedom. Perhaps this was what had really happened, before the War. She put down her bag to ease her aching arms and shoulders, and squeezed Amma's hand as they stood and took it all in.

Jedan tried to walk round the house, but came back shaking his head. "There's no way in; the undergrowth is too thick all the way round. But if this is the beginning of the village, ladies," he added, "there will be more houses. We just need to keep going. It may not be much further now."

He was right. After a few more paces he dumped his bags again and ran to a rusting piece of metal tangled in a bush at the side of the road. "Tadworth!" he called, sounding both relieved and excited as he pushed creepers away from the old sign. "We've made it!"

"Oh, praise the Lord," said Amma with a sigh, stopping to tuck a blanket over Mikiah as the temperature continued to drop. "I really do need to rest my weary bones. I have never felt so sorry for the Israelites in the desert, as I do right now! So many times I have wanted to complain today and remembered them and tried so hard not to."

"How are your sandals?" asked Jedan with a grin.

Amma laughed. "Shoes! They've not worn out yet!"

"Shall we sing again?" suggested Chella, as more dark dwellings began to loom up out of the gloom. "This place is so lonely. So empty." She gazed from left to right, swallowing hard at the strangeness of it all.

Amma nodded. "That's my girl! What shall we sing? I'm so tired I'm not sure I have the breath to sing, but if you do, it will bring such encouragement."

"I wonder if we should approach quietly?" suggested Jedan. "Just in case there are people living here?"

"I hadn't thought of that," Amma replied in alarm. "I hope we haven't made too much noise already."

Chella felt a sudden wave of panic, and looked around for moving shadows. But Jedan smiled, and pointed out a low stone wall in front of what must have been, at one time, a house or a garden or a park, or perhaps the village square.

"Why don't you three wait here, while I check things out? I won't go far, and I won't be long," he promised. "Perhaps there will be a church building we can sleep in!"

As Jedan walked away into the darkness of the night, Amma and Chella made a pile of their luggage at the foot of the old wall. They quietly got their warm cloaks out of their bags and wrapped them round themselves, as a blackbird sang its final evening song. Chella held the cross her dad had made her in the palm of her hand as she and Amma settled on the ancient wall.

The fragrance of the night air hung around them. Amma picked up Mikiah and cradled him as he began to stir, then rocked him in her arms while Chella sang gentle lullabies, until he fell asleep again. When she stopped singing, the hugeness of the darkness filled her soul. Somewhere nearby a fox barked, and another returned its call, further away. It made goose bumps prick up on her skin, and she shivered as a chill breath of air ruffled her hair and skirt.

"Chella, can I share something with you?" Amma asked softly.

"Of course."

"Look around you, Chella – everything looks so dark, doesn't it?"

"Yes, I hope Jedan comes back soon; the night is deepening," Chella agreed, gazing around at the fearful, solid darkness of the forest, and the looming shadows of the unknown village, hiding who knew what terrors? It was dark in every sense of the word.

Amma breathed in deeply. "Every so often, in the last

few years, I have had a recurring dream. It may be nothing more than a dream, but it has been a comfort to me."

"A dream in your sleep?"

"Yes. In my dream, I'm sitting on a bench, in a garden – not exactly like this, but close enough. I'm not in the Area, anyway – I can feel the space. As I sit on the bench, the sun sets, and darkness begins to close in around me. I feel how the bushes and trees are getting dark and cold, surrounding me, pressing in. There's a feeling of foreboding as I sit there in the gathering darkness."

Chella nodded, looking around. It was so dark, she could almost feel the dream herself. "Like this?"

"Yes, so very much like this. But then, in my dream, I look up, and the sky is still light. Look up, Chella – see how different it is?"

Chella looked up and opened her eyes wide in surprise. She expected the sky to be black, but it was a glorious shade of turquoise blue. "That's amazing," she whispered. "It's so light up there!"

"In my dream, I know I need to keep looking up, no matter how dark it seems here on earth."

There was a silence as both women gazed up at the sky, then around them at the darkness, then back at the night sky again.

"It's as if the Lord has been preparing me for this time," Amma continued. "I feel like this is it, this is my dream. I need to keep looking up."

Chella's eyes widened. "So you think the Lord knew this long ago? That we would be here? That this was all part of his plan? That he gave you this dream in advance?"

"Yes, Child, it does seem so."

"Amma, do you not have any doubts about what we are doing?"

Amma pursed her lips and was silent for a moment before speaking. "There have been times today I have wondered if I have made a terrible mistake. Everything happened so quickly... us leaving... we hardly had time to think. Lavitah was absolutely right about the pramcot – it wasn't made for a journey such as this, yet I simply dismissed her sensible objections. What was I thinking of?"

Amma tucked Mikiah's blanket closer around him and shook her head slightly. "Here we are, in the middle of nowhere, with dangers on every side and only enough food and milk for a couple of days. Yes, I have doubts. And if I'm honest, at times I do feel afraid. But now, sitting here, remembering that dream... it gives me courage. Chella, we need to remember we were sent with the blessing of the church. And we must never forget the Lord is our everlasting light. We need to keep looking up, even when the darkness seems to be falling around us, surrounding us."

"It is so dark here!"

"There's nothing we can do about that. But look up, Child, look again."

Chella had looked down, but looked up again to the heavens, and kept her gaze there for a while. "So many stars!" she breathed. As she kept her gaze upwards, more and more stars appeared, until it seemed as if the sky was full of light and she felt a deep stillness reach out and touch her soul. She could almost hear Jesus saying, *"Why are you afraid, O you of little faith?"*

How amazing that Amma had had that dream! Surely there was no place on earth they could flee from the presence of God – even here.

SEVENTEEN

The Past

Jedan was in the year below Chella at school, but she didn't remember him from their school days. After their first meeting at the Christmas service, Amma had encouraged their friendship. She knew how lonely Chella had been since her father had died, and knew her brief fling with Solod had ended badly.

Chella hadn't noticed Jedan watching her during the service, but as she prepared to leave with Julip and Nidala, he had asked to walk her home. Old Erimah had smiled at her, and nodded, and she had blushed.

Even on that first walk home when they were both too shy to say much, there was an energy between them she couldn't explain, and she knew she had met the man she would be with, until Jesus came or called them.

Their friendship grew as they met and talked. They ate together in the Dining Hall, spent time in her apartment or walked in the Parkland, and Jedan joined her history group.

Jedan wasn't new to the faith, exactly. He had heard the good news of Jesus through Amma, many years ago.

Many parents shooed their children outside to give them a bit of peace and quiet, but Amma often spent time in the Playpark. Occasionally she told a story about Jesus; not that she could ever mention his name, of course: she called him the Good Shepherd.

The children in the Playpark got to know Amma: they would come to her when they fell over, talk to her when they felt alone, ask her to be the judge when they had disputes about whose turn it was to be the queen, the pirate, the teacher, or the Head of the Council.

"She had the friendliest face I had ever seen," Jedan told Chella once. "I was jealous of Nidala, having a mum who spent time with her, and laughed, and sometimes joined in the games." They wondered if they might have met back then, because Nidala and Chella had often played together, but neither of them could really remember.

They laughed together as they reminisced about those days. The swings, the slide, the roundabout and the climbing frame would be a desert island, or a dragon's lair, or a hospital where the patients died of the Plague, or were nursed back to health.

Amma used the opportunity when she was sitting in the park to pray for the children, but not openly. Only to those who seemed that the Lord was drawing to himself, would she speak more freely, and then only a little at a time. Jedan was one of those. He was constantly asking questions, Amma told Chella. He wouldn't be fobbed off with anything that didn't seem quite right, and wanted to know if the Good Shepherd was real. So Jedan had heard the gospel, little by little.

"He thought deeply about everything I told him," Amma had told Chella with a smile and a shake of her head. "I could see the Holy Spirit was at work in him. So when he asked if he could be a follower of the Good Shepherd, like James and John, Andrew and Peter, I didn't feel I could refuse. So I taught him to pray the prayer of Jesus, as Jesus taught his disciples."

"Amma, you are a fisher of people, and you have fished me," he had said afterwards, before running off to play. She admitted afterwards that she feared for Jedan's young faith, and for her own safety, but continued to pray that the Lord would preserve them both.

One day Jedan stopped coming to the Playpark. Amma didn't know it at the time, but when his parents found out that he had been listening to religious stories, they withdrew all privileges for a long time, and forbade him ever to mention anything to do with religion ever again. Amma didn't know why he no longer came, but she continued to pray that his faith wouldn't fail and that he would keep, and read, the handwritten Bible stories she had given him. He did read them in secret for a while, with his brother, although he admitted to Chella that it was partly because they were forbidden that they were alluring!

Then he had met Amma again by chance, last summer, in the Library. His faith had taken a step back over the years, but after talking with her again, he re-dedicated his life to Christ and joined the church in his Block. He was baptised in secret, over the far side of the lake, with just two witnesses, as every new believer had been since the New Order.

After he and Chella started dating, Old Erimah had taken him under his wing. "Our Lord is the one who is able to keep anyone from falling, and to complete the work he has begun in us," Erimah reminded Chella one day. "He kept Jedan, when humanly speaking, all appeared to be lost. It is a great encouragement." It seemed, even then, that the Lord had something special for Jedan to do.

At first, Chella was reticent to open up her heart to him, but Jedan was so different from Solod, and she allowed herself to fall deeply in love. She loved his energy and earnestness, the way he threw himself wholeheartedly into everything he did.

Chella did mention her relationship with Solod, without saying his name, but skipped over that period of her life as quickly as possible. How she wished that she had told Jedan everything in the beginning! However painful it might have been at the time, it couldn't be as bad as carrying this awful secret in her heart. There were things about Jedan's past he didn't want to talk about, either, Chella guessed. He had admitted to being a rebel in the past, but if she pressed him he always changed the subject. She understood. Some things were just too painful to put into words.

Chella's heart beat faster as she heard Jedan's footsteps running back to where she and Amma still sat on the strange old wall. "Good news and bad news!" he called out. "The bad news is, the church building has long been abandoned, along with the rest of the village. The good news is, I've found a dry place for us to sleep, in a house!"

Amma let out a big breath. "Praise the Lord, Jehovah

Jireh, our Provider," she said, sliding off the wall and placing Mikiah gently back in his pramcot. "Knowing He is taking care of us out here is a great comfort."

"It is," agreed Chella, and meant it with all her heart.

Jedan nodded as he helped Chella with her bags. "I must admit, I'm looking forward to getting settled for the night, however strange. It's been a long day."

The house was in a turning just off the main road; it was the first in a group of several houses in a semi-circle. "This is what they used to call a close," Amma told them, looking round. "The road doesn't go anywhere, it's here for access to these houses."

"How strange," said Jedan, but Chella just looked. Now dark and overgrown, the houses surrounded them as if they were begging for help. Some of the dark windows had jagged edges; they looked as if they were silently screaming, forlorn and abandoned, slowly being strangled by the jungle that must have once been neat front gardens. The front of the first house had fared better – an old, gnarled tree had broken up the concrete, but the jungle hadn't yet claimed the house itself.

"We need to go through here," Jedan explained, indicating a dark passageway at the side of the first house. "I couldn't get in the front door, but there's another door round the back."

Chella's heart beat faster as she turned to follow the others in the dark, over the tree roots and broken concrete, under a little arch, into the narrow passageway and round to the back of the house. *I'm going to sleep in a house*, she thought.

EIGHTEEN

Sleeping in a House

The back door creaked and groaned as Jedan pulled it open. "The lock gave way," he explained to the others. "It was the first wooden door I came to. Most of them round here seem to be made of plastic; impossible to open, even after all these years."

After helping Amma up the step with the pramcot, he led the way into what had once been a kitchen, through a dark hall, then into one of the downstairs rooms. "It's the best room here," Jedan informed Chella and Amma, upending the torch on the window sill, then lighting a candle and setting it carefully down on the mantelpiece. "I could only open one window, but I hope it will get rid of the dusty smell a bit. We can close it later, if you like."

"This will be fine," said Amma with a sigh and a smile. "You've done well, Jedan. It's shelter from the elements, and it's only for a night."

It would have been a fabulous room many years ago, Chella decided, catching her breath as she looked round it in the flickering candlelight. It was rectangular, and spacious, with two large windows to the front and a smaller one to the side. It was empty now, apart from a fireplace with a simple wooden mantelpiece, and the remains of curtains hanging in tattered shreds at the windows. It was evidently a shadow of what it once had been. Long, thick cobwebs vied with peeling wallpaper for wall space. Chunks of plaster lay in heaps where they had crumbled away from the walls, and a layer of dust covered the threadbare carpet. The air smelt damp and stale. It was still, though, and even with the window open it was warmer than outside, and peaceful, and safe from wild animals. The silence almost sang.

Jedan lit another two candles, so they could see a bit better. Mikiah woke, so while Amma fed and changed him, Chella and Jedan set to work to clean a bit of floor space for them to sleep on, with a broom and a dustpan and brush Jedan found in a kitchen cupboard.

"Our first ever holiday!" said Jedan after a sneezing fit, as he swept up the debris Chella had gathered in a heap.

She smiled back, and Amma said, "The only people in the world to be having a holiday, perhaps!"

Chella thought about that while she swept — the world was so vast. Was it really possible that everyone in the whole world now lived in Areas? That nobody lived outside of the World Council's law? That nobody had holidays? What about in other countries, other continents? Did the World Council's laws really extend over the whole globe? Or were there people still living independently in houses like these? Or in any sort of dwellings, come to that. Was it possible that the Old Church in Anderley lived in houses like these, still today? Did they have holidays? She knew the loudspeakers told lies. Perhaps there was a lot more truth that the Area Council either weren't broadcasting, or didn't know. Maybe there were other people going wherever they wanted, outside of the official Areas. There was no way of telling, but the thought gave Chella hope.

It was a strange feeling being inside an old house; almost like they had gone back in time, to an era of freedom Chella had never known. Now she and Amma and Jedan could pray out loud, make choices, go where they wanted to go, do what they wanted to do, and surely no one could find them here? Sleeping in this ancient house would be odd, but in a strange way she might be safer here than in her old apartment, Chella decided. She stopped sweeping for a minute and touched the top of her arm where the Correctioner had pinched it. It was still sore. Maybe she would never see a Correctioner ever again. She could almost *feel* that freedom.

A cry made her turn round. "Oh!" said Amma, lifting her hands in the air. "I don't know why I didn't think of it before! There may be emergency supplies in a cupboard somewhere."

Jedan had turned round, too, from where he had been sweeping the floor in front of the hearth. "Did you say *emergency supplies*?"

"Yes, I can't believe I've only just thought about it – it shows how tired I am. It was standard practice for every household, even after the war was over, to keep a supply of things like tinned food and bottles of water, bedding, medicines and toiletries and all those sorts of things, in a sealed chest. Then if you had to evacuate in a hurry, you had the essentials to hand."

Jedan's eyes gleamed. "Really? I'll go and look. Any idea where I might find the box, Amma?"

"Well, we had ours in the cupboard under the stairs, but it might be in an outhouse or something. It would definitely be on the ground floor, so it could be picked up quickly."

Chella frowned. "But wouldn't the people who lived here have taken the box when they left?"

There was a pause. "They might have died," Amma said, then added quickly, "or gone to stay with relatives."

Chella nodded. "That's true, but all the furniture has gone. . ."

"Yes, I expect the furniture was used for firewood, but many people left the emergency boxes, if they didn't need them, in case someone came in and needed shelter in a hurry."

"Well, that's us!" said Jedan with a grin. "I'll go on a search, see what I can find. There are a lot of things left in cupboards all over the house." Picking up the torch he headed for the door, and returned a few minutes later dragging a wooden chest. "This it?" he asked, pulling the box in front of the hearth. "It looks like a treasure chest!"

Amma laughed. "Yes, that's it!" she said, running over with Mikiah in her arms. "Smaller than I remember, but that's definitely it! They were standard government issue."

The chest was so tightly sealed it took Jedan a few minutes to prise it open. They all sat round on the floor and peered in as he took out one item after another, all sealed up in thick, clear plastic bags. Chella took Mikiah from

Amma, who opened each bag carefully. "Oh, look at this!" she exclaimed at every new find. A cake of soap wrapped in a flannel, four new toothbrushes, a tube of toothpaste that had gone hard, a first aid kit, plastic bottles of water, canned food and a can opener. There were four soft grey blankets at the bottom of the chest, with a satin edge which had begun to disintegrate, and four blue towels which still looked as good as new.

"It's all exactly as I remember," marvelled Amma, shaking her head, as she reached the bottom of the chest. "We had a box just like this one. Even after the War ended, we kept it, just in case. We used to check it every year, and replace all the perishables. In fact, it's probably still in our old house!"

"It's amazing," whispered Chella, as Mikiah snuggled into one of the blankets. He laughed and smiled, sensing the others' excitement. And suddenly Chella was glad they were taking Mikiah to a place where he would be safe. *Lord, if nothing else*, Chella prayed silently, *please help us for Mikiah's sake.* The Church had to exist, it had to.

"I don't think we should attempt the food," Amma warned, as Jedan turned his attention to the cans. "Goodness knows how long they've been here."

"Good point," replied Jedan with regret in his voice as he checked the labels on the cans by the light of the candles on the hearth.

Amma smiled. "There should be a use-by date stamped on them."

"I can't make anything out," he admitted. "The labels are too faded. Shame. You're right, Amma; better not risk it. We might end up eating pet food!" They all grimaced at each other and laughed at that thought.

"The blankets are a blessing though," said Chella, holding one up to her face. "They smell a bit of the plastic, but they're so thick and soft."

"They are the best find, for sure," agreed Amma. "We can lay them on the floor in place of a mattress. Keep us off the dust a bit."

Chella nodded, clapping hands with Mikiah while he babbled away, stopping him from crawling on the dusty floor. "Mikiah can play on one for a while, and I can use these towels for cleaning!" she added with a smile, getting up and handing Mikiah back to Amma.

There was a buzz of excitement at their find. Jedan shook the blankets outside to air them a little, then he lit a fire in an old metal fire pit he had found in the garden, to heat up some water for a cup of tea. Chella tied one of the towels on the end of the broom to get rid of some of the biggest cobwebs off the ceiling, so they didn't fall on them as they slept, while Amma kept an eye on Mikiah. He was mesmerised by the candles, staring at them like a moth to a flame, and watched everything with round eyes.

When they had done what they could to make the room habitable, and the water had boiled, the travellers sat by candlelight on the soft blankets, drinking their tea and enjoying a final meal of bread and butter, and the hard boiled eggs that Lavitah had cooked that morning.

They talked over their day as they ate: the early morning prayer meeting; Jedan's escape and arrival at Amma's flat; packing up and leaving the Area; Chella's talk with the

Correctioners; Jott's pancakes; their long walk. What an eventful day it had been! "The Lord is still with us, even here!" said Amma, with a mixture of awe and wonder in her voice. It sounded silly, because of course he was, but Chella knew exactly what she meant. When they had finished eating, Chella gathered all the food they had left; it fitted easily into one bag, and the cheese was soft. Still, by the Lord's grace they had already done well.

When Mikiah had finished his milk and Amma had tucked him up in his pramcot, Jedan got out the map again. "We've come over a third of the way," he decided, measuring out the distance with his finger and thumb. "Now we're on proper roads, we'll be able to go faster. The forest slowed us down, for sure."

Chella nodded, and yawned as she leaned over his shoulder. They would have to stay on the same country road for a little while the next day, then they would meet what looked like a wider, straighter road and turn on to it. Anderley still seemed like a long way off, but Chella felt encouraged. "Do you think we might make it to Anderley tomorrow?"

"I'd like to think so," replied Jedan. "We'll be passing through several other villages, by the look of it, so there will be options if we need to stay somewhere overnight again." Chella vowed to herself to walk as fast as she could the following day, and help Amma with the pramcot any time she looked tired. The sooner they got to Anderley and the Church, the better.

After washing with bottled water from the chest, they got on their knees to pray. They started with thanks to the

Lord for helping them thus far. They moved on to praying for safety for their journey. They prayed for the church they had left behind, for the Old Church they were heading towards, and for the worldwide family of believers in Jesus, of whom they were a small part.

Mikiah still hadn't fallen asleep, so after their prayers Chella rocked the pramcot and began to sing gentle songs of worship. The others joined in – Amma with her sweet alto and Jedan finding the deep notes, until Mikiah's eyes closed and his breathing became deep and peaceful.

A beautiful silence filled the room after they finished singing. The stillness was so complete that it almost seemed as if the angels were singing with them. They prayed the Evening Prayer aloud together before Jedan blew out the last candle, then they settled down to sleep on the soft blankets, with the towels rolled up for pillows, and shawls and cloaks to cover them.

There were no loudspeakers, no neighbours in the flats above or below or next door, nobody talking outside, no footsteps on the walkways. A whole new world beckoned.

NINETEEN

Plan for the Future

Chella slept fitfully. Her arms and legs ached, and all the sounds of the night were unfamiliar – the rustling of the bushes, the night animals' calls, the scraping of the branches of the trees on the windows. The air was dusty and damp, and the floor was hard.

As Chella slept, she dreamt that Odina was calling her home to work for the common good, that Jedan had left the Area without her, that Mikiah was screaming as he was taken away from Amma, that she was alone on the path surrounded by dogs in the woods. The cold didn't help. She woke up in the middle of the night with a draft round her neck. She dozed back off after a while, until the hoot of an owl woke her again, just as the first light of dawn was beginning to paint the sky blue. Her back and hips ached where she had been lying on the floor, and the top of her arm still throbbed. The musty smell of the room was all-pervading despite the open window, and a black cat staring at her with big moon eyes made her jump.

The room looked dingy and dismal in the half light

of dawn. The streaked windows were almost as murky as the night, and the tattered curtains shuddered in the faint breeze from the open window, as if fearful of what might happen next. Still, thought Chella, as Jedan suggested they make an early start, although it wasn't the best night's sleep she had ever had, at least they were all still alive. Then, in spite of herself, she smiled. For the first time in her life, she wasn't going to hear a loudspeaker!

Jedan went outside to light a fire to heat some water, but a minute later he came rushing back in. "There's a water butt in the garden!" he sang out. "We can wash properly – come and see!"

His energy and enthusiasm were infectious. Amma and Chella followed him outside.

Chella caught her breath as she stepped into the garden. It was like stepping into another world. "Paradise lost," she thought to herself as she blinked in the first light of the day and filled her lungs with the gloriously fresh air. The sound of birdsong filled the air. The dawn was filling the world with a newness, glory and purity that could only come when untouched by mankind.

"Look at that!" Jedan said with a flourish, pointing to the water butt on the side of the house.

"I can't believe I'm so excited to wash outside!" said Amma with a laugh, and Chella laughed with her. They all breathed deeply of that glorious morning, then Chella took first turn to wash, in the chest that Jedan brought out for them to use in place of a basin. The water was cold, and it made her shiver at first, but then she felt fresher, and more alive.

Never had the Lord's promise of his mercies being new every morning seemed as relevant as it did that day, Chella decided, as she spread her towel out on a bush to dry and whispered the morning prayer on her own. *"As we lift our hearts to you at the beginning of this new day, may the wonder of your presence fill our lives with love for you, now and always."*

The sky was a fresh, clear blue, and the sun's first rays were beginning to shine through whispers of mist, bringing out the fragrance of foliage and flowers that grew in a tangle beyond the broken concrete strip that surrounded the house.

Instead of going straight back inside when she had finished washing, Chella couldn't resist pushing her way down an overgrown path that led away from the house. Shrubs and trees exploded with life and colour all around her. Bugs scuttled at her feet, bees buzzed in the bushes, a thrush sang in a tree nearby and the heady scent of wild roses filled the air. The garden wasn't decorous and neat, like the gardens at home, but it was... Chella struggled to find the word she wanted, and decided on *free*. It was free. And it was thrilling. Not so long ago men and women had cultivated this garden, trapped it and made it work for them. Now, with all the exuberance of creation, it had fought back and won.

When thorny brambles prevented Chella from going any further, she stopped where she was, closed her eyes and filled her lungs with that wonderful fresh air.

Opening her eyes, she saw with a thrill that some of the blackberries on the bushes were ripe! She pushed her way back to the house to get a bowl, and was met by the smell

114

of wood smoke and the crackling of flames from Jedan's fire. He came to meet her as she reached the paved area, drew her to himself and she allowed his love, and the love of God through him, to seep through her body into her soul.

"God is helping us," Jedan murmured, letting her go a little, and looking into her eyes.

She smiled back. "I know," she agreed, and Jedan grinned, then ran back to the fire, as the water bubbling in the old can began to hiss and spit.

For breakfast they ate the fruit Chella picked, with their bread. It made a delicious start to the day. Despite her weariness, Chella felt something new and beautiful filling the air. Although she had never known anything but the Area, she felt a bit like the garden — as if she was beginning to throw off a heavy covering that had been holding her down.

Chella looked after Mikiah while Amma washed: he was happy crawling on the blankets and knocking down the towers of toys she made for him. She pushed away the thought that Nidala was missing this precious moment with her cheerful, chubby-cheeked baby son — it was too painful.

Just before leaving, Chella couldn't resist having another quick look round the rest of the house in the daylight. The upstairs was damp where a creeper had somehow managed to work its way into the house and left a gaping hole, like a wound. Still, it was a graceful ruin, and so incredibly spacious. Perhaps, one day, she might even live in a house like this... the thought thrilled her heart. She tried not to think of her past, and how that might affect her future. She made up her mind that she must tell Jedan about Solod as soon as she found a good opportunity.

It didn't take the group of travellers long to get ready. They had less food now, but the bags were now stuffed with the blankets and towels. They set off cheerfully, though quietly; even Mikiah dozed in his pramcot. As Chella pulled the back door closed behind them, she felt a lightness in her spirit, mixed with a hint of regret at leaving the first house she had ever slept in. Perhaps tonight they would reach their destination, and sleep in a house that wasn't falling down!

She was surprised, too, as they reached the road, to find the desolate houses in the close had lost their creepiness. Now, in the glorious light of day, they just looked empty, and the bushes and blossoms were transformed from menacing to triumphantly vibrant.

"How will we know where to find the Church, once we reach Anderley?" Chella asked Jedan, as they turned on to the main road.

"It shouldn't be difficult," Jedan replied. "Anderley doesn't look much bigger than this village, on the map. But we'll cross that bridge when we come to it. Actually, it looks from the map as if we will be crossing a real bridge!" He grinned at her, and she smiled back. She didn't like the unknown, or not having a plan, but what could she do? After all, she reflected, she had promised she would go with Jedan wherever he went, even before he had asked her to marry him.

A few weeks after their first meeting, Jedan had asked Chella a question she had never considered. They were walking round the frozen lake in the Parkland, arms linked, enjoying the sharp winter frost on a Sunday afternoon. "What are your dreams for the future, Chella?"

"What do you mean?" she had replied. She wanted to be with him, of course, but that was difficult to say, as he hadn't yet asked her to marry him!

"Don't you ever daydream? Wish you were doing something else? Hope for anything?"

Chella frowned. "Not really. I like my work in the Studio. I hope one day to have a family..." She could feel herself blushing.

Jedan grinned at her and put his arm round her shoulders. "Of course!" he said. "But that's not what I asked. Not what I meant, anyway. Don't you ever dream of not being here, of being free, of being able to do what you want instead of what you're told?"

Chella had frowned. What a question! "No, I've never thought about anything like that. I like my apartment. I like it that the windows look over the Parkland. I wish the church could meet in safety, of course."

"Nothing for yourself?"

"Well, nobody ever asked before and I've never seriously considered it because it's impossible, but I guess if I had the choice, I would like to work in the Nursery for the common good instead of in the Studio. Actually, if I could really have anything I wanted, I'd be in charge of the Nursery. I'd make the rules. I'd make it so it wouldn't be compulsory to leave your children there. Mothers would be allowed to stay at home with their babies if they wanted to. Or the fathers." She surprised herself with the audacity of her thinking. She

117

even looked round, to see if anyone had heard her, but nobody was following them on the frozen path.

Jedan grinned at her. "Wow, you'd be great at that! You've got a quiet strength and you're great with people."

Chella smiled and nodded, warming to her theme. "I could at least pray silently for the little ones while I was with them. And maybe when they're older I could teach them stories from the Bible, like Amma does. But in freedom." Chella shocked herself by thinking something so outrageous. "Yes, I would like that," she declared. "Imagine being able to tell children stories from the Bible freely, and take them to church meetings! That would be amazing. I should hate to put my children in the Nursery," she added.

Jedan grinned at her. "That's my girl!" he said. By his face she knew he was proud of her, but still, she had surprised herself with her own daring thoughts.

Suddenly she made a face and squeezed his arm. "But what's the good of having an idea if you can't do it? In fact, now I've thought about it, it makes it worse, because none of it can happen." She had frowned at him, but he smiled back.

"Pray about it; the Lord does miracles!"

"Yes, but nobody can choose their work. And you know we can't freely share Bible stories with anyone; children or adults." She was getting fed up with this ridiculous conversation, but suddenly she stood stock still.

"What?" asked Jedan.

"Do you think there will ever be a day when people won't live in Areas?" The awesomeness of what she was asking rushed through her like water rushing down a stream.

Jedan didn't reply immediately, then he asked her, "Do you like being here?"

"I've told you I do."

"But I mean here in Area IF208."

Chella dropped her voice to a whisper and looked around again. "I don't think about whether I like it or not. It's my home! It's not like we have a choice – and I haven't been anywhere else to compare it with."

"But we've heard stories of what it was like in the Old Days, and we've studied it in history. What if we could go back to those times? What if we could leave the Area, and start up a new style of dwelling area, where Christians could live in peace?"

Chella frowned. "Leave the Area? You know that's against the law. Why are you asking such questions? What's the point of considering things we can't do?" *Or too scared to think about*, she added to herself. They were quiet for a minute as another couple walked past in the other direction, then Jedan drew her by the hand.

"Let's go look at the fields," he suggested.

In silence, with her gloved hand in his, he drew her away from the lake, to the edge of a ploughed field. Chella thought the conversation was over, but apparently not. Jedan sat her down on a fallen tree, checked all round to make sure nobody could hear, then sat next to her, putting his arms round her and drawing her close. "I have heard there are people living outside, in places that are not proper Areas," he whispered.

Chella's eyes opened wide. "Where did you hear this?"

"A colleague in the Stables heard it from his dad, who cleans in the Area Hall."

"But that can't be true! You know what people are like for making up stories. How could groups of people survive alone, without food and medical care?"

"I think it must be possible. People used to do it all the time, before Dwelling Areas existed. We've all heard stories of the Old Church, living and worshipping in peace."

"I know, but nobody really believes it. It's just rumours..." Chella's voice trailed away.

"We don't believe it because it's what we've been told, but why couldn't people live in groups on their own? Think back to the Old Days – people lived in towns and villages and managed perfectly well for thousands of years!"

"Yes, but those times have long gone! Now there's a World Council, and everyone lives in Areas."

"How can you be sure everyone left their former dwelling towns and cities? People governed themselves in the past – throughout history each dwelling area had its own elders, or some other form of government. Even in Bible times. Maybe they still do."

Chella was silent, but she thought it through. "I see what you mean," she agreed eventually. "But what about wild beasts? And they had the knowledge then, how to grow food, build houses and that sort of thing."

"We have it now! See the fields around you? Next year we will have wheat and barley and vegetables, and fruit, and meat from the animals. How did we do that? We still have farmers! How hard can it be to grow crops, if you have the seeds? We may not know everything here, but we can get the

120

knowledge back. We can learn! Perhaps, in the early years of the New Order, certain groups of people stayed where they were. Perhaps there are still whole villages and towns of people outside, living perfectly happily in communities. Or on farms. And having church meetings."

"Do you talk like this to anyone else?" asked Chella. She was alarmed at his thoughts.

Jedan laughed. "I wrote an essay on the idea of future freedom, in my final year of Second School. I was hauled before Mr Rusitschabe, who told me not to write such ridiculous nonsense. And he told me to be careful, which is interesting. I could see by the look on his face and the tone of his voice, that he was saying one thing and meaning another. He agreed with me, I'm sure he did, even though I failed the Final Exam. I think he had to fail me, or he might have lost his job. Or disappear."

Chella nodded, but tears came to her eyes. Nidala and Hamani's disappearance was too fresh, and now Jedan was saying such things! Where would that lead? Trouble, for sure.

"Don't be afraid," said Jedan, stroking her face. "You're thinking of Nidala, and others you love. But think, maybe the Old Church is out there somewhere, worshipping God freely."

"Why are you so interested? You shouldn't be talking like this, it's not safe."

Jedan paused and stroked her hair. "Somehow I feel that my destiny lies outside. When I think about it, when I pray about it, I know it."

Chella frowned and shook her head. "But nobody leaves their Area!"

"I think I'm going to. One day. I don't know when."

She looked at his face, searching for any sign of amusement. "Are you serious?" She saw no sign of jest; only earnestness shone from the light in his eyes.

"Chella, I really like you – I've liked you since the day I saw you. I love you, actually." Chella nodded, her heart beating faster. He loved her! Was he going to ask the question she had longed for? His eyes searched her face. "But my wife would have to come with me wherever I went. If I left here; left the Area, would you come with me?"

"What do you mean?" Go where? she wanted to ask. Was this a marriage proposal, or something different?

He squeezed her hand, sensing her confusion. "Think about it, let me know. I have heard you pray, I have seen the way you care for people, I have seen your hunger for the Word of God. These things are precious. And you have a gentleness and strength which I admire. I don't deserve you, but even so I'd like to be with you, Chella, forever, and I don't have the right to ask you this, but I have to obey the Lord. If he calls me to go, then I have to go. And if you were my wife, you would have to come with me. I want to ask you to marry me, but first I needed to be honest with you."

Chella was stunned. Jedan looked hopeful and sincere, but his grey eyes held an edge of determination. To be with him was all she wanted, and he had said he loved her, but she was not expecting this! "Where would we go, what would we do, how would we live – how would we get there? And what about the common good?"

"I don't know." He waited for her response and loosened his hold on her a little. Chella began to panic. If he was watching to see how she reacted, she hoped he wasn't going to be disappointed. This was totally crazy – nobody left the Area! OK, it wasn't easy living here as a Christian, but it was possible – lots of people did it, and had done so since the beginning. People from other religions, too, probably. But she so wanted to be with Jedan! When she wasn't with him she felt as if a part of her was missing. She needed to be with him, and had dared to hope she might make him a good wife. But talking about leaving the Area... that was crazy!

"This is... this is... so sudden," she managed eventually, lamely. Tears pricked the back of her eyes. This wasn't the romantic proposal she had been hoping for.

"Think about it," he said, drawing her close again and kissing her gently on the forehead.

They walked home in silence, hurrying to get back before the curfew. Their breath came in mists; Chella's fingers and toes were numb with the cold, and the last streaks of daylight were fading in the western sky by the time they reached her apartment.

Jedan held her close, as he left her, then a few minutes later there was a knock on the door. By the time Chella opened it, Jedan had gone, but a bunch of snowdrops lay on the doormat, with a note. "I will come tomorrow for your answer."

TWENTY

Outside

The first thing Chella saw as she opened her eyes the following morning was the vase of snowdrops on her bedside table. Her heart leaped and she knew she would say yes to Jedan. He loved her – he had said so, and she knew it was true. A lightness came to her spirit as she washed and dressed and put up her hair in a knot for work. Jedan wanted her to be his wife! She danced at the thought! She was glad Lavitah was still on Shift One and she had the apartment to herself – it was a special moment, just herself and the Lord.

Maybe all the talk about leaving would fizzle away, Chella decided. It would probably never come to anything, and they would live the rest of their lives in the Area, happy together, secretly worshipping God in the quiet way all Christians had had to do since Year 0001.

Still, in her lunch break she went to the Library to look at some history books, to find pictures of what the world used to look like before the World Council took over. Could it be true that there were people living outside of the protection and law of the World Council, even now?

As she turned the pages of books of old photographs, she was struck by the beauty of variety in the Old Order. The gardens and parks were vibrant, the clothes of every style you could imagine, the houses and other dwellings full of brightly coloured fabrics and quilts and toys for the children. The Area looked drab and faceless, compared to the images of the dwellings, shops, castles and gardens she was looking at. Of course, there wouldn't be places quite like those any more. Still, it would be wonderful to be free...

But as she put the books back on the shelves, and turned back to reality, it all seemed so remote. Perhaps Jedan was mistaken, and they would never leave, or perhaps there would be a time in the future when everyone could leave freely.

When Jedan came round that evening, she was ready with her answer. This would be her second engagement, but this time she would be married. This time she was loved in return.

Now, here they were, walking further and further away from the Area on an ancient road, and they weren't even married yet! They couldn't hold hands because they were carrying too many bags between them, but they smiled at each other from time to time, and despite all the uncertainty, Chella felt she was doing the right thing. Whatever happened, she determined to do her best, as much for Amma and Mikiah's sake as for her and Jedan's. What they were walking towards she didn't dare think about. Surely Jedan had to be right. Surely the Church must exist, and they would be safe once they got there. Surely Old Erimah wouldn't have let them go if there was any doubt.

Walking through the remainder of Tadworth only took a few minutes. Moss and creepers covered remains of stone walls, and every so often bits of ancient buildings and paving were visible under the all-pervading green, but gradually the forest took over completely from the work of mankind.

The joy of the early morning quickly fizzled out into hard work, as the road continued to climb uphill. The sun had burnt their faces and arms the day before; their legs ached, and the bags seemed to get heavier and heavier.

"Tell us some more stories of the Old Days, Amma," suggested Jedan, as they paused for water after a particularly steep incline. "I'd love to hear more about what it was like. You mentioned that you used to get Messengers from the World Council in your town where you lived. We still have Messengers come to the Areas — I've looked after their horses, but no one knows where they come from. None of the Workers, anyway. Where did your Messengers come from, do you know? I was thinking about it as we went to sleep last night."

Amma shook her head. "I'm embarrassed to admit I don't know. I never paid that much attention. I was young, then, and it didn't seem important. I can tell you, though, that they used to come in pairs, on horses, with a posse of guards to keep them safe."

"Interesting," said Jedan. "It's not that different now, except of course they only talk to the Elite."

"Yes, that's a big difference. They came to speak to us all then. They announced their arrival with trumpets, so everyone would know they were there. As soon as we heard them, everyone would drop whatever they were doing and run to the town square – we all did. To be honest, as a child, I didn't really take in most of what they were saying; we just wanted to see those beautiful horses! All through the War they came with news and supplies, then there was a gap of about three or four years, because of the Plague. Nobody travelled during that time, of course, for fear of spreading disease.

"So when we heard the trumpets again after all those years of silence, we ran to the town square with a mixture of thrill and dread, not knowing what the news would be. Not that there were many of us left – the square seemed almost empty. I still remember how my heart thudded, though! We could have been the only people left in the world, for all we knew, until they came. And there they were, out of the blue, wearing the purple New World Order livery and carrying the harlequin banners, to cover all the colours of the old flags of the world, as you know. We were totally amazed and dazzled by it all."

Jedan nodded. "You can see why they'd do that, with the colours."

"Yes, after the greyness of the terrible years we'd been through. . . just seeing them felt like hope rising. Then they told us about the new World Order that had been set up, and that a World Council had taken charge and were sorting everything out for the survival of humanity. They told us about the new Areas that were being set up, where there would be medical centres and schools, and jobs for everyone. Food production was going to be organised so nobody would go hungry. There would be a home for everyone, and everyone would work together for the common good. Most of us cheered and cried and clapped and hugged each other – we were dancing and shouting and jumping up and down. After all the terrible things we'd been through, it felt that at last, our heavy burdens would be lifted. We had no idea, of course, what it would really be like."

Jedan screwed up his face. "Didn't people realise they were going to lose their freedom?"

"The Messengers only mentioned the banning of religions briefly, and made it seem like it would be a big step forward for world peace. You have to remember, we were so beaten down after years of struggling; so many deaths, so much sadness, so much loss and grief, and so much effort just surviving, that for the most part, all we could think of was having our basic needs met – food, safety, schools, medical facilities, clean water, that sort of thing. Some people had a bit more discernment. . ."

"But most people thought it was good?" asked Jedan.

"Yes, they did. I did – I was one of the ones who danced in the square! Of course, once we had time to think it through, certain things were a concern, like the loss of democracy, and religious people were worried about what would happen to them – not just Christians. Some were our friends."

They walked in silence for a while, then Jedan said, "I can see how the Areas would seem like an attractive proposition, after everything you'd been through."

Amma nodded. "It really did. It was like a miracle. We were living hand to mouth. Any kind of help was welcome."

128

"So how did the Messengers know how many people were going to go to the Area?" asked Jedan. "It wasn't compulsory at that point?"

"I don't think so. After their speech, they took everyone's names. We all had to line up in family groups and give our details, then they took away all the builders and doctors and teachers and farmers. The following day, I believe, or very soon afterwards. I don't think they had the choice, although I can't be sure. You know old Dr Bane from the medical centre? He was one of those who was taken."

"Goodness!" said Chella.

Jedan raised his eyebrows. "Did their families go with them?"

"I believe so. The rest of us were told that they would come back for us in six months, when the apartments and the basic structure of the Area would be ready to receive us. Almost everyone was packed and ready to go when they came back, in the September of Year 0001. Life was tougher than ever after they'd taken the doctors and farmers." Amma shook her head and sighed. "You can't imagine! When the Messengers came back they gave everyone a map, and people left in groups, travelling together, taking as many of their belongings with them on carts and donkeys and wheelbarrows and bicycles as they could. They had to give up everything except their personal possessions, of course, when they arrived at the Area, but everyone was given a free apartment and a job to do. But you know all that."

"Did most of the Christians stay in your town?" asked Chella.

"Probably about half left that first autumn. Every six months the Messengers came to give updates on how wonderfully the new Areas were working, and to take whoever wanted to go with them. My family struggled on as long as we could, then we left in Year 0003, as I said."

"Just your family?"

"No, a group of families left together, mostly from our church. We were all desperate by then. My parents had been determined never to give up, but my brother and sister became ill. In the end getting to see a doctor in the Area seemed like our only hope." Amma was silent for a moment, then shook her head. "But I told you about that yesterday. The World Council were clever again, you see. Nobody was ever forced to leave – we came to the Area of our own free will. But what choice did we have? There was no schooling, and children had to work to help grow food. Seeds were even harder to come by than ever before, and there was not even the most rudimentary help if you were sick. And so many of the houses were empty. We felt so alone."

"I can't imagine what that must have felt like," said Chella, thinking how lonely the village of Tadworth had seemed. She tried to imagine what it would have been like to be just one of a handful of people living there, with everything crumbling around them.

"Christians argued over it in the beginning," said Amma. "Some said the World Council was the Beast and we shouldn't have anything to do with it. Others said that God in his grace was giving us another chance at life."

"What do you think, Amma?" asked Jedan. "Do you think the World Council is the Beast?"

"Honestly, Jedan, I don't know. But any power that tries to annihilate the church is not from God, that's for sure."

"I think I'd have wanted to stay," said Jedan. "To be able to live freely. Share the good news, sing and pray out loud."

"That sounds noble, Jedan," said Amma, "and we have the benefit of hindsight. But you have to understand, our churches had already been closed and two years on there was pretty much nobody left in the town – so there wasn't anyone to share the good news with! Plus, it wasn't until we reached the Areas that we had to sign a declaration saying we wouldn't join in or organise any religious activities, or keep or read any religious writing. We knew things wouldn't be easy, but didn't know how strict the declaration would be – that we would have to give up our Bibles. . . and by then it was too late. Things weren't as simple as you might think."

Chella thought about that time, long ago, before she was born. "My dad was born just before the war, like you, Amma, but I don't remember him ever talking about those times. I wish I'd asked him. I don't even know the name of the town he used to live in."

"I'm afraid I can't help you there. As I said before, we pretty much stopped talking about the Old Days once we got to the Area. We didn't want to make things difficult for anyone, if we were overheard."

"Grandad didn't mind!"

Amma smiled. "Your grandad was something else! He never minded about anyone or anything. How he managed to live out his days in peace without ever being reprimanded I will never know!"

"Good on him!" said Jedan. "I wish I could have met him!"

Amma laughed. "Yes, you two would have got on well. But he would probably have led you into a lot of trouble!"

"More trouble than I'm in now?" asked Jedan with a grin, and they all laughed.

"No, I suppose not, when you come to think of it," admitted Amma, looking round with a big sigh. "Look at us out here, in the middle of nowhere!"

"It's funny to think these roads were once full of people," Jedan agreed. "Talking of which, we should be passing through another settlement soon."

Not long after he had finished speaking, he pointed out a rusting signpost, then the first buildings appeared. They passed various ruined dwellings, a school called Owen Academy, a crumbling statue, a Baptist church building, and a row of what looked as if they may have been shops – all being swallowed up by the never-ending tide of green. Chella looked at everything in awe as they walked past, trying to imagine living there, going to that school, shopping in those shops, attending meetings in that church building. Many of the roofs of the buildings had gone, and some of the walls, but at least some of the bricks still stood, full of silent secrets of times gone by.

Jedan suggested they stop for a break when they had left the settlement, a little way into the trees, so they could rest in the shade for a while. It was quite early for lunch, but they were glad of a rest, and decided a meal would give them energy. Amma spread out one of the blankets for them to sit on, and after a simple snack of bread, cheese and apples, Chella offered to look after Mikiah. Amma gratefully laid down on the blanket and closed her eyes, while Chella followed Mikiah as he crawled in the leaf litter.

If they had been at home, Chella reflected, as she made a big effort to smile and clap and sing nursery rhymes with Mikiah, this would have been her day off. Right now she would have been getting ready to go to her sewing group. Her friend Julip would be there. Julip had helped her choose the fabrics for the bag she had brought with her; she would be praying for them along with all the other ladies. Tears came to Chella's eyes as with a pang she suddenly missed her friends, and wished she could have said goodbye. Geraldith, Grace, Jeana. . . they were like sisters to her. Just as well they knew nothing, though, for their own safety – if anyone was questioned about her disappearance, they could honestly say they knew nothing. Maybe one day they would all be together again. If not in this world, in the next.

Yesterday evening she and Jedan should both have been at their history group. It cheered her to think the group would have been meeting around the same time they had settled for the night in the house in Tadworth. She mentioned it to Jedan and he laughed. "I'd forgotten about that! I don't suppose they studied much history, do you? Garem would have told them why we weren't there. They would have been praying for us!"

The group was a history group in name only; after everyone had opened up their history books and they had a brief discussion about a pre-arranged topic, they quickly turned to prayer and a Bible passage; the real reason for their meeting. The older Christians shared their Bible knowledge and wisdom with the younger ones. And occasionally a newly baptised believer was added to their number, despite the difficulties, which brought great rejoicing to them all. Assuming there weren't any unexpected newcomers, of course. That did happen from time to time. In the event of a visitor attending, the original discussion would continue, but the members made it as dull as they could. It invariably worked; visitors never stayed more than a week or two, and the believers would laugh and get back to prayer and Bible study as soon as possible.

Before her father's illness and death, Chella had loved both her groups – they were the highlights of her week. She only stopped going when her dad injured his leg in the Woodwork Studio, where he worked. The wound seemed to heal at first, but after a while his calf became swollen, red and painful, and he found it increasingly difficult to walk – towards the end he could barely get round the apartment. Chella had stayed with him then, to look after him. Deep vein thrombosis was diagnosed. He was given advice on exercise, and extra credits for ginger, cinnamon and garlic, but he collapsed a week later; a blood clot had broken off and lodged in his heart.

Chella was at first numb with the shock, then grief took over. The emptiness and pain were all-consuming, and blaming God for taking her dad, she shut herself away.

Until Solod found her.

TWENTY-ONE

Half a Romance

Solod was Elite, but Chella hadn't known that to start with, because the Elite didn't usually mix with Workers. She knew that Workers weren't allowed in the Elite Zone – everyone knew that, but Chella didn't know that Solod wasn't allowed to be in the Workers' Zone, either. She hadn't known how often he broke the rules. She hadn't known his charm was merely a covering for the wolf underneath.

After her father's death Chella walked in the Parkland every evening after work, to fill the hours and exhaust herself, so she wouldn't have to think, and to avoid sitting alone in her empty home. She stopped going to church meetings, cut herself off from Christian friends, and banished her scripture portions to the bottom of a drawer. How could there be a god who cared, Chella had railed with anger, if he took your mum away when you were little, then your dad? How could there be a god who cared who allowed wars, famines, plagues, and so much suffering? How could there be a god who reigned supreme if he allowed his own people, the very ones who loved him, to be persecuted?

Why, God? she said every morning as she got up to aching emptiness, went to work, walked until she could walk no more, then went home to eat her evening meal alone.

Solod stopped to talk to her one evening, in the Parkland. She hadn't seen him following her, but when she paused to watch a moorhen bobbing in the lake, he stopped next to her, and asked her why a beautiful girl like her should look so sad. She was so surprised, she couldn't reply at first, but he had seemed genuinely concerned. And he was good looking. A little taller than herself, dark skin and hair, piercing blue eyes, close-cropped beard, soft leather jacket.

How could she not have seen how dangerous he was? That very first evening she had opened up her heart to him. He had held out his arm for her. She took it after only a brief moment's hesitation. As they walked arm in arm on the gravel path around the lake with the leaves on the trees beginning to turn and a chill in the air, she told him about her dad's death, about her mum disappearing all those years ago, about the aching loneliness of grief, and feeling so alone.

He had seemed so understanding. His grandad had died, he told her, when he was younger, because some youths had set fire to his home for a bit of fun. He had never been able to get it out of his mind, he said, seeing his grandad coughing in the smoke. She was horrified to the core that anyone could do such a terrible thing as to set a home on fire for fun. On the other side of the lake, where nobody could see, he took her into his arms, and she sobbed on his shoulder, and he shed a tear or two on hers. She felt his pain, and she thought he felt hers. When they got back to the apartment blocks, he pulled her a little closer, and held her longer than he needed to. The comforting smell of his leather jacket, the softness of his shirt, the tenderness of his touch, the briefest whisper of a kiss, and her heart was stolen.

She dreamed of him that night, and wondered if she would ever see him again. She did – the very next evening. He smiled as he approached, and her heart flipped, then when he drew her to himself without a word and gently brushed her lips with his, she was his to do with as he wished.

The third evening they held hands like a proper courting couple, walked round the lake, watched the windmills turning and the sheep grazing. They lingered by the woodland glade as the sun began to set, marvelling at the changing colours of the leaves after the first frost of the season. Sometimes they talked, sometimes they just walked. It felt so good. They had to run home to avoid missing the curfew.

As he left Chella that third evening, Solod told her he had a secret to tell her that she must tell no one. He was Elite, and worked in the Trade Department, but he wasn't allowed to talk to her about his job, as he had signed the Secrecy Law. She was shocked, and questioned his presence in the Workers' Zone, but he assured her that the Elite were allowed to do anything they wanted, and she believed him. How wrong she was! She thought he cared about her. She was wrong about that, too; he cared only about himself.

It was a whirlwind romance – from her point of view, at least. For the next three weeks he came to see her almost every day. Sometimes they walked out, if the weather was kind; sometimes he came to her apartment. They talked, they laughed, they cuddled and kissed. He and Chella were made to be together, Solod said. They were soul mates, he told her. He had had a girl before her, who had broken his heart, he said. He whispered how much he wanted Chella and needed her, how she was the only one for him – that now, at last, with her by his side, he felt comforted for the loss of his grandad. He brought her luxurious treats: flowers, sweetmeats, white bread and cakes, and for the first time in weeks, she smiled and laughed. The aching void of loneliness was pushed aside for new love.

It was all so fascinating; so different. Solod made her feel special, and she was under his spell. Being with him quickly took over her life. He made her promise to tell no one she was seeing him, because of the delicacy of his secret job, he told her, so she didn't. Ena and the others at the Studio remarked on the new sparkle in her eyes and were glad for her, but she told them nothing about the real reason for the change in her life.

About her faith and the church she said nothing to Solod – the silence was too deeply ingrained, and it felt like another life, anyway, that she no longer belonged to. Sometimes Chella thought of Amma, Nidala, Julip, Grace, and her other Christian friends, and would have loved to tell them about her new love, but kept away from them. How could she talk to them without giving away Solod's secret? And deep down she knew they wouldn't approve of her seeing someone who was not a believer. Whenever anyone called, she pretended not to be in, even when she could hear Nidala's voice at the door, calling her. Nidala didn't need her now, anyway, Chella reasoned; she had a husband, and a baby on the way.

Three weeks after their first meeting, Solod brought a bottle of wine to Chella's apartment, along with two vintage wine glasses. They must celebrate being together for twenty-one days, he told her, as he handed her a delicately embroidered bag containing the gift.

Chella was speechless with amazement as she opened the package. The bag was exquisite, the glasses so fine, and wine was an almost unknown luxury. Solod wouldn't tell her where he got it, but she deserved the best, he assured her.

She jumped when he popped the cork, which made them both laugh. "Watch this my Beauty," Solod instructed her, as the deep red liquid glugged sensuously out of the bottle into the delicate round glass Chella held in her hand. Solod showed her how to swirl the wine to release the aroma, and to enjoy the way it sparkled in the light. She didn't like her first sip, but pretended she did, and he insisted she drink it all. It made her giggle, then he gave her more, and he took her to bed. She didn't want to at first, but he was so tender, so gentle, so insistent, and the wine was so heady, she gave in.

The following morning, when she woke up to find Solod gone, she hadn't known whether to laugh or cry, but got up for work as usual. That evening he assured her they were bonded now; that they were perfect for each other, and she must marry him. He had come to take her to meet his parents, he announced, and had brought along with him a twisted leather band for an engagement ring. She was puzzled when he didn't ask her to marry him, merely

139

assumed she would, but the ring fitted perfectly and she didn't question him. Surely he could have had the pick of beautiful Elite girls? But he had chosen her! And even if he had asked, she had reasoned, she would have said yes. Surely his family would want him to marry an Elite girl, though? she had asked him, her heart thumping with the twin emotions of thrill and alarm at the suddenness of it all, and what they had done, but he shrugged and said he didn't care what they thought.

She only found out later that they had instructed him to find a respectable wife, because his ways were bringing them into disrepute, and because they wanted a grandchild. She was nothing more than a convenience.

TWENTY-TWO

How Things Used to Be

After a short rest, the travellers set out once more. It seemed to Chella that every muscle in her body screamed for her chair in the Studio. She had never walked so much! What a strange thing it was to be walking further and further away from the Area, towards something unknown. She tried not to think about that too much.

"Are we going to make Anderley by nightfall, do you think, Jedan?" Amma asked, as she settled Mikiah in the pramcot, voicing the question Chella wanted to ask but almost didn't want to know.

Jedan shouldered as many bags as he could manage, to relieve Amma. "I think we might. It's only just after noon, and we're walking much faster than we did through the forest. If we do get there tonight, it would be good, as it will give the church extra time to decide what to do, when we tell them they've been discovered."

"It's never been a crime to live outside the Area, though, has it?" asked Chella, stretching her stiff legs and arms and stifling a yawn.

"Not as far as I know," replied Jedan, and Amma shook her head as the pramcot wheels began to turn once more.

"It's only a crime to leave an Area once you're there. Meeting to worship in a church building is definitely against the law, though."

"What I don't understand," said Jedan, "is why the World Council was so keen on getting everyone to go to the Areas. Why didn't they just leave the ones who didn't want to go? Or let them leave the Areas if they didn't want to be there any more?"

"Oh, that's easy – they needed as many workers as they could get," replied Amma, "to make the Areas work. Simple as that."

And so the Elite can live in luxury, Chella thought, but said nothing.

"But surely it wouldn't matter to them now, who does what outside of the Areas?" persisted Jedan.

"Well, for one thing there's a spiritual battle, don't forget," Amma reminded him. "Satan wants to crush the Church. And perhaps, from a purely human point of view, they'd be worried about opposition – uprisings, that sort of thing."

"I see. That makes sense."

"Yes. Because believers in Jesus have a higher authority than the World Council – they don't like that. I don't know when the Messengers stopped visiting the old towns and villages, though."

"You mean to get people to go to the Areas?"

"Yes." Amma paused. "I suspect they gave up eventually, assuming everyone outside would die with no fresh water and medical help. It's wonderful to think that's not the case. And I've been telling you about all the bad times when we lived outside, but I really should tell you about the church, before it closed, because perhaps we are walking towards times of being able to worship in freedom again."

"Oh yes, Amma, that would be such an encouragement," agreed Jedan.

Amma smiled back. "Every time I think how much my legs ache, I think of that and it helps!" she said. "So, our church building was just around the corner from where we lived. There was a big old car park round the back, so I guess back in the day some people must have come in cars."

"How many people were in your church?" asked Chella.

"About three hundred, I would guess, during the War – numbers dwindled, of course, as people died."

Jedan whistled. "So many Christians!"

Amma laughed. "Ours was only one of several churches in our town."

Jedan's mouth dropped open. "Really? How many?"

"Goodness, a dozen or so, probably! When I was little there were services every Sunday morning, with Sunday School for us children. We took it for granted, of course, like you do when you don't know any better."

"Didn't you have to worry about the neighbours?" asked Chella.

"Not at all! There weren't any restrictions on religion, then, and the church was known for doing good things, generally. Old people's lunches, baby and toddler groups, soup kitchens, help for veterans, after school clubs – lots of

143

things like that. And before we lost contact with the outside world, aid for poor people in other countries, too.

"Sounds amazing!" said Jedan.

Amma nodded and smiled as a pair of squirrels chased each other across the road in front of them, then disappeared in the trees. "We were as free as those squirrels," she said with a smile. "And there were lots of other church meetings, as well as the services on Sunday. Prayer meetings, men's breakfasts, women's meetings, groups that met in homes for Bible study and prayer. And there was lots going on for us children, too – not just on Sundays, but clubs in the week. Our leaders made it fun for us, with games and talks and walks and treasure hunts and quizzes, barbecues and bonfires... looking back on it now, our leaders gave up so much for us, even through the dark times. It was because of the children's workers that I first learnt to trust the Lord for myself. I grew up on the Bible stories, of course, but it was at a special youth weekend I saw my sin for the first time, and asked Jesus to forgive me."

Chella smiled at Amma. "That must have been a very special time."

"Oh it really was, I can't tell you. Children's and youth camps were some of the best times in my life. I've just had a thought – imagine if Mikiah was able to go on church camps when he gets a bit older!"

"That would be amazing," agreed Jedan, then he turned to Chella with a big grin. "We could be leaders together!"

Chella laughed and shook her head. "Let's get there first," she said. "I can't think that far ahead!"

Amma laughed, too. "We called it 'camp' but it wasn't

in tents – we stayed in our church hall – there were enough rooms in the annexe for us all to bring our sleeping bags and we slept on the floor. Volunteers fed us – it must have been a mammoth task! I cried the first year it was cancelled, because of the Plague – then it never happened again."

"What did your church building look like?" asked Chella.

"It was one of those old-fashioned ones, made of grey brick. It had a ground floor extension with loads of extra rooms, and a clock with a chime in a tower which rang out on Sundays to call people to worship."

Chella tried to imagine what that might be like. "That must have been lovely," she said.

"It was! Hearing the bells ringing week by week reminded us somehow of God's faithfulness, all through those terrible years. When the church was closed, the silent bell was a symbol of us having lost our freedom."

"So," said Jedan, "you began meeting in secret, even while you lived in your old town?"

"Yes, we did. Those first New Order Messengers left a foreign man in charge. Mr Carshena, his name was, or something like that. He took over from the Town Council, which had pretty much fallen into nothing anyway. He was frightfully efficient. He closed up all the churches and other places of worship straight away. It was all so sudden, and scary. I remember it well – the confusion and the fear. We weren't prepared for it."

"But not everyone minded?" asked Jedan.

"It didn't impact most people, because if you weren't part of a religious community, it didn't matter. It was a big subject of discussion in those first few months, though, while people were waiting to leave for the Area, but most people were happy to side with the 'religion causes war' line. Whether they really believed it, or feared the consequences if they spoke against it, I don't know. Some and some, probably."

"Did you see your church closed?"

"You mean the building? No, my dad thought we ought to keep away."

"But you heard about it?"

"Yes. All the doors were boarded up, the gate padlocked, and notices were put up within a very short space of time. Anything of value had already been removed, though. Some of the church leaders went straight to the building after the Messengers had finished their announcement in the town square, and took away everything they could carry. Lots of church members helped, once they realised what was going on. We hid everything between us. The communion cups and plates, the altar cloths and candlesticks, hymn books and prayer books, pictures and vases and the lectern and all sorts of bits and pieces from the kitchen and Sunday School rooms, and all the books and Bibles, of course."

"Where are all those things now?" asked Jedan. "We ought to go on a treasure hunt!"

Amma laughed. "Maybe one day someone will! Those things don't really matter though, do they? I don't know why we bothered, really, looking back on it. The Word of God is precious beyond compare, and some of the books have been a great encouragement since our exile, if you can call it that, but the rest – we don't need any of it."

"We've all benefited from the books," said Jedan.

"Absolutely," agreed Amma. "We got good at swapping covers, even then, so from the outside they looked like novels or whatever. It was a fiddly job, finding books that fitted perfectly – the spine was often the worst thing, because you had to have the same width. But I was telling you about what happened after the church building closed. Bible study and prayer groups were set up straight away, and we met every day somewhere, so it would look like dropping in for a cup of tea – never more than five or six people at a time. Till someone hit on the idea of the groups as you know them, so we set up the first sewing, history, music, art and literature groups. The rest is history, as they say!"

Chella smiled. "Goodness, our groups go back that long!"

"Yes, it was a brilliant idea and we loved it! But suddenly having to hide our faith was a huge change. We had to be so careful. Many people who used to come to church with us didn't join the small groups, and if they met us in the street, didn't stop to chat. It is written, as you know, that the love of many will grow cold in the last days – that certainly happened. Those of us who held on to our faith still tried to do what we could to help the bereaved, and visit the sick, but we were no longer able to talk about our faith – not openly, anyway."

"Was there still electricity then?" asked Jedan.

Amma shook her head. "No, no, we hadn't had that for a long time. Way back. I hardly remember electric lights. One of the major benefits of the Areas was that there was going to be power. People were so excited about that, after

147

having to collect wood for so many years. The winters were so cold, and the oil lamps so dim and smoky."

Amma fell silent and they all returned to the thoughts of their tired minds as they kept walking on that long, silent, uphill road. From time to time one of them would carry Mikiah to give him a break from the pramcot, but as the afternoon wore on the heat intensified. The hotter it got the stickier they got, and the more fractious Mikiah became. When he finally fell asleep, Chella draped her light shawl over the pramcot as a makeshift sunshade. She wanted to talk to Jedan about Solod, but he was so totally focused on the journey, she wasn't sure he would listen. She thought about it as they walked. Should she insist? No, perhaps, after all, she decided, it would be better to talk after they reached their destination. What must happen, must happen.

If only she had clung to God after her dad's death, instead of turning away, she sighed to herself. Regret had to be the worst pain in the world.

TWENTY-THREE

The Elite Zone

The Elite Zone was out of bounds for Workers. Although Solod had told Chella it would be fine because she would be with him, and he could do whatever he liked, she couldn't help worrying she would be stopped and arrested. The high, wooden gate into the unseen land on the other side was guarded day and night. She knew the law.

Of course when she was younger she had peered through the thick, high, hedge of conifer trees that separated the Elite from the Workers. All the children did, although it was a lot higher and thicker now than it had been then. Chella had heard about a boy who had once dared to squeeze though a gap in the trees. He had returned with a black eye, covered with scratches from the branches, and refused to talk about his adventure. As far as Chella knew, he was the only Worker who had gone in and returned.

Despite Solod's assurances that everything would be fine, his parents would love her, and she looked amazing in her best dress and shawl, she was nervous as they approached the Elite Zone. She felt swept along out of control, and suddenly Solod began to act differently, too, although she couldn't put her finger on the reason at the time.

She had given herself to this man, in the most intimate way. She was wearing his ring, which bound him to her, and it seemed that now she must follow him. Half of her didn't want anything to be different, but the other half wanted everything to slow down – it was all going so fast.

She thought of the boy with the black eye as they approached the security guard at the Elite entry point, and her heart banged in her chest as they drew level. But the man on duty merely winked at Solod, opened the gate in silence, and closed it behind them.

Chella's eyes widened at her first view of the Elite Zone, as she heard the bolts in the gate slide back into place behind her. It was like being transported into a beautiful dream – a fantasy adventure, a fairytale. A faint mist hung in the still air in the gathering dusk. They were the only people on the road. Beech trees on either side of a gravel lane spread their leafy branches high above them. Solod led her by the hand down the middle of the lane towards the Elite dwellings. Every so often a golden leaf drifted down, to land on the frosty ground. Only their cold breath condensing in the chill of the evening air, the crunch of their feet on the gravel, and Solod's warm hand in hers, reminded Chella this was real.

As they reached the end of the avenue, two-storey apartments came into view; white-washed and clean, with neat gardens boasting all manner of wonderful shrubs.

"What beautiful dwellings! Who does the gardening?" Chella asked in amazement.

Solod shrugged. "I don't know. Foreigners. Why would anyone care who the gardeners are?"

"Why are you nervous?" she asked, picking up on the tension in his voice and noticing his sweaty hands. "You promised me everything would be all right!"

He gave a stilted laugh and squeezed her hand. "I'm taking my girl to meet my parents, Chella!" he said, and she forgave him for sounding snappy – of course he would be nervous! She resolved to make him as proud as she could.

They walked past several rows of pretty apartments. Chella could hardly believe that housing as beautiful as this existed so close to the drab, grey Workers' apartments she had lived in all her life. Would she one day live here? she wondered, her heart beating faster as she marvelled at the neatly clipped hedges separating the clean white blocks. Or would Solod come and live with her? He hadn't mentioned it, and she didn't want to ask, for fear of sounding grasping. She would find out sooner or later. Anyway, just to be with Solod would be enough. She squeezed his hand and smiled up at him and he smiled back, but his smile looked wooden, Chella thought.

A few people were coming and going on the neat walkways, but nobody looked at them, and after a couple of minutes, Solod led her to the left and into his apartment, on the ground floor.

His mum came to meet them as they stamped the frost off their shoes on the door mat. "You must be Chella," she said warmly, taking her hands in her own. "Come in, come inside, out of the cold. I can't tell you how glad I am to meet you! I'm Sheva, Solod's long-suffering mother, as I'm sure you will have realised by now. Take the girl's cape, Solod, for goodness sake."

Sheva was tall and attractive, but older than Chella had imagined, with greying hair cut in a neat bob. She was wearing a simple navy dress with lace at the collar, and a blue velvet jacket with pleats and frills. The colour reminded Chella of pictures of the sea. It was the most beautiful outfit she had ever seen in her life, and she told Sheva so, who laughed. "Oh, these are only old rags. If only we could go back in time. The dresses we had! The parties we went to! But we mustn't talk in the hall. Come, you must meet Walt." At that moment, Walt came into the hall from another room, and shook Chella's hand. He was a taller, older version of Solod, and had a commanding look about him, but his smile seemed genuine. His suit was made of the finest cloth Chella had ever seen. No doubt it was vintage, and carefully looked after.

Chella's eyes opened wide as Walt showed her into the living room. It looked more like something out of a book than reality. A welcoming fire crackled and spat in a fireplace, surrounded by a stone mantelpiece. Two proper brown leather settees stood opposite each other, one each side of the fire, with a highly polished wooden coffee table on a patterned rug between them. Matching bookcases full of old books stood on each side of the chimney breast. Various other elegant pieces of furniture adorned the room, decorated with exotic ornaments. Sea-green drapes at the window hung in luxurious folds, floor to ceiling: there was nothing out of place, nothing that looked home-made. Where was the kitchen area? Chella wondered, then realised; there must be a separate room just for the kitchen.

"Come, sit!" Sheva commanded Chella, and as if in a dream, Chella sat down on one of the settees next to Solod; Sheva and Walt settled themselves opposite them. Chella could barely speak. She knew the Elite lived differently, but she hadn't expected the difference to be so dramatic. Her eyes were drawn to the fireplace, over which hung a large mirror with an elaborate gold frame.

"It's from our old family home," Walt explained, following her eyes.

"It's exquisite," breathed Chella. "Everything here is! I have never seen such a beautiful room, such lovely things!"

"Oh my dear, you haven't lived!" exclaimed Sheva. "It must be so dreadful for you in that awful Workers' ghetto. Solod has told us some fearful tales of the poverty over there. That old mirror is nothing compared to some of the things of beauty we used to own. Oh, if only we could go back to those wonderful days!" She launched into a monologue on how appalling life was now compared to what it had been before. Chella hardly heard her, but nodded and smiled as she tried to gather her racing thoughts. Could this be real? Did all the Elite live like this?

To add to Chella's confusion, a maid in black uniform came in while Sheva was still talking, carrying a tray with a pot of tea, four china cups and saucers, and a plate of little white cookies. She gently placed the tray on the coffee table. Chella's eyes opened even wider. Was this girl from a *servant class*? She couldn't be! Surely this was everything the World Council was against?

The maid left after a brief curtsey. Chella smiled at her, but she didn't notice, and none of the others even looked at her. Sheva poured the tea. As they sipped it, and crunched the sweet cookies, Sheva recounted tales of the Old Days when she and Walt had lived in luxury, in a castle, no less. Chella looked at Solod with wide eyes, when Sheva told her that Walt was a descendant of a Scottish lord, and she herself was the daughter of a baron. Solod rolled his eyes as his mum listed everyone in their family and their titles and achievements – she couldn't tell if he he was pleased or embarrassed. Either way she resolved to remonstrate with him later for not telling her that he was the descendant of real nobility.

When Sheva eventually paused, Walt asked Chella about her life – her work, her friends and her family, and the things she liked to do. When she had told everything, carefully leaving out her previous involvement in the church, Sheva and Walt nodded and smiled at each other, then at her.

"I'll be honest with you, we weren't best pleased when Solod insisted on bringing home a girl from among the Workers," Sheva admitted, pouring a second cup of tea. "But I have to say, my dear, we're impressed by what we see. Aren't we, Walt?"

"Yes, we are," Walt replied, with an indulgent smile in her direction. Chella smiled back, but her heart hammered in her chest and she wondered what they could possibly be impressed with, after knowing her for such a short time. "I see now why Solod wanted to spread his wings a bit!"

154

added Walt, with a wink in Solod's direction. It was slightly disconcerting; Chella felt as if she was being weighed up in a balance. At least she seemed to be passing the test. She clung to Solod's hand and tried not to look around the room too much.

Everything was so breathtaking, it was hard not to stare. The curtains shimmered in the light of the lamp; the bookcases held hundreds of old books. The pictures on the walls were real paintings − a boat on a stormy sea, flowers, people. Chella longed to have a closer look at everything. That they came from a time long ago was evident. She carried on nodding and smiling, hardly taking in Sheva's tales of the Old Days and how many precious artefacts they had had to leave behind when they had finally had to leave their castle home, but when she eventually stopped, Chella remarked on Solod's resemblance to his Dad.

Sheva smiled, got up, and brought one of the photos from the mantelpiece over to show Chella.

"No, Mother, no, not now!" Solod groaned. But Sheva just laughed as she held out the photograph to Chella. "We need to let you in on a secret. We need you to carry on the family line. We need a grandchild, my dear. An heir. You do want children, I assume?"

Chella was so taken aback she could barely speak. "Yes, yes, oh yes, I do, but, well, I hadn't really thought..."

"Move up, Solod, make room," puffed Sheva, signalling him for him to move up and make room for her on the settee next to Chella.

"Mother, we've only just got engaged," complained Solod. "Leave the poor girl alone!"

155

But Sheva waved his objection away with her hand. "She's joining our family, so she needs to know what a vital role she will be fulfilling."

Chella's heart was pounding as Solod moved up to make room for his mother, who showed her the old photo in an ornate silver frame, which was of a wedding. A family group, dressed fabulously, was posing in front of a castle, no less. That it was Walt and Sheva's wedding was evident. They were younger then, but they still looked the same. Chella looked up at Walt and he smiled indulgently as Sheva explained who everyone was. The parents, the siblings, the bridesmaids, the important people. "Walt's real title is *Lord*," sighed Sheva. "And I *was* a Lady, once." She sighed. "Now such things have no meaning; they're not permitted."

"Oh!" exclaimed Chella.

Sheva patted her hand. "But in our hearts, that's what we still are. And maybe one day, things will go back to the way they were and we will return to our inheritance. Get rid of these wretched foreign servants and hire decent people who speak English properly."

Walt nodded encouragingly. "Solod is our only son, so you see how important it is that we have grandchildren to carry on the family line?"

"And of course," added Sheva, "you and Solod will carry on our title, when we're gone. You will be a Lady, too."

Chella couldn't reply. She stared at the photo for a minute, then turned to look at Solod, who had his face in his hands. "Parents!" he groaned, shaking his head.

Sheva cuffed him behind Chella's back. "Mind your manners!"

TWENTY-FOUR

Horses

From time to time the travellers could see evidence of the Old Order; rotting gates and fences, road signs, hints of minor roads leading away from the main road, and lengths of crumbling walls, which Amma told them marked the boundaries of fields long abandoned. But mostly it was just the road and the forest. The only sounds were their footsteps, the chirping of birds, the rustle of the wind in the trees, and the pramcot wheels turning.

The hint of a breeze that had begun that morning was getting stronger. It brought relief from the heat, but it was bringing clouds with it. If it rained, Amma observed at one point, looking up at the gathering clouds, she hoped it would be after they had found shelter. Chella agreed wholeheartedly. If they got wet, it would be impossible to dry out. And what about Mikiah, if it rained?

In some places the road had been nearly swallowed up by bushes and trees, so walking side by side was impossible, but when he could, Jedan walked next to Chella. They talked little, but Chella loved him to be near.

"What are you thinking about?" he asked her once, as they paused to shift the bags on their shoulders.

"I was wondering what sort of buildings the Old Church live in, in Anderley, and hoping we'll reach there before nightfall. You?"

There was a short silence. "I've been thinking about my family."

Chella's heart gave a flip for him. "You miss them?"

"I didn't think I would, but I do."

"You wanted to make it up to them, I remember you saying."

Jedan nodded. "I can't do that now."

"You never know what God will do."

Jedan smiled at her. "True," he agreed, and smiled back at her, but she saw him blink his eyes. They both knew there was no going back.

Chella had only met Jedan's family twice, and then only briefly. After they had been seeing each other for a couple of weeks, Chella asked him if he'd told his mum and dad about her.

"To be honest, we don't talk much now," he had replied, as they sat at her dining table, finishing their evening meal with a bowl of warm stewed apples. "I told them I had a girlfriend when we first started seeing each other, but they didn't reply. I think they'd like me to just go away. I think they're glad I'm not at home much now. All their hopes are fixed on Vasilus, since I failed the Final Exam."

"But that wasn't your fault!" she said, drizzling a little more honey on the sharp fruit.

He shrugged his shoulders. "It was. Writing about freedom was a risk, I knew it was, but, I don't know, I felt I had to say it. I was always a rebel – always getting into trouble, and they hated me for it. Failing the Final Exam was the last straw. If anyone ever accused me of being a Christian, I think they would disown me."

"They still don't know?"

"I tried to talk to my dad once, when I was little, but he cut me off and said he never wanted to hear me talk about God again. So I didn't."

"Even when you came back to the Lord last year?"

"Thought it better not to. I think they suspect it, but they've never said anything."

"What about your brother?"

"He used to read the Bible stories with me when we were younger, in secret, but that was a long time ago. To be honest, we don't have anything in common. He's quiet, studies hard, keeps his head down, tows the party line. He's never given mum and dad any trouble. Not like me!"

"Even so..."

"I let them down. It's my fault. Because of me, dad didn't get the promotion he should have got, and mum had to go back to working with the juniors. They both had pay cuts."

Chella got up to put the kettle on. "Love loves anyway, no matter what."

Jedan sighed. "They were humiliated. Mum is ashamed of me and what I have become. I can see it in her eyes when she sees me in my work clothes. And she sniffs when I get home from work, smelling of the yard."

159

"The system is harsh."

Jedan nodded. "It is, but you have no idea how awful I was. Maybe one day I'll tell you everything."

"Tell me now," she had said as she fetched two cups from the kitchen cupboard, but he shook his head.

"I don't want to spoil us, what we have." He got up, walked round the table, and put his arms round her. "I have you now, and the church. That's all the family I need. I'm not the person I used to be. The past is the past. I don't even like thinking about it. And maybe one day I can make it up to them."

Later, Chella had wept. Jedan's parents were alive, but they didn't care. Her parents were gone, but they had both loved her. God's purposes were a mystery: beyond understanding.

They missed the wider road – on the map it looked as if it should have been obvious, but it was only when Jedan noticed a rusting road sign wrapped up in a creeping vine, that they realised they must have walked straight over the crossroads. Jedan walked back to check, then called Chella and Amma; they had indeed missed it. Once they knew it was there they could see it all too clearly, despite the overgrown bushes that were masking the way.

With a beating heart Chella realised they could so easily have walked for hours on the wrong road. Seeing Amma's wide eyes, she knew Amma was thinking the same thing.

As they turned on to the new road, her stomach still churning with the shock of their mistake, Chella stopped in surprise as she saw faint horseshoe-shaped tracks in the dust on the broken tarmac. "Look!" she exclaimed, pointing them out.

"Horses have been here!" exclaimed Jedan in amazement, looking first at the prints Chella had noticed, then scanning the road up and down. "And carts, too," he said, pointing out the tracks on the ground.

"Goodness!" exclaimed Amma, following his gaze. "Horses and carts, right out here? That's something we weren't expecting."

A chill suddenly touched Chella's soul, as if she had been hit by an arrow. She could hardly speak. "How old are the tracks, do you think?"

Jedan frowned in concentration as he studied them. "Impossible to say, but the newest ones have been made since the last rainfall, for sure."

Chella swallowed hard. "You mean there's more than one set?"

Jedan walked down the road a little way, studying the tracks closely. "Yes, it looks like a regular route."

"You don't think this could be the road the Elite take to visit another Area, do you?" asked Chella, her voice shaking with emotion. "Messengers, or traders, maybe?"

"I hope not," said Jedan, with feeling, crouching down to study the nearest marks more carefully. "The prints are so faint, I can't tell if they're ours or not."

Chella's voice cracked as she spoke. "If it's Elite from our Area, visiting another Area, we need to be careful..." She couldn't finish her sentence, but strained her ears, in case she could hear anyone approaching. She suddenly felt sick.

Surely, surely, they couldn't have come this far, to fall into the hands of Elite from their Area – or even Solod himself?

Jedan frowned. He got out the atlas, flipped the pages back and forth to the relevant places, then smiled and shook his head. "I can't see any reason why anyone from our Area would come right out here – it's just an old country road. See this big red straight road? Elite would use that road, surely, not this little one that winds around."

Chella let out a deep breath and Amma shook her head. "Well, that's a relief!"

Jedan nodded. "Yes! Plus, look. This road passes right through Anderley. The church building is on the main road – see the mark of the cross on the map? Logic dictates that the Church wouldn't be worshipping there if Elite regularly went through. It wouldn't make sense."

"Well in that case these horses must belong to people from the Old Church then, surely?" said Amma with a smile. "Oh, praise the Lord if that is so..." Then she suddenly stopped and her face dropped. "It could be other people outside, though? Not believers, I mean. Just people who never moved to the Areas?"

Jedan pursed his lips. "Either's possible. There's no way of knowing. And now I think of it, when the guards were talking in the prison, they were talking about the Church being watched in secret. We'd better listen out – maybe we shouldn't sing. And if we hear horses, we'd better hide in the woods, and not make ourselves known unless we're sure they're safe."

"You're right. Better safe than sorry," agreed Amma.

"I don't know why I didn't think of it before," said

Jedan, shaking his head. "There might be guards around or something. We've not been as vigilant as perhaps we should have been."

They all nodded soberly to each other then set off again, quietly. "I wish we knew for sure who uses this road," said Chella, thinking how loud the rumble of the pramcot wheels sounded in all that emptiness.

"Don't worry, it'll be fine!" Jedan reassured her. "The Lord wouldn't bring us right out here to fall into the hands of our enemies! Don't forget, he has given us an important job to do. We just need to be sensible."

Chella smiled back, but didn't reply. The forest was thicker in that area. The trees were taller and closer together. Their shade was darker, almost as if they were hiding a secret. Even the noise they made in the wind was different, and the atmosphere somehow heavier. Not long after that, Chella heard a regular beat in the distance, a bit like drums, far away. She frowned and stopped to listen. Jedan, seeing she had stopped, listened, too, through the noise of the wind. "There they are!" he exclaimed.

Chella's heart began to pound. "Is that the sound of horses?"

"Yes."

"Are they coming this way? They all listened again, straining to hear the noise above the wind. "Yes, I think they are," said Jedan.

For a second they all froze, then Amma grabbed Mikiah from the pramcot. "Run!" she said, heading for the forest. Jedan dropped all his bags into the pramcot, picked it up and followed. Chella picked up the bag Amma had dropped and ran, too, crashing through the undergrowth.

Amma ran to a length of broken-down wall a little way from the road, and crouched behind it, holding Mikiah tight, who was looking at her with wide eyes, his lower lip trembling as if he were about to cry. "His drink, quick!" Amma whispered to Chella, who fumbled in his bag and found his cup. Chella stared in shock at Amma's white face, as she threw herself down beside her with the bags. Jedan quietly placed the pramcot next to them.

"I'm so sorry, leaving you with the pramcot and all the bags," whispered Amma, once she had settled Mikiah with his bottle. "I don't know what came over me – something just took over and I had to run, with the baby." Chella clung to her and Mikiah together as they heard the sound of the horses' hooves getting closer.

"It sounds like there are only two of them," whispered Jedan, pulling the pramcot further round the broken wall. He peered above it, straining to see the road through the layers of trees. "Horses, I mean. With riders."

"Will they see the marks of the pramcot wheels, do you think?" asked Amma. Jedan made a face and shrugged his shoulders. Chella closed her eyes as the sound of the horses, and men talking, got louder and louder until they seemed to fill her soul.

And then they had passed, and she opened her eyes.

"I wish I could hear what the riders are talking about," whispered Jedan. "They might be from the Old Church." Chella didn't reply. They might. Or they might not.

TWENTY-FIVE

Diamonds and Emeralds

At the end of Chella's first visit to Solod's apartment, as they were saying goodbye to his parents at the door, Sheva told Chella she must go for dinner the following day. It didn't sound like an invitation: more like an order, but Chella accepted gladly, and a little later, her head spinning, she almost danced as Solod walked her home down the lane of beech trees. The lane was even more magical in the light of the moon. Solod laughed and spun her around, as if a load had been taken off his shoulders, and when he drew her close she hardly dared to believe she could be so happy. She was in love, with an Elite man, who was the descendant of a real Scottish Lord, and who lived in luxury she hadn't even known existed. Any doubts about their relationship she pushed aside. Did she not have the right to be happy, after all she had been through?

Solod stayed with her that night — to keep her out of trouble, he said. He seemed animated, too, and the night was one Chella would never forget.

The following morning Solod told her he had something

to do for an hour or two, and she mustn't go out or open the door to anyone. He didn't say why, and was a lot longer than the time he said. Fortunately it was her day off, so she kept herself busy tidying and cleaning, ready for his return. She'd have loved to have shared her happiness with her old friends, but didn't dare to disobey him. She wondered why she shouldn't go out. Perhaps it might have had something to do with his secret work? She hadn't asked, and it hadn't seemed to matter at the time. She brushed away any niggling thoughts that what she was doing was against the moral law she had stood by for so long. Why should she care? At last things were working out for her! She had a new life – all the old hardships were being swept aside. Who needed God, or the church, and all those restrictions?

As on the previous day, Solod waited until dusk to take her to his home. As before, the security guard let them through, and once more, Sheva and Walt welcomed her warmly.

Over a sumptuous dinner in their dining room, on plates edged with gold and glasses to match, Chella told them a bit more about her work in the design studio, and her colleagues who worked there. Walt nodded politely, but once more Sheva's main topic of conversation was the Old Order. Chella could hardly believe how wonderful it all sounded – soirées, shooting parties and card parties, swimming parties and cocktail parties and so many other sorts of parties her head began to swim. Sheva talked about the food they used to eat: the desserts, the cakes and chocolate and buns and spices – the fish and meat and trifles and pastries and all sorts of delicious sounding delicacies.

"One day I'll get all the old photos out and show you, when I can bear it," said Sheva with a sigh. "To be honest looking at them depresses me. We stayed away from the War, of course, but when food became scarce, and all the servants died or left. . ." She took a swig of wine and dabbed her mouth with her napkin. "Just look at us now!" she added gloomily, waving her hand at that room filled with more expensive things than Chella had ever seen in her life.

"I think it's beautiful here," Chella dared to say, and meant it with her whole heart.

Sheva looked at her with pity. "Thank the stars I can't see your apartment, if you think this is beautiful. Must be as dull as ditch-water."

Chella opened her mouth to protest, but changed her mind. Compared with this room, her living area was basic. . . and how could Sheva understand, coming from nobility as she did, and being used to living in a castle, no less?

Solod was silent through most of the meal. Walt didn't speak much, but smiled pleasantly enough, and as the maid came in to clear away the dessert plates he opened a second bottle of wine. After filling everyone's glasses, he announced, during a pause in Sheva's reminiscing, that he should be able to get Solod and Chella an Elite apartment by the end of the month.

Chella couldn't speak, overwhelmed with the thought that she would be going to live in such luxury as this herself, with the man she loved.

Her eyes shining, cheeks flushed with the alcohol, she lifted her glass with the others as Walt proposed a toast. "To our new, beautiful daughter-in-law-to-be, and her handsome groom," he said. Chella followed their example as they clinked glasses, and they smiled at each other as they sipped the smooth, heady liquid.

As she put her glass down, Chella, still smiling, fingered the leather ring Solod had given her. Sheva, nodding towards it from the other side of the table, said, "We'll have to get rid of that rubbishy old leather thing and get you a proper ring."

Walt nodded. "A pretty girl like you needs a ring as beautiful as you. What are your favourite stones?"

"Stones?" asked Chella, shaking her head.

"Yes, you know, diamonds, rubies, emeralds, sapphires..."

"I...I don't know, I've never seen jewels in real life," she stammered.

"Oh my dear, you haven't lived! Come with me," Sheva said, wiping her mouth on her napkin and sweeping her away through the entrance hall to the bedroom she shared with Walt. "You know what they say: diamonds are a girl's best friend!"

Chella's eyes opened in awe as she stepped into that beautiful bedroom, mostly in black and grey, with deep red curtains and a white fur cover on the bed. Old photographs and carefully placed ornaments adorned the walls and the polished surface of a chest of drawers. A real glass chandelier full of twinkly lights hung from the ceiling, the likes of which didn't even exist in the Area Hall.

"Of course you shouldn't really be here with us so-called Elite," crooned Sheva, gripping Chella's arm and drawing her further into that sumptuous room. "But we won't tell, will we? Such a ridiculous distinction."

Dread suddenly filled Chella's stomach. She knew she shouldn't have come; she didn't belong here – this wasn't the world she knew. "I knew I shouldn't be here," she stammered. "Solod said..."

Sheva made a sound like a puff of air and waved her hand dismissively, as she seemed to do a lot. "There are way too many rules; frankly I'm sick of them. Walt will pull some strings. And we'll make sure you get married as soon as possible, so you can become one of us." She looked at Chella's frightened face and laughed her tinkly laugh. "Don't worry," she said, going over to the chest of drawers. "Everything will be fine. Now let's look at rings."

Chella swallowed hard and stood in that grand room, feeling slightly light-headed and more out of place than anywhere she had ever been in her life. The room even smelled of luxury, like fragrant flowers on a summer evening.

"Do you like emeralds?" asked Sheva. She strode over to a dressing table and picked up a wooden jewellery box, with little drawers and bead handles. Taking it over to the bed, she sat down. "Emeralds would pick out the green in your eyes. Come and sit here, girl, come, next to me," she ordered, patting the cover next to her.

She's not used to being disobeyed, thought Chella, as she submissively took her place. Thrill and dread coursed through her as she realised that from now on she would have to do whatever this woman said, and she wouldn't ever be able to tell anyone she had been here... but the fur bedspread was so unbelievably soft, and the room so incredibly beautiful!

"Solod had another girl before you, but she didn't suit him," Sheva said airily, lifting up the lid of the box to reveal a mirror on the inside of the lid, and four separate sections. Each was lined with purple silk and filled with necklaces, bracelets, earrings and brooches in neat rows. Chella had never seen anything like that jewellery, or that exquisite box. She couldn't take her eyes away. The gold and gems sparkled in the light, and the purple set them off like a frame around a painting. Leather rings, armlets and necklaces were the best jewellery she had ever possessed. "You are so much more his type than that horrid girl, I can see that straight away," continued Sheva loftily. "And you and me, we're going to be the best of friends, I can see that, too."

Chella didn't dare reply. Solod had told her about the horrid girl, and she was glad Sheva liked her better, but wasn't sure about being friends with this imposing woman – not yet, anyway. Maybe in time...

"Come closer," commanded Sheva. Suddenly Chella felt tatty in her best dress and shawl. She felt like an oaf sitting next to a princess. She obediently moved up a little, and stroked that wonderful fur bedspread with the tips of her fingers.

Sheva showed Chella each piece of jewellery, one by one, and told its story – how much it was worth; where it came from; where she had worn it. When she had exhausted the top compartment of the box, she opened one of the little drawers underneath the main compartment. It was full of rings in neat rows.

"These are all antique, of course," sighed Sheva, shaking her head, which made the silver bells on her earrings tinkle, "from the good old days when having jewellery meant money and privilege. Some of them have been in our families for countless generations, but have hardly seen the light of day since we came to live in this godforsaken place. Now let's find you a nice ring. Which do you prefer, emeralds, sapphires, rubies? Or just diamonds?" She stopped talking and caressed the rows of rings.

"They are all so beautiful," breathed Chella.

"They are. Diamonds are traditional for an engagement, but emeralds would match your eyes. Oh, how I miss the outside world," sighed Sheva. "I wish you could have seen it – you have no idea what you are missing. I had such a wonderful life spread out before me, before the war started. Well, you know how it was. I'm sure you have heard a million times how lovely the world was in those days. The fun, the travel, the clothes and lovely things... Oh the stupidity of man and his pride, causing wars and death and destruction. If only women had been in charge, things would have turned out so differently. Try this ring on," she said suddenly, picking up a gold band, alternately studded with diamonds and emeralds. "It belonged to my great aunt, the Countess of Arrandale, God rest her soul."

Chella shook her head as Sheva held out the ring for her to try on. "No, no, I couldn't, it's yours! And it belonged to a *countess*?"

"But you must, you silly! I have so many of these, look at them all, and no occasion to wear them. And you will be keeping it in the family. Auntie would be pleased. Anyway,

I want you to have it. Perhaps it will bring you some luck. It's no good to me, so I might as well have the pleasure of seeing you wear it. If it fits, of course."

As she spoke, Sheva grasped Chella's left hand, peeled off her leather band and slipped the diamond and emerald ring on her finger. Chella snatched her hand back and was about to take it off, but as she did so, the diamonds caught the light and she gasped and looked again, twisting her hand to make the diamonds flash. The ring glistened and shone, and Chella laughed, entranced.

"It fits perfectly," crowed Sheva, pleased with herself. "It must have been meant for you. Just look at it!"

"Is it real gold? And are those really diamonds and sapphires?"

Sheva laughed at her. "Emeralds! Sapphires are blue. Would you prefer sapphires? You can have any of these rings you like... although the emeralds do bring out the green in your eyes. I was right."

"No, no, this is beautiful..."

"Of course it is, you silly, and it's perfect for you. A leather ring indeed," she scoffed. "Solod's nothing but a mean cheapskate. All we need to do now is get you two married. Let's go and show the men!"

Suddenly Chella wanted to put the leather band that Solod had given her back on, but Sheva snatched it up. Grabbing Chella's elbow, she marched her back to the living room.

"Just take a look at this!" she said to Jedan and Walt, pushing Chella in front of her. Walt was adding another log to the fire; Solod was sitting slouched on the furthest settee, swirling the wine in his glass. Sheva triumphantly showed Chella's hand wearing the ring on her engagement finger, in place of the leather band.

Chella looked at Solod's face. She tried to make an apologetic smile, but for the first time ever he frowned back at her. Chella was mortified. She hadn't intended to upset him. She turned to Sheva in desperation, her heart banging in her chest. "This is the most beautiful ring I have ever seen," she said, "but please can I have my leather one back?"

"What do you want that rubbishy thing for?" snapped Sheva.

Chella felt close to tears. "Please," she begged, taking off the diamonds and emeralds and holding it out to Sheva.

"Well, keep them both then," said Sheva after a difficult moment's silence, and gave her back her leather band. Solod got up and put his arms around Chella's waist, then helped her put the leather band back on, smiling at her again.

"Mother you're an old hag, giving my girl a ring when I had already given her a perfectly good one."

"A bit of old leather," mocked Sheva. "You can't call that a ring. Now that's a proper ring," she said, pointing to the diamond ring which Chella had changed over to her right hand. "It belonged to your great aunt, so show a bit of respect."

"You're an interfering old busybody and you should mind your own business," Solod retorted.

"Oh stop being a bore, for goodness sake," sighed Sheva, sitting as close to the fire as she could. "You should be pleased I've taken to your choice of wife. Tell him to shut up, Walt," she said to her husband, who had been watching the proceedings with apparent amusement.

Walt went to the drinks cabinet and chose the third bottle of wine of the evening. "Come on, both of you," he said mildly. "I think we should celebrate, have another drink. Bubbly this time. It's not every day your son gets engaged!"

Walt popped a cork from another bottle he chose from a cabinet, then handed tall glasses of the sparkling wine to everyone. Chella accepted her glass with a smile, and was relieved to see Solod grin at his dad as he took his own.

After another toast to *the happy couple, and grandchildren to carry on the family name*, Chella sat down next to Solod and sipped the golden liquid, admiring the delicate colour, and the way the bubbles rose up in the glass. How easily it slipped down, and how cosy it was, with the crackling fire, surrounded by extravagance she had never dreamed she would ever see, let alone be part of! Walt winked at her before topping up her glass, and she smiled warmly back.

Sheva quickly went back to talking about the Old Order; the properties their families had owned and the places she had visited as a child. After she had exhausted that subject, she moved on to the cities and countries she had travelled to. Chella tried to take it all in, but it was hot in the room, and her head was swimming with the unaccustomed alcohol. She struggled to understand where all the houses and castles were situated, and all the twists and turns of the holidays and trips abroad.

"Well, Solod, you'd better show Chella your room, where the two of you are going to be sleeping for the time being," declared Sheva, eventually, when everyone's glasses were finally empty. She turned to Chella. "In the morning we can discuss the wedding, and furniture for your new home."

Chella stared at her. "I think there's been some mistake," she stammered, swaying as she got to her feet. "I. . . I need to go home."

"This is your home now, you silly," said Sheva, getting up and putting her arm around her. "You can't go back to that old apartment now, can you?"

"But I must!" Chella looked at Solod, hoping he would back her up, but he was looking at the floor. "I have to get up for work tomorrow. Today was my day off."

Sheva waved her hand dismissively. "Don't worry about that, I'll send a message to say you won't be going in any more."

Chella's head thumped. She desperately tried to keep her balance. Her head swam, and she tried to think straight. "But I must go in to work, for the common good!"

Walt smiled and winked at his wife; Sheva gave a tinkly laugh. "But now you're one of us," she said indulgently. "Or you will be very soon. You won't need to work any more – we'll look after you. Anyway, you're in no fit state to go anywhere tonight, are you?"

TWENTY-SIX

Approaching Storm

Chella began to breath again, as the rhythmic sound of the horses' hooves disappeared into the distance. Relief flooded through her soul. They were safe!

"Well, there's a thing," said Amma, breathing out a huge sigh of relief. She shook her head, and put Mikiah down to crawl on the leaves while she got out her water bottle. "What a journey this is turning out to be!"

Jedan stood up and craned his neck, then ran stealthily towards the road, evidently hoping to see the back of the horses. He rejoined Chella and Amma as they were quietly sorting out the bags between them. "I wish I got a better look. I wonder if we should have made ourselves known? If they were from the Old Church, they would have been able to help us."

Amma shook her head. "I think we did the right thing. By God's grace we'll reach Anderley tonight, and if they weren't from the Church..."

"True," Jedan admitted, but he didn't look happy.

Chella swallowed hard. In her gut she could still feel

the dread that the horses were from their own Area. What if the men on the horses were spying on the Old Church, or Correctioners out looking for them? They could easily be either. Jedan was an escaped prisoner, after all, and somehow the Church had been observed in secret. How? By whom?

Chella and Amma waited at the edge of the road while Jedan examined the horses' tracks, but after a little while he shrugged, shook his head and they set back off.

The rest of the afternoon passed slowly, mostly in silence, apart from Mikiah's babbling and toy-rattling. At one point a herd of deer bounded across the road in front of them, making them jump, and another time they heard dogs barking and howling in the distance. They walked a little closer to each other for a while after that, but the noise drifted off into the distance, and it came to nothing. The cloud cover grew, and the breeze blew stronger, bit by bit, until it became a proper wind, whipping their hair and clothes as it gusted around them. It was relief from the sticky heat of the morning, but Jedan smiled less, Amma looked weary, and Mikiah became fractious and more difficult to entertain until he finally dozed off.

As the sun started dipping towards the west, Amma declared she couldn't walk any further. "I'm so sorry, I really can't take another step," she said, and let out a big sigh. "I'd love to make the most of it and have a short rest, while Mikiah is asleep. Just ten minutes. If you don't mind? I wish I could keep going, but I just can't," she apologised.

"Of course, Amma," said Jedan after a short pause. "I

was thinking we ought to stop and have a meal, as we had lunch so early."

He forged a way off the road into the forest, and spread out one of the blankets under a fir tree, where they were hidden from the road. The ground was soft and dry, and the air was warm and sheltered from the wind. After finishing off most of the food they had brought with them, keeping only a bread roll each for breakfast, and a handful of sweet biscuits for Mikiah, just in case, Amma made her shawl into a pillow, lay down and closed her eyes.

"Oh, this is just what I need!" she sighed. It had indeed been a long couple of days. Chella yawned, too, and after a little while she curled up herself, leaving Jedan on guard, leaning against the trunk of the tree, studying the map.

A far away rumble woke Chella a little while later. "That wasn't thunder, was it?" she asked, yawning and blinking as she looked up at the gathering clouds through the waving branches of the trees.

"Actually, I think it was," said Jedan, jumping up and tucking the atlas back into the pocket of his bag. "We'd better move on."

They all felt better for a rest, and sang quietly as they walked, to help them keep up a rhythm and amuse Mikiah, but were careful not to make too much noise. Fortunately, although the clouds were getting darker, the thunder rumbled only in the distance, then disappeared altogether, and the rain held off.

After a while the trees began to thin out. Prickly yellow gorse bushes and thick tufts of wild grass took over from the trees. Chella noticed Amma checking the pramcot wheels as they bumped across that ancient road, and silently prayed they would hold up until they reached their destination.

"It looks like this road turns into a river when it rains," observed Jedan. "See the gulleys at the edges? I'm so glad the rain's kept off."

"It would be slippery, too, if it was raining," Amma agreed, and looked up at the thickening clouds. "Praise the Lord for keeping us dry! His hand is upon us."

And then, suddenly, as the road turned a corner, there were no more trees. "We're nearly at the top of a hill," cried Chella in surprise, holding her hair out of her face as the wind struck them at full force.

Not far off the road, an ancient concrete post marked the peak of the hill. Jedan grinned. It was his turn to push the pramcot. "Ready for this, Mikiah?" he asked, as he ran off the road to the very top of the hill. Mikiah laughed as the pramcot bounced and jolted over the rough ground, and the wind whipped around them.

Chella and Amma followed more slowly, picking their way through the clumps of grass, rabbits bobbing away as they approached. "Look, wild ponies!" said Chella, pointing out a group of about a dozen, a mile or so away. "They must be what keeps the grass short!"

Her eyes opened wider as the view opened up in every direction. Ponies were scattered in groups over that high moorland, then mile after mile of forest stretched out on hill after hill below and beyond, right into the grey distance, where the sky melded with the land. The wind whistled round them, whipping their hair, their clothes, and the long grasses all around.

Chella let her bags fall to the ground and turned all the way round in open-mouthed wonder, holding on to her shawl to stop it blowing away. She had never in her life imagined she would see such an awesome sight with her own eyes. The energy of the wind and the immensity of the space took her breath away. She had seen photographs of beautiful places like this, of course, but the reality was infinitely more glorious. "Such vastness..." She breathed it in, and felt a shiver of thrill at the enormity of it all.

Jedan put his arms round her. "I knew about hills, but this is truly incredible! It hardly seems real, it's so – I don't know, I don't think I've got words for it! You know, I'm starting to feel the freedom. I know we are free inside, but here it feels like the chains of the old ways are dropping away. For so long we've had to fight against everything the World Council has told us to think, but still it's kind of invaded us. Our thinking."

Amma breathed in deeply. "I know what you mean. And to think the Lord God made all this!" She spread out her arms towards the view before them, then making the most of the opportunity, took Mikiah out of his pramcot, and sat down with him on the tussocky grass. They laughed together as the wind blew around them and made the grasses wave wildly.

"It makes me feel I could fly!" said Chella with a laugh, holding out her arms in the direction of the wind. Her clothes streamed out and flapped behind her.

Jedan grinned. "You look like you're on a washing line!" He pretended to put pegs on her shoulders and they all laughed together.

Amma shook her head. "I can hardly believe, all my life, this was here all the time, but we never knew it. And look at the sky! It's so huge! Mind you, goodness me," she said, getting quickly to her feet, "we'd better not stay here too long, look — look at those dark clouds over to the west!"

"That's probably where that thunder came from," agreed Jedan, looking in the direction Amma was pointing. "It does look black. See how the world is round, though?" he added, pointing out the curve of the earth.

"Yes!" gasped Chella, tying her hair up in a knot as it continued to blow over her face. As she did, she noticed a small group of dwellings clustered together in the valley ahead, on the edge of the forest. "Do you think that's an old farm?" she asked.

"It might be," replied Jedan, squinting at the group of ruined buildings. "Let's see if I can find it on the map." He frowned, then whooped and shook the atlas in the air, making Chella jump. "It is a farm, according to the map, and if I'm right, we're almost there! See that line of trees there, heading towards the buildings? That must be what remains of the track that leads to it. When we get to the bit that joins our road, we'll be nearly at Anderley!"

"Oh praise the Lord!" said Amma. "That is good news indeed. And is that a river? My eyes aren't what they were." A curving line snaking into the distance suddenly sparkled in the light, as a shaft of evening sun broke through the scudding clouds.

Jedan took a sharp intake of breath and whooped. "Yes! That will be the river we'll need to cross to get to Anderley! If we follow the line of the river. . ." He looked up and gazed into the distance, then gasped as he pointed out a stone tower rising just above the line of trees. "Look, look, look, Chella, look, Amma, look, that must be Anderley – see the church tower through the trees? *That's where we're going!*"

"Goodness," said Amma, squinting into the distance. "I can't make it out, Jedan, my eyes aren't good enough, but oh, thank you dear Lord, the end is in sight!"

Jedan grabbed Chella and whirled her round. "We're nearly there!" he crowed. "We've made it! Well, nearly!" Chella laughed as he put her back down, then she gazed at the solid stone of that ancient strong tower, where believers had met together to worship for hundreds of years. Relief flooded her heart. Surely, soon, they would be safe.

"Oh, praise the Lord," said Amma. "Despite our rest earlier – I felt so bad about that, holding you back – we will surely reach Anderley tonight. Shall we kneel and thank the Lord? It seems fitting on the top of this hill."

"Yes," enthused Jedan, stuffing the map back in his bag once more. "This old post can be our Ebenezer stone – thus far the Lord has helped us, and delivered us from all our enemies. Just think, there may be people in that church building right now! When we join them, Chella, we'll get married. Next month, yeah? We'll have proper Bible readings," he continued, dropping to one knee in front of her, "and music and psalms and hymns! We'll have prayers and blessings and we'll all sing out loud!"

Chella opened her mouth to grab the opportunity to tell Jedan about Solod, but Amma, who had turned to face the way they had come, suddenly cried out.

"We'd better pray quickly. That band of dark cloud is

coming this way fast...and oh my goodness!" she added, with a note of alarm. "You can actually see the rain dropping from the clouds. Look at that!" Even as she spoke, the sky darkened as if someone had put out a light, and a smattering of raindrops blew in the wind.

"Oh, no!" gasped Chella. A sheet of dark cloud was coming their way, emptying its load as it came. A faraway flash of light lit the sky, followed a few seconds later by a low rumble of thunder.

Amma grabbed Mikiah from the grass. "We need to go now. We'll have to pray as we walk."

TWENTY-SEVEN

The Road to Anderley

The road led the travellers along the ridge of the hill, then started to drop down into the valley. Chella was relieved for two reasons: walking downhill felt good after the uphill climb of most of the day, and it was good to be heading into the forest again, for cover. Imprints of horseshoes still dusted the road. Would the horses they had seen return this way before nightfall? Might there be others? There was no doubt this road was used by someone on a regular basis, but who?

As she walked, Chella's heart thrilled at having stood on the top of that hill, and seen that view. *Even if I never see it again, I will always remember it,* she thought. She stood still for a moment, with the wind on her face, thinking of that view, and letting the knowledge – the *feeling* of the knowledge of the vastness of the glory of God, wash in and through her.

Noticing she had stopped, Jedan looked back at her quizzically. "God knows everything," she managed, by way of explanation, and he smiled at her, and nodded, but she knew she wouldn't be able to explain how she felt, even to Jedan.

As she caught up with the others, Amma smiled at her. "We have an awesome Saviour, my dear." Chella nodded. How wonderful it was to know God and be part of a living Church! And surely, soon, they would be joining their brothers and sisters; unknown, but still family. What a wonderful thing that was – and maybe, one day, the other members of their church back in the Area might be able to join them, too.

The group spoke little as they descended the hill, but when they did, despite their tiredness, it was with a new energy. Even Mikiah picked up on the new mood. He blew raspberries, waved his toys and babbled cheerily. Chella kept an eye out for somewhere to shelter in case the rain came, or the horses came back, but, miraculously, although the thunder still rumbled in the distance, the spitting they had felt on the top of the hill came to nothing, and they saw and heard no one but themselves.

"Maybe the rain clouds will blow right over us," commented Amma. "If so, I will be truly grateful. If the pramcot gets wet, Mikiah will have nowhere to sleep."

Chella was the first to see the turning off the road – a spur of grey tarmac heading into the undergrowth. "Isn't that the old track to the farm we saw from the top of the hill?" she asked.

Jedan stared at it, then checked the map and grinned. "Yes! It must be! Oh, ladies, we are so close!"

They all grinned at each other. "I hope they have nice

comfortable chairs in the church!" said Amma with a laugh. "My feet do ache."

Jedan grinned. "Oh yes! And a nice hot rabbit stew and potatoes would be perfect right now..."

"You've only just eaten!" Chella said.

"True," admitted Jedan. "But a man can dream!"

They all laughed and Chella admitted, "A hot meal would be wonderful."

"Oh, yes," agreed Amma. "Not much longer now, surely. And here's the most important thing. Whatever the chairs are like, and the food, there will be no World Council Nursery to teach Mikiah that anyone who thinks that God exists is a fool, or a danger to mankind."

Chella nodded in agreement, then as she bent down to remove a twig from one of the pramcot wheels, she noticed an unusual mark on an old wooden post. It looked like someone had carved something into it. "Look at this," she said to the others, stepping off the road into the waving grasses to uncover the carving from the weeds that were partly masking it.

"What it it?" asked Jedan.

"Someone's marked the post." As she uncovered it, she stared. "It's a fish!"

"The ancient symbol of the Church!" said Amma with awe in her voice.

Jedan ran over to see for himself. "Someone must have left it here for... for other Christians to find... I guess."

"Another encouragement!" agreed Amma with a weary sigh and a smile.

Jedan ran back to the road and grabbed the bags. "Come on ladies, let's go!" he sang out. They heard the rushing water before they reached the river. The ancient bridge was a stunning work of art, made of stone in a span of three arches. If only it could have spoken, it could have told so many secrets, thought Chella. She imagined the Messengers riding on horses over this bridge, in times gone by, and before that, metal vehicles. If only the stones could speak! Chella touched the mossy sides of the ancient, cold stones as they passed over, and felt the firmness beneath her feet. Even their footsteps made a different sound as they passed over – it felt like arriving.

As they stepped off the bridge, a ray of sunshine suddenly shot through the clouds in a silver arc, and gave such hope that Chella's heart leaped. She would have loved to have stopped to watch the rushing river dancing over stones, making rivulets and eddies and little fountains and waterfalls on its way to the sea, but they were all so keen to finally reach the end of their journey. Perhaps they would live here in Anderley, near this bridge, and be able to come and watch the river whenever she wanted. Perhaps she would be able to walk out to the hill sometimes, and see the ponies. Of course, it would depend on what the elders of the church decided, once they knew the World Council was watching them. . .

Jedan cried out as he caught sight of buildings. "This is it! This has to be Anderley!" At first they all walked quickly and cheerfully towards the village, but gradually their optimism began to turn to puzzlement. Jedan had to push his way through a tangle of bushes to reach the

187

village sign. "It does say Anderley," he assured the others as he pulled creepers away from the letters, but something didn't feel right. Where were all the people? This village looked as abandoned as every other dwelling area they had passed through.

As they passed the first house on the main road, with a hole in the wall where a window had once protected its inhabitants from the elements, a light drizzle began to fall. "Why don't you three take shelter in that house, and I'll run on to the church building?" suggested Jedan. "I'll come back and get you when I've found it."

Chella looked up the road. "The church can't be far," she said, wiping her damp face with her hand. "What do you think, Amma?"

Amma pursed her lips and looked round at the desolation. "Perhaps we should stay together." Even Mikiah was quiet as they walked on. Amma stopped to put on his coat and hood, tucked a blanket round him, then covered the pramcot with her shawl.

So they walked on in the darkening sky, the wind whistling round, the endless trees and bushes waving in the incessant wind and the spitting rain. Chella shivered and looked up. The sky was ominously dark, which wasn't encouraging. She shivered. She needed to get out her warmer cloak, but didn't want to stop. What was wrong? Where was everyone? She felt a heavy bubble of fear creep up and settle in her stomach.

Their footsteps and the pramcot wheels echoed on the empty buildings. "I wonder if people only come here once a week, to meetings?" wondered Amma out loud. Chella's heart sank further. Surely, surely, Amma couldn't be right? Sunday was days away, and they only had a bread roll each left for breakfast!

They passed a whole street of ancient buildings – all of them forsaken and neglected. Still the only signs of life were the birds and the waving trees, bushes and creepers.

"Perhaps everyone is in hiding, because of the evening," said Jedan, but Chella knew, even as he spoke the words, that it was wishful thinking. It was obvious that this village had been abandoned long ago.

Puzzlement was turning to dismay by the time they reached the gate to the ancient church building. Chella felt dizzy as she gazed up to the top of the grey tower that they had seen from the top of the hill, encircled by cawing rooks. Jedan kicked open the rotting wooden gate, then fought his way through the overgrown path towards the building. Chella followed, holding back the undergrowth so Amma could pass through with the pramcot.

They joined Jedan on a stone pavement in front of the ancient door. The church was as desolate as the rest of the village. "This can't be right," Jedan said, frowning. The door was padlocked with a rusting chain, smothered in ivy. Most of the lower storey of the church was only visible in snatches through a blanket of waving green. The windows had creepers growing in and through them, and a silver birch tree had taken root right in the sanctuary and had burst out through the roof. Now it was shaking in the wind, and even as Jedan spoke, a tile slid off the roof near the hole made by the tree, and thudded to the ground.

They all took a few steps backwards, but carried on

staring at that building. Amma eventually broke the silence. "What exactly was it you heard about Anderley and the church, Jedan?" she asked.

Jedan frowned. "People were living in a place called Anderley, and they were heard singing hymns in the old church building. They were seen going in and coming out." He shook his head, still staring at the ruin in front of them. "I don't understand; it doesn't look like anyone has been here for years." Chella looked at his face, his brows knit together, his hair glistening with the dampness from the drizzle. A knot twisted in her belly. Surely this couldn't be right?

"What about round the back?" asked Amma, fighting to keep the wind from blowing her shawl off the pramcot. "Perhaps there's a church hall?"

Jedan went off to look, fighting his way through the undergrowth that was strangling the lower storey. Chella got her warmer shawl from her bag and helped cover Mikiah with the lighter one, but didn't dare catch Amma's eye. The rain started to fall more steadily, and the wind whistled as it whipped round the church building. The trees creaked and shook their leaves as if in pain. This couldn't be happening. This couldn't be what they had come for. *Lord, what is this?* Chella silently prayed, shivering, not just from the cold. *Where are your people?*

"Perhaps it was a different church building?" asked Amma eventually, as Jedan returned from his tour of the church, shaking his head and sucking his hand where it had been scratched by thorns. "A Baptist one, or a Catholic one, perhaps, somewhere further on?"

190

Jedan nodded and grabbed his bags. "Yes, of course! Maybe this isn't the one. Let's go look."

Amma shook her head. "There must be an explanation, but for now we must find shelter from this rain."

"Yes, yes of course," agreed Jedan. "Do you two want to take Mikiah to that first house we passed on the way in? I'll find the church, then I'll come and get you."

TWENTY-EIGHT

Shelter

Amma and Chella ran the last few metres to the ruined house as lightning lit up the sky and a clap of thunder rolled around in the darkness above them. Rain began to fall in earnest. Chella lifted the pramcot in the window hole, then took Mikiah before helping Amma in.

"I'm getting a bit old for climbing into abandoned buildings," Amma said, trying to smile, but she shivered as she spoke.

Chella's heart sank as she turned and saw the state of the room. Vegetation was claiming the floor, and debris of all kinds littered what must have once been a carpet; broken slabs of plaster, twigs, leaves and rabbit droppings. Dirty shards of glass showered the ground near the window hole. Their shoes crunched on it as they stepped further away from the window. The only furniture was an old garden bench, but even that was covered in a layer of green.

They didn't talk for a few minutes, as Amma changed Mikiah into his nightclothes, then changed into dry clothes herself. While Amma was busy with Mikiah, Chella checked out the door at the back of the room, which wouldn't open, then silently cleared the old garden bench of debris as best she could and rubbed it with a towel to get the worst of the dirt off. At least they would have somewhere to sit. The work made her a bit warmer, but she couldn't shake a feeling of foreboding. Amma helped her to move the bench to the side wall, where it was sheltered from the wind and the rain.

"Amma, what are we going to do? Where do you think the church is?" she asked, trying to sound light-hearted as she shook the towel out of the window hole.

"Don't let's think of that yet. Perhaps Jedan will find something."

Chella nodded. "Maybe," she said. "But what if..." She wanted to say *what if we never find them*, but she realised even as the words formed in her mind that it was better not to say them.

Amma knew what she was thinking though. "I can't bear to think..." she said, as she wiped her eyes. "We have to trust God," she added, and hugged Chella. "You ought to put on some dry clothes, Child. Goodness that rain is really coming down cats and dogs now. And oh, listen to that thunder!"

Chella did as Amma suggested, then joined Amma and Mikiah on the bench. The blankets made it slightly cosier. Chella took a turn with Mikiah, jiggling him up and down on her knee, playing peek a boo with the toys as if they were at home, not sheltering in a cold, dark, abandoned building.

"I hope Jedan comes back soon," Amma worried, when

he still hadn't joined them after several nursery rhymes. "He'll catch his death of cold out in that rain."

Chella couldn't answer. What was going on? What was happening? She tried not to cry; to keep her hope alive, but even while she smiled and carried on singing rhymes to keep Mikiah entertained, she felt numb inside. Mikiah wriggled and fretted; he wanted to get down and play on the floor, but he couldn't in all that mess, and now, to make matters worse, a puddle was beginning to grow where the wind was blowing the rain in through the window hole.

"Lord have mercy," whispered Amma as Mikiah's grumblings turned to proper cries.

"Jedan, hurry up!" Chella added, but as soon as she saw him, she knew he wasn't bringing good news.

He threw in his bags, jumped in through the hole, then wiped his wet face with the back of his hand. Chella looked up at him, hoping, desperate, but his white, grim face said it all. "There's nobody here. Not anywhere.

Rain continued to beat against the walls and through the window hole while Amma handed Jedan a clean towel, which he ran over his face and hair. "Are you sure?" she asked.

Jedan collapsed on to the bench and sank down, his face in his hands. "Everything is deserted. Everywhere. There's no sign that anyone has been to this village for years. Apart from the horses that pass through." He shrugged. "But even they don't go off the main road, as far as I can tell."

Chella shivered, even in her blanket. *No*, she thought, watching Mikiah push away his milk that Amma was offering. *This can't be happening.* He didn't want it cold. "But what about your dream, of the church worshipping?" she asked.

Jedan got up, grabbed his bag where he'd dumped it in the middle of the floor and pulled out the atlas and his torch. "I don't know..." he began, crouching on the floor, and flicked to the back of the book. "What if..."

"What is it?" Chella asked, as Jedan crouched over the atlas.

"I've had a thought..."

Chella watched the circle of torchlight move down the list of names in the index in alarm, as Jedan's shoulders dropped, and he started to breathe faster. Then he turned off the torch, threw it on the floor along with the atlas, stood up, and covered his head with his hands against the back wall.

The torch hadn't given out a lot of light, but now the darkness was complete. Chella passed Mikiah to Amma, picked up the torch and the atlas, and went over to Jedan, her heart thumping, not knowing what to do or say.

Amma rocked Mikiah in her arms, trying to get him to take his milk. "Jedan?" she asked. He turned and slowly took the atlas and the torch from Chella, and found the index again. The wind from the hole in the wall fluttered the pages, as he pointed out names on the list, one by one.

"Look. There's an Adderley, then here there's an Amberley and an Anterley. And more like it..."

Chella leaned against him and closed her eyes. Surely, surely, they couldn't have come to the wrong place? Jedan dropped the atlas again and held her tight.

"When it stops raining I'll find us a better place to stay for the night," he promised, "and light a fire."

"A hot drink would be most welcome," agreed Amma.

So many thoughts were going through Chella's mind, she couldn't speak. What would they do now? They couldn't go back, but they had nowhere to go, and precious little food. With a baby! How could this have happened?

Jedan led her back to the bench, squeezed her hand in his and hung his head against her shoulder. Chella had never seen him like this before. She felt like sinking to the ground, but gripped his hand instead. She couldn't give up. There had to be an answer.

"I'm so sorry, Jedan," exclaimed Amma, trying to distract Mikiah with a wooden rattle, as he wriggled and fought to be free. "I should have checked for other similar names when we first looked in the atlas..."

Jedan shook his head. "It's not your fault."

Amma's voice sounded wobbly, over Mikiah's cries and the gusting wind. "We'll decide what to do tomorrow."

Jedan nodded. "And if we hear horses, I'll go out and talk to the riders. Wherever they're from, they might help us."

Chella's heart lurched. "But what if they're from the World Council, spying on the Old Church?"

Jedan put his arms round her and stroked her hair. "There's no Old Church here, Chella."

So they sat there on the filthy bench, wrapped in blankets and cloaks to keep them warm, waiting for the storm to pass. The wind and rain thrashed on the walls and blew in through the window hole in cheerless gusts, as if trying to reach them with their miserable tentacles. Mikiah eventually drank his milk and fell asleep in Amma's arms. Jedan searched through the atlas to see where each of the similar names were, but eventually switched off the torch and said nothing, and neither Chella nor Amma made any comment. Jedan tried to light a candle, but a gust of wind blew it out, so he gave up.

It seemed to Chella that it was darker in that filthy room than she had ever known darkness before. It seeped into her very soul. And she couldn't even look up, as she and Amma had in Tadworth. She kept looking through the hole in the wall, hoping to see a glint of light, but there was nothing but the dark sky.

Chella tried to be strong, and remind herself that God was with her, and everything would be fine, but it didn't feel honest – everything in her longed to be safely back in her old apartment. She longed for her own bed, a hot meal, for safety, for warmth, for her cheerful colleagues in the Studio, whom she had abandoned, her friends in her groups, and all the things she had left behind.

How could they have made such a terrible mistake? What would they do now? Chella went back over snatches of the last couple of days in her mind – Jedan's arrest and escape, his visions, the prayer meeting. What had gone wrong?

The thunder and lightning moved slowly away, but the rain continued to fall, sometimes harder, sometimes letting up a bit, and the wind continued to blow through the hole in the wall. Mikiah woke and cried again when Amma tried to lay him in his pramcot, and Chella noticed Amma wiping tears from her face as she picked him back up.

Amma's tears were the last straw. While Jedan still sat with his head in his hands, Chella curled herself up in a blanket on the floor, and allowed her own tears to fall, until she was spent. Then she tried to think of nothing. She didn't even really want to pray, but just so she wouldn't have to think, she prayed the evening prayer over and over again in her mind: *"Shine your light into our darkness, Lord, and by your grace protect and deliver us from all evil this night; in the name of your Son, our Saviour Jesus Christ, we pray."*

By the time she got to the third repeat, she began to mean the words, and by the fifth, she had never meant them so deeply. Never, ever had that prayer seemed as relevant as it did at that moment. She carried on praying the words over and over again in her mind, with all her heart and soul, until Mikiah stopped crying, or perhaps she no longer heard him, and she dropped into an uneasy sleep.

Chella woke when Jedan moved. She watched him walk quietly over to the window hole. Amma was lying on the bench with a rolled up towel for a pillow; Mikiah was asleep in his pramcot. The wind had died down somewhat, and a flicker of the sun's final rays shone on the horizon in the western sky, under a purple cloud tinged with gold. Jedan walked over to Chella, crouched to kiss her hair, and gently tucked the blanket around her shoulders. "The rain's stopped," he whispered. "I'm going to see if I can find us a better place to stay."

Amma sat up slowly and yawned. "But it's so dark!"

"I'll take the torch. We can't stay here."

"Shall we pray together, then, before you go?" Amma suggested. "If ever we needed the Lord's help, it's now." Chella spread out the towel she had been lying on and they knelt close together, with the cold seeping round them.

Chella's teeth chattered. Her mouth felt dry and stale. Her hair needed brushing, let alone washing, and she was hungry, thirsty and chilled to the bone.

She didn't feel like praying, but as Amma began to ask quietly for guidance, Chella felt a sudden trust in God, like a flash of light, pierce her soul. Surely, whatever happened, God *would* protect and deliver them from evil. He *would* shine his light into their darkness. Amma's dream of looking up surely meant looking to Jesus, the light of the world, not at the sky! As she thought about it, Chella could almost feel the true light lightening her darkness. She knelt up straighter, then a thought hit her, like an arrow, just as Jedan said *Amen* to Amma's desperate prayer for help.

"The fish," she exclaimed. "We need to go back to the fish."

TWENTY-NINE

The Fish

Amma looked at Chella in sudden remembrance, and Jedan stared at her. "Of course," he said, his face lighting up. "The fish!" Chella smiled back. She had surprised herself as much as the others.

Amma clasped her hands together. "Oh! The carving on the post! Maybe there *are* Christians nearby somewhere. Where was it, Chella, do you remember?"

"Near that turning to the farm."

Jedan was already grabbing Garem's old jacket and the torch from their pile of things in the middle of the floor. "Yes, yes, I remember where it was now. Perhaps it was an indication for the lane?"

"It's a good thought," said Amma, heaving herself up from her knees. "Well done Chella! That's exactly what we need – a bit of hope."

Jedan leaped out of the hole in the wall, landing with a thud on the other side. "I'll check it out. There have to be Christians here, right?"

The little room was as dark as an underground cave by

the time Jedan returned. Chella was stiff with the cold, and with fear and hope churning together in her belly. She and Amma had spent the time sitting on the bench, rocking the pramcot backwards and forwards, talking about old times. They both knew it was to keep up the other's spirits, but they didn't say so.

Chella had been straining to hear Jedan return for what seemed like ages, her heart lurching every time she heard a rustle in the bushes outside. At last she heard his footsteps approach at a run, then saw his form appear outside the window hole. She and Amma rose as one as he climbed in. Chella hardly heard his actual words. He was smiling, and his tone was jubilant: that was all she needed to know.

"Guess what?" he crowed, hugging her and Amma together. "I've found a place, a kind of house – Christians are living there! There's no one there at the moment, but I think this must be the right Anderley after all!"

Amma took in a deep breath and clasped her hands together. "Oh, Jedan, that's such good news!"

Chella's stomach did an astonished flip, as she clung to Jedan and tried to get to grips with what he said. "So you've found the Old Church?"

"Yes!" replied Jedan, his eyes shining. "Well, one of their dwellings. And the house is warm and dry. Let's just take the essentials," he added, as Chella quickly bent down to start gathering up their things. "It's not far. We can fetch the rest tomorrow."

Chella wanted to dance and sing and laugh, so great was her relief, but Amma suggested they go quietly, as they still couldn't be sure who may be around, so only the rumbling of the pramcot wheels disturbed the night. Nothing could stop them smiling at each other, though, as they made their way back down the road they had arrived on so full of hope not so long before. They held hands and linked arms wherever there was space. The air smelt fresh after the dingy dampness of the ruined house – the walk felt like a fresh start; an exciting new beginning. The rain clouds were blowing away, and stars began to appear in the sky; bright and jubilant, as if glad to light their way.

Chella couldn't see the river as they crossed the bridge, but heard the water tumbling and falling over the rocks below. Wild animals cried in the night, bats flitted around them and night birds hooted and screeched, but Chella felt the light within and was glad to the depths of her soul. Even the frame of the pramcot snapping as Jedan pushed it over a big tree root didn't faze her. Surely, now, it wouldn't matter. They had prayed the pramcot would last the journey, and it had. Chella made her shawl into a carrier for Mikiah, who stayed asleep through it all, and tied it round her. After saving the bedding, Jedan threw the pramcot as far as he could into the undergrowth, so it couldn't be seen from the road.

Near the sign of the fish, Jedan led the way up the narrow side road, which had been almost completely reclaimed by the forest. Dripping trees pressed in on every side. The undergrowth was sodden, so Chella's dry skirt got wet up to her knees, and her feet slopped in her shoes, but she didn't care. Surely now they would be safe!

After walking in single file for a few minutes, a ruined house loomed up out of the darkness. Jedan shone the torch on to another fish carved low on an ancient wooden gate post. "I nearly missed it," he whispered to Chella with a grin, squeezing her hand. "Then it took me a while to work out the fish points the way you need to go!"

"Wow, that's brilliant!"

"Yes! Imagine, Chella; in this new first century we're doing exactly the same as Christians did in the last first century in Rome!"

Chella smiled back – what an amazing thought!

The gate to the old farmhouse was rotting where it stood, and was almost completely overgrown with nettles and brambles, as was the house itself, but Jedan led the way round the side, down an almost-overgrown concrete path, until a one-storey stone outhouse came into view.

"This is our home for the night," Jedan said with a grin. "What do you think?"

"It doesn't look like a house," whispered Chella, staring at the strange building, then round at the dark forest.

Amma opened her eyes wide, as Jedan flashed the torch over the outside. "Is this the house you meant? People are living here? Really? Are you sure?"

Jedan nodded and grinned.

"Well," said Amma, "I've never seen anything like it! Perhaps this used to be a barn or something."

From the outside, the building looked as abandoned as the main house. The slate roof was green with moss. Dirty wooden shutters with cracked and peeling paint covered the windows. Overgrown shrubs and creepers hugged the stone walls. With a grin, Jedan indicated to the others to follow him, then as he reached the middle of the building he slipped round a bush and pushed open a door, which brushed on the wooden floor. He had to go in first, as there was no room for anyone to pass, but he held the door open as Chella and Amma followed him inside.

Chella grasped Amma's hand as Jedan closed the door behind them and flashed his torch around. The light revealed another world. It was one large room, a bit like their apartments in size – but what a room! Chella took a deep breath of that warm, still air, which smelled faintly of herbs and vegetables, and looked round in the dim light. A stove stood against the wall opposite the door. Two easy chairs stood in front of the stove, with a low table between them, on which lay a pile of books and a box of candles. A kitchen area to the left held a larger table, with wooden chairs, several cupboards and a sink. To the right, behind a carved screen, Chella could see two beds. As Jedan flashed the torch into the corner, she could see they were made up with patchwork quilts, with a woollen blanket folded neatly across the bottom of each one.

"There's a larder with food, a bathroom area out the back, and a well in a courtyard," Jedan told them, speaking in his normal voice at last. "Horses come here from out the back somewhere – there's a stable and a paddock, I think, though it's difficult to see much in the dark."

Chella stood there in amazement. "But how do we know this belongs to people from the Old Church?" she asked.

In answer, Jedan walked over to a picture hanging on the wall. It was a simple embroidered picture of two fish looking at each other. The picture was held up by a cord on a nail in the whitewashed wall. Jedan turned it over to reveal an exquisite painting of a group of sheep on the other side, with the words *The Lord is My Shepherd* across the top, and a hidden recess behind the painting, on which lay a Bible. "The fish are pointing, inwards, see?" explained Jedan.

"Oh my goodness!" breathed Chella, feeling her panic subside, and amazement and relief taking its place.

"I can't believe it," whispered Amma.

Jedan laughed at their open-mouthed wonder. "Is this like your old house, but without the stairs, Amma?" he asked.

"Well, no, not really," Amma replied, looking round in amazement. "We lived in a town house. I've never seen a country house like this before, but there are still so many things the same." She gazed around. "The cupboards, the chairs, the books, the beds..." She slipped off her shoes, blew her nose and walked over to the kitchen area, where crockery on a shelf glinted in the light of the torch. "Look at this pretty milk jug! My grandma had one a bit like that. . . I'd forgotten such pretty things existed. And oh, look at this!" she exclaimed, picking up a slate from the kitchen table. "There's a note! Jedan, could I borrow the torch for a minute?"

He passed it over, and Chella joined them by the table, cradling Mikiah, who stirred and sighed in the sling.

"If no one is here when you arrive, please make yourselves at home," Amma read. There was silence while the three of them took in the message. "Do you think this is a hut for travellers, then?" asked Jedan slowly, looking round as if seeing the house in a new light.

Amma breathed out. "Travelling preachers, maybe? Oh,

this has to be the most beautiful place I have ever seen in my life! Thank you Lord, oh thank you, thank you dear Lord Jesus," she said, tears beginning to stream down her face.

Jedan whooped. He couldn't hug Chella because of the baby, but he grabbed her hands and jumped up and down, which made her laugh. She could almost feel the nightmare of the last few days beginning to melt away as she continued to gaze round that amazing house. So they had finally found the Old Church!

"That note would explain why the door wasn't locked," said Jedan, winding up the torch, then up-ending it on the table to give light to the room. He grabbed a handful of candles, and went on a search for candlesticks and matches. "Can you believe how well hidden it is here?"

"I feel like I'm in a dream, and might wake up at any minute," Amma said, wiping her eyes. "And I don't mind staying here either, after that note – walking into someone else's house without an invitation didn't feel quite right!"

Chella laughed, properly, for the first time in a long time. "Just think – we're here! We're really here." She walked over to the beds and sank down on to the nearest one. "I can hardly believe it."

Jedan grinned. "Oh you of little faith!"

Chella flashed back a smile. "These are real beds!" she exclaimed, gently taking Mikiah out of her shawl and placing him, still sleeping peacefully, on one of the hand-knitted blankets. "Look at the quilts, with such pretty fabrics. And everything is so neat and clean!"

Amma joined Chella and shook her head as she looked round at the cosy room. "So much reminds me of my

206

childhood. So many things I had forgotten. To think the Lord has kept a remnant of his people alive, living like this in freedom. And now we will join them. Truly He is faithful!"

Jedan laughed aloud, as he searched for matches. "Yes, He is! I really thought for a while, down there in the village, that we'd got it all wrong, but here we are! I know it's late, but when I've got these candles going, I'll get the stove going for that cup of tea I promised you."

Amma gave a huge yawn. "Oh, that would be absolutely lovely! Then we can sleep." She stroked Mikiah's curly black hair, as he lay peacefully on the bed.

"He will be safe now," said Chella with a sigh.

"Yes, he will. Thank you for all your help, Child. I wouldn't have made it here without you. And thank you, too, Jedan for all you've done. The candlelight is beautiful, as well – so gentle. If I never had to step out of this house ever again, I don't think I'd mind!"

Jedan grinned as he piled wood from a basket into the little stove. "I know what you mean. It is amazing here, isn't it?"

Chella nodded. It was exquisite. Like a dream. But they still had their main mission to accomplish. "I wonder how the people who come here will take the news about them being watched?"

Jedan looked up from blowing the fire. "You know, I can't help wondering if they already know, somehow."

"I was thinking that myself," said Amma. "There must be a reason this place is so well concealed. One house, on its own, in the middle of the forest, with the Bible hidden behind a picture, and the front of the house looking as if it's

207

uninhabited? That must be deliberate. It's a strange thing. But where do they get their provisions? And I wonder where they meet, because it's not in that old church building."

Chella nodded slowly, and Jedan shrugged. "I don't get it at all. It's a complete mystery."

"Oh well," declared Amma with a sigh, "in the Lord's good time we'll find out, no doubt. Did you say there was water, Jedan? Perhaps we could take it in turns to wash?"

While Amma prepared a drawer for Mikiah to sleep in, Chella spread out the pramcot bedding in front of the fire to dry out, along with her shoes, then wrapped herself in a blanket and wriggled out of her damp skirt, and put that out to dry, too. Tomorrow surely would bring answers – or perhaps the next day.

As she sat in one of the old armchairs and gazed into the crackling fire, watching a curl of steam rise from the kettle's spout, a deep, comforting stillness began to fill her soul. It had been a difficult journey, but the Lord had done a miracle and given her Jedan back from prison, after she'd thought she'd lost him. And now here they were, together, in this beautiful place; warm, safe and free, with Amma and Mikiah as well. She allowed her thoughts to drift back to the day when Jedan had told her that one day he thought he would leave the Area. It had seemed so far-fetched at the time! She smiled as she looked at him now, searching in the cupboards for cups for their nettle tea.

"Oil lamps!" he exclaimed with a grin, holding one up to show Chella. "We can use these tomorrow instead of the candles, if we're still here."

Chella smiled back. Would they still be there tomorrow?

A tiny chink of uncertainty made its way into her thoughts, but she brushed it away. The Lord knew. Even if they had to flee with the Church, He would work it all out. He would guide them with his light.

THIRTY

Back in the Village

Chella slept the whole night through, waking to the sound of birdsong and Mikiah's gentle snores as he slept in his drawer between her bed and Amma's. Amma was still asleep, too; her breathing regular and deep.

Chella lay still for a minute, savouring the precious new feeling of freedom, and the scent of lavender on her pillow. She felt rested. Chinks of morning light slipped in through gaps in the shutters on the front of the house, and windows at the back, with the merest breath of wind rustling the leaves outside.

The house looked even more beautiful in the gentle morning light than it had the night before. The whitewashed walls looked fresh and clean. Rag rugs gave the room a homely feel. The wind had blown itself out, and there was a calm, a peace, a warmth and a beauty that was beyond words. No loudspeakers. No fear. Everything was so natural. Jedan must already have gone out, Chella realised, seeing the empty space where he had made a makeshift bed in front of the stove.

Creeping out of bed, Chella pulled on her clothes, and opened the front door with a heart so light she wanted to dance and sing. The chill of the early morning and her bare feet on the stone path made her shiver, but a burst of newness hit her senses as she stepped into the sunshine. The fresh, earthy scent of the forest filled the air. Rays of sunlight streamed through the tree canopy, and birds sang everywhere. She couldn't see Jedan, but stood still for a minute, closed her eyes, and breathed deep. *Weeping may tarry for a night, but joy comes in the morning*, Chella remembered with a smile.

Going back inside, she found Jedan cheerfully laying the table for breakfast and Amma following Mikiah, who was babbling cheerfully as he crawled round the floor, exploring the new territory. Amma was wiping her eyes. "It's the relief and all the emotions," she apologised, as Chella gave her a hug and took over watching Mikiah so she could wash. Chella guessed with a sudden pang that Amma was thinking of Nidala, and she prayed silently in her heart for her friend, but didn't dare keep her thoughts there too long. With a lump in her throat, she asked the Lord to have mercy, and sang happy songs to Mikiah, as much for her own sake as for his.

Jedan suggested they go back to the village straight after breakfast, to collect the bags they had left in Anderley, and to check they hadn't missed any signs for the Old Church. "After all," he pointed out while they ate together at the table, "it was dark last night. There may be more fish carvings we didn't see, pointing to other hidden homes like this. You never know, we might even find people at home!"

211

"We might!" agreed Chella. "I hadn't thought of that. I'd like to wash my hair, but I can do that when we get back."

"Yes, let's go early, if that's OK," said Jedan, topping up her tea from the pretty green teapot, "in case people go out to work or something."

"Would you mind if I might stay here?" Amma asked, jiggling Mikiah on her knee.

Jedan nodded, but Chella stopped with her cup half way to her mouth. "We can't leave you here on your own, Amma, in the middle of the forest!"

Amma reached out and squeezed her shoulder. "I think it would be better if I stayed here with Mikiah," she said gently. "Why don't you two go, spend some time alone together? I've got Mikiah for company, and the Lord will be with us." She let out a big sigh. "Honestly, I feel like I've done enough walking. Especially as we've lost the pramcot. Plus, if any Christians come, I'll be here to explain everything."

Jedan nodded. "That does sound sensible. We can always come and fetch you if we find anything."

"Yes, indeed," said Amma, clapping hands with Mikiah, who gurgled and blew bubbles. "Tell you what, I'll make hot soup for when you get back – how about that? There are plenty of vegetables in the pantry that need eating up."

"Ooh, hot soup!" said Jedan, smacking his lips, and so it was decided.

When Chella and Jedan were ready to go, Amma and Mikiah waved goodbye at the door with cheery smiles. "Take care," said Amma. "The Lord be with you!"

"And also with you," replied Chella, giving her and Mikiah both a hug.

It felt strange leaving them behind in that lonely house, but Chella told herself she worried too much. Surely there could be nothing to fear now?

Jedan took Chella's hand as they set off together down the little path, but soon had to drop it as the road narrowed. "Can you believe we're really here?" he asked, holding a thorny branch out of her way.

She shook her head as she gazed round at the vast forest. "No, it hardly seems real. I feel like I might wake up in a minute and it will all be a dream. I think that's partly because everything happened so quickly. Do you realise, it's only two days since the prayer meeting?"

Jedan laughed. "This is exactly the sort of adventure I always dreamed I'd have, though." He squeezed her hand and suddenly turned serious. "I'm so glad you're with me."

Chella smiled at him, then carried on smiling to herself as she followed him down the track, avoiding the muddiest puddles. She had never dreamed she would have an adventure like this! But she was glad to be there. Of course she missed her friends, but no doubt she would soon make more, and there were so many things to be thankful for. She and Jedan were together. They had found that beautiful house. They had all stayed fit and healthy. They had hot soup to go back to, and now there was hope for the future, with the Old Church.

Once they reached the main road Jedan took Chella's hand again. They didn't talk much, but once again Chella felt the bond between them. Soon they would be married, and now they had a new life to look forward to together.

The bubbling river sounded like the greeting of an old friend, but Anderley looked no different than it had the day before. As they made their way down the main road, and hunted down side roads and entrances to what might once have been large homes, they found no evidence of current human habitation. Birds cheeped and cawed, squirrels raced around in the trees and a feral cat peered at them with wary eyes from a moss-covered wall, but although Jedan and Chella searched the whole village, they found no footprints, no cleared paths, no fish carvings. Ancient posts leaned precariously against trees. Rusting gates and crumbling buildings showed this had once been a thriving community, but everything looked as abandoned as every other settlement they had passed through.

"Something doesn't add up," said Jedan, shaking his head as they reached the far end of the village, where the forest once more took over. "That house we found can't be much more than a mile away, but there's nothing here in the village. Nothing. It's weird. What about shops, schools, a meeting place? Where are all the people?"

Chella squeezed his hand. "If the house is for travellers, maybe no one actually lives there."

"But what about what I heard about the Old Church?"

Chella shrugged. "When the people from the house come back, or the next set of visitors, whichever it is, they'll explain everything."

"I'm sure they will, but I don't like not knowing. This

afternoon I think I'll follow the path the horses take from the back of the house, see where it leads."

"I'll come with you if you like."

"Thanks, if Amma doesn't mind being left on her own again. The horses must go somewhere! Maybe the two riders we saw yesterday were from our house. I wish we'd stopped them."

Chella made a face. "Surely it's better to be sure first?"

Jedan laughed out loud. "I guess. You're going to make me a good wife, Chella. Stop me from acting without thinking!"

The ruined house they had sheltered in the previous evening was on the shady side of the road, and was every bit as damp and miserable as Chella remembered it. "Let's be as quick as we can," she suggested with a shiver, as she climbed in, avoiding the puddle by the window hole.

Jedan nodded as he wiped a spider's web from his hair and picked up a grimy blanket. "Yes, the thought of Amma's soup is making me feel hungry. My stomach's already rumbling in anticipation!"

"Mine, too!" agreed Chella with a laugh.

"Finding that house last night was amazing, wasn't it? Imagine if you hadn't remembered that carved fish on the post?" Jedan made a face as he picked up another one of their hastily discarded blankets and shook it outside. "Imagine if we'd had to stay here?"

Chella shuddered as she rolled up the filthy towel she had used to wipe the bench. "We're going to have to find out how they do their washing..." she began, but stopped as a faint, unexpected noise drifted in through the window

215

hole. She stood up straight, and looked at Jedan. He lifted his eyebrows and looked back. Chella's heart began to beat faster. "Is that horses?"

Jedan listened for a few more seconds, dropped the blanket back on the floor as he whooped and punched the air. "It is! Just one I think, and... yes, it sounds like it's pulling some kind of cart – a farm wagon, I think!"

"Oh Jedan!" breathed Chella. "They're coming from beyond the village, right? The other side? Maybe there are more houses like the one we found, but farther on!"

Jedan nodded, then a smile lit up his face. "Do you think the Church might be meeting today?"

"Maybe." Chella could barely breathe as she walked over to stand on the opposite side of the window to Jedan. "Shall we stay here till we're certain who it is? Do you think they might be spies?"

Jedan's face fell. "Good thought. I can't imagine what spies would be doing with a wagon. But you're right. We'd better stay hidden until we're sure they are believers."

As the sound of the horse's hooves rang louder, Chella closed her eyes. Could these people really be from the Old Church? This could be the end of all their troubles... or it might be the beginning of something else awful. *All this uncertainty must be over soon, surely,* she thought, as butterflies danced in her stomach around heavy stones. "We need a sign," she whispered to Jedan.

Jedan nodded and reached out to hold her hand across the gaping window hole. His hand was trembling, but his eyes were twinkling full of hope as the sound of singing drifted in through the window. Chella held her breath and strained to hear over the sounds of the wagon wheels, the horses' hooves, and the summer leaves sighing in the breeze. It was a song she had heard before but couldn't place, then suddenly the singer changed his tune, and Chella and Jedan recognised the ancient hymn at the exactly same moment. Chella's mouth dropped open. "Amazing Grace," she whispered.

"Yes!" yelled Jedan at the top of his voice, making her jump as he punched the air with his fist. "Can you believe it? This is it! Thank you Lord!" He grabbed her and hugged her before helping her climb out of the hole in the wall. "This is it, Chella," he repeated as they ran together to the road and stood at the edge, hand in hand. He had to wipe his eyes. "This is it. The Old Church! We've done it! We're here!"

Chella couldn't help laughing out loud, but tears came to her eyes, too, as she clutched Jedan's hand, waiting for the horse and wagon to come round the corner. Her voice cracked with emotion, but with all her heart and voice, she joined in with the hymn she had had to whisper all her life.

So this was the end of their journey. Through many dangers, toils and snares they had already come! God's amazing grace had brought them safe thus far, and surely now he would lead them home. They had achieved what they had set out to do. Now she and Jedan, and Amma and Mikiah, too, could start a new life together. They could have beautiful pictures on their walls that declared the truth, pray in freedom, read the Bible without fear, sing Amazing Grace whenever they wanted, wherever they wanted, as loud as they wanted, with other believers. They would be free.

At last the wagon appeared, pulled by a chestnut brown horse with a plaited mane, walking at a steady pace. Two men sat on the wagon seat, wrapped in hooded brown cloaks. The one who wasn't driving raised his hand in welcome as Jedan and Chella waved to him.

Chella's heart thrilled as the horse drew closer. She had seen horses in the fields before, of course, but never pulling a wagon. Its coat almost glowed with glorious light from the sun's rays. Chella felt relief and joy surging through her whole body as she and Jedan sang along:

I once was lost, but now am found,
Was blind, but now I see.

But as the cart pulled up to a stop beside them, Chella froze.

THIRTY-ONE

The Wagon

Chella realised half a second before Jedan that the singer was changing the words of the song into blasphemies, and she knew even before he threw back his hood, that he was the person she least wanted to see in the whole world, and that the driver was his vicious friend, Toy. She stood there, rigid, too shocked to speak or move.

Jedan's face had turned ashen grey. "Run!" he yelled, pulling her away from the road.

Toy threw off his cloak and jumped off the cart with a grunt as Solod finished the gruesome song. Chella could hear Solod laughing behind her as she and Jedan fled. She had barely gone a few paces when Toy caught her.

Jedan yelled and tried to pull her away from him, but Toy was in another league when it came to violence. He slugged Jedan in the face with his fist as if he were nothing more than an annoying insect, then punched him in the stomach and kicked him to the ground. Chella screamed and fought to get away as Jedan struggled to get to his feet, but Toy tore off her cloak, twisted her arms behind her back and tied her wrists together as calmly and efficiently as if he were tying up a dead deer.

Solod, who had jumped down from the wagon, stood in the middle of the road smiling at the mayhem; arms folded, legs astride. Chella continued to scream and fight as Toy put the finishing touches to his knots on the cords around her wrists, then pushed her towards Solod. She cried out in pain as she stumbled and fell at his feet, winded, shocked and sobbing.

Solod laughed out loud. "It's good to have you back, my Beauty," he crowed. Jedan tried to get to her, but having sorted Chella, Toy turned back to him. This time Jedan hit the ground first time. Chella screamed and tried to get up, but Solod put his foot on her and crushed her down on to the road with his boot. The tiny stones from the hard tarmac bit into her face as she watched Toy tie up Jedan's arms and legs, kick him until he lay still, then nod at Solod.

"Job done."

Solod grinned back, then turned his attention to Chella. "Well, my dearest," he crowed, hauling her to her feet, "I have you back at last! A bit dirty, but nothing that a good wash won't clear up. With your new beloved, I see! Exactly as planned."

Chella's breath was coming in gasps, and her whole body was shaking with the shock. She turned her face away from Solod and desperately struggled to free her wrists from the bonds. "I'm not your dearest," she cried. "Let me go. Let us both go! Please, please, please, let us go!" She would have collapsed if Solod hadn't been holding her up.

"Not expecting me, eh? You didn't know I was coming

for you, did you? You always were gullible. I can't believe your own stupidity — falling right into my trap with one of your own songs!" Chella's heart thumped with the realisation that she had never spoken of the church to Solod. How did he know she was a believer? And how could he have known she was coming here? She stopped struggling and stared at him. Solod laughed. "Think I'm stupid?" he scoffed. "Lavitah told me of your penchant for religion."

It took a few seconds for the information to sink in. "Lavitah?" Chella whispered.

Solod was grinning in triumph. "Yes, my Beauty, she works for me. She makes a good snitch," he added, with a sneer.

"Ready to go then, Sol?" asked Toy. "I reckon we could turn the wagon round here. We could get the horse into that side road, then back the wagon up. Save us going up to the moor."

"OK. If you think it will work." Solod let Chella go and she sank to the ground, her breath coming in gasps, her heart racing. She half saw, half heard Solod go over to Jedan, and began to drag him off the road, into the bushes. "Make sure nobody sees him," he explained to Toy. "Just in case."

"OK mate," Toy said, going over to help. Chella sobbed and rocked her body backwards and forwards on the muddy road as Jedan's groans of pain echoed around the old buildings.

"Right, let's go," said Solod, when Jedan lay out of sight. "The wild beasts can have the loser."

Chella nearly fainted as Solod forced her to her feet

again and hauled her to the back of the wagon. Now Jedan would die a horrible death, if he wasn't dead already, and it was all her fault. And Lavitah? *No, no,* she thought, closing her eyes. Her head was spinning and she felt sick. She had left everything in her apartment to Lavitah. Lavitah was her friend, or so she had thought. She knew everything about her, and everything about the church in their block. They had left her with the Bible and the children's work. She knew all the church members — she knew their secret tap, their meeting places outside of the Area... everything. But she had been at the prayer meeting on Monday. She had been there when they talked about going to Anderley. She had heard what Jedan said about the Old Church. *She had been the one to tell them of Jedan's arrest.* Surely, surely, though, she couldn't have, wouldn't have betrayed them?

"Lavitah is a good friend of mine, in case you were wondering," Solod told her. "I'm so glad you got to know her. Actually, her name's not Lavitah, it's Marith. Not that it matters."

Chella felt herself retch, and was suddenly filled with rage. "No!" she screamed, kicking out at Solod. "No, no, no!"

"Quit the dramatics," Solod said through gritted teeth, gripping her tighter as he waited for Toy to let down the tailgate at the back of the wagon. "You ought to be pleased to be coming back with me, where you belong."

"I don't belong with you," cried Chella, her voice shaking along with her body.

"Of course you do! You said you'd marry me. You broke your promise. I'm merely holding you to your word."

"You can't make me," Chella said, knowing that he could. This proved it. He could do anything.

"I can," said Solod, echoing her thoughts. His eyes narrowed, and he pulled her face close to his. In the months she had been away from him he hadn't changed. His blue eyes and dark hair were so familiar, yet now she saw them so differently. She used to caress his face, stroke his hair, stare with love into the eyes that now stared at her with power, jealousy and revenge. She wondered fleetingly how she could ever have thought she loved him. Solod returned her gaze. "Why would you choose this loser over me?" He pointed to the place where Jedan lay in the undergrowth. "You had everything with me."

Toy helped Solod lift her up into the empty wagon. She cried out as she landed with a thud on to the rough wooden boards. "I didn't have everything with you. You never loved me," she sobbed, crawling backwards as far away from the men as she could.

"Whatever," hissed Solod. "But you *will* marry me. Have you any idea how it made me look, when you ran away?"

Chella turned her head away, and as she did she saw movement in the undergrowth, where Jedan lay. Her heart leaped as she realised he was still alive, then for a fleeting moment she remembered she had never told him about Solod. Well, now he would know this was all her fault.

"Please, please let us go," she begged Solod. "Don't take me back. Please don't take me back. I didn't meet Jedan until after I left you."

Solod lifted his hand to Toy, to stop him lifting the

223

tailgate, and sneered at Chella. "Do you think I'd ever let you go with *him*, after what you did to me?"

"What *I* did to *you*?" Chella's voice trembled with emotion. "I saw you, with the maid. You didn't need me. What does it matter to you who I'm with now?"

"I did need you, to keep my parents off my back," he spat out, then as she tried to push past him, he grabbed her and pressed her body close to his. His face was so near she could feel his breath on her face. "Did you really think you could walk away from me? And you're prettier than the foreign trash," he crooned. "It's good to have you back at last! Oh, I can't wait to have you again." He slapped her face when she closed her eyes. "Look at me!" he commanded. She opened her eyes to see him smiling a cruel, wicked smile of victory.

Chella desperately tried to wriggle out of his grasp, but Solod pulled her back and forced her to look at him. "Please don't make me," she begged. "I gave your mum her ring back."

He hit her again, harder this time. She could feel the blood trickling from her nose. "You failed me, but now, my Beauty, you *will* give me a child."

"No, please," Chella pleaded as he pushed her back into the wagon. "I'll run away again!" Her breath came in short, sharp bursts and her whole body shook.

"If you do, I'll find you. I know everything."

"Only God knows everything!" she cried out, as Toy slid the bolts on the tailgate into place with a squeal of rusting metal.

Solod turned to leer at her as he climbed up on to the

wagon seat. "Maybe I'm God then!" He laughed as Toy climbed up next to him. "Your God doesn't exist."

"He does," Chella whispered, as much to herself as to Solod.

"Where is he then? Not helping you now, is he?"

Chella couldn't reply. *Where was God?*

"Ready then, Sol?" asked Toy.

"Yes, let's go. Can you believe how easy that was? I love it when a plan falls perfectly into place."

Toy slapped the reins and clicked to the horse. Chella slid back with a jolt as the wagon began to move forward. *"Jesus, help me!"* she cried out in fear.

"Jesus?" scoffed Solod as the wheels ground on the worn tarmac. "Do you really believe in those old legends? I can't believe so many people believe in the Old Church. Good plan of mine, though, to get you out here. It's taken a while, but finally we're all even."

Chella braced herself against the back of the wagon, almost paralysed with fear, and looked over towards the place where Solod had dragged Jedan. He had managed to sit up, and was looking towards her in horror; his face white, shocked, and bleeding.

"In case you were wondering," Solod called back, turning his head to make sure Jedan could hear, "I orchestrated the loser's arrest, and got the guards to talk about the rumours to get you out here. Old Church at Anderley! The Old Church doesn't exist. The doddery old fools in the Council worry about everything. It was convenient though, you've got to admit that. And now I have you exactly where I want you."

225

Jedan fell forwards with a cry of despair.

Solod laughed. "I'm a genius!" The wagon stopped as the horse had gone as far as it could, which made Chella slide across the boards and hit her head. In a moment of panic she tried to scramble over the tailgate, but with her hands tied behind her back the wagon made an efficient prison; it was impossible to get a hold and she fell back with a thud.

Solod turned round. "Try to escape again and I'll come back and kill him slowly and painfully," he hissed, pointing viciously towards Jedan.

A howl of anguish escaped from Chella's soul, as the horse's hooves began to clop again and the wagon wheels moved backwards. She stopped struggling, sank down on to the wooden planks, closed her eyes, and allowed the darkness to fill her soul.

So it had all been a lie. Jedan's arrest, the journey, everything. Then she sat up with a jolt. What about the house in the forest, and Amma and Mikiah?

THIRTY-TWO

Broken Wheel

As the horse began to walk forwards, a loud crack from somewhere under the wagon split the air. Chella grabbed the side of the wagon in fear. Solod yelled and Toy jumped down to reassure the horse, who was stepping all over the road, making the wagon shake.

Solod ran round the wagon to see what had caused the problem, and looked underneath. Chella heard the sound of metal scraping against wood, somewhere beneath her. The wagon juddered and listed to one side. "See this?" Solod hissed at Toy, as he joined him. "In the spokes. Look what it's done!"

Toy swore as he pulled out a long metal bar. "Looks like a bar off an old gate or something."

"It doesn't matter what it is!" seethed Solod.

"It's done a lot of damage. See this crack?"

"Of course I can see it, you idiot!" Solod yelled at him. "You must have picked that thing up in the wheel when you backed up!"

Toy stared at him, then looked behind into the bushes

that edged the road. "Well don't blame me, it's not my fault! Do you think I wanted this to happen? You and your fancy plans and schemes, always getting us into trouble!"

"We should have gone up to the common. Turned round where there was room. You said it would work, turning here. You're just a stupid waste of... ugh!"

Chella shuffled as far away from the metal bar and the two men as she could, and huddled in the corner, shaking from the shock of all that had happened since she had recognised Solod in the wagon. She couldn't even stop her teeth from chattering. She had heard the fury in Solod's voice. She had seen what he could do when he was angry.

Toy bent down. "We're going to have to get a new wheel. This one's completely bust. See this bit here?

"Can't you do something to fix it?"

There was a pause. "Well I can try..."

Toy disappeared under the wagon. Solod kicked it, cursed, swore and spat. Toy yelled back. Every time Chella felt the wagon jolt, a bolt of fear ran through her. She pressed herself in the corner against the hard boards and squeezed her eyes closed. Thoughts and images continued to whirl around in her mind. Jedan in the bushes. Amma and Mikiah waving goodbye. Lavitah helping to pack her things. Solod in bed with the maid. The wagon approaching in the sunshine. Surely this wasn't real?

Tears dripped down her face, but she couldn't pray. Where was God? Where was the light of His presence now? How could He have let them fall blindly into this trap? She tried to imagine going back to live with Solod. It made her retch.

"There's nothing I can do. We need a new wheel," Toy said eventually, coming out from under the wagon.

"Wouldn't it hold till we got back?"

"No, you see, the..."

Chella heard Solod swear and mutter and stomp and curse. "I'll get a wheel from the quarry. Help me unhitch the horse."

"You can't leave me out here on my own!"

The rattle of buckles and the stamp of the horse's hooves sounded loud in the silence of the empty village. "I'll be back as soon as I can," Solod yelled, as he swung himself up on to the horse's back.

"How will you explain it at the quarry?"

"I don't know but I'll think of something."

"You'll kill yourself with no saddle, if you fall off."

"I'm not even going to bother to answer that."

"I'm not staying out here on my own."

"You have no choice."

"I'm not doing this!" Toy argued.

"There's only one horse, idiot," Solod shouted back. "If you weren't so pathetically incompetent, you wouldn't have to stay."

"But it wasn't my fault!"

"What do you want me to do, sit and cry?"

Chella heard the horse's hooves return the way they had come, and Toy swear and spit and thump the cart with his fist.

After a brief silence Toy strode into the forest. "Don't get any ideas of escaping, woman," he warned her, yelling over his shoulder. "There'll be a price to pay if you cause me any bother. Sit there and *don't move*. Actually..." Chella froze in fear as he turned and stomped back to the wagon. He shot the bolts back on the tailgate, and banged it down. "I'm going to tie up your legs, so you can't run away. Give them here. I'm not in the mood for trouble, so just do it, OK?"

Chella complied. When Toy had left her, she couldn't stop the sobs any longer. She couldn't stop them any more than she could stop the sun from shining or the rain from falling. She lay on the rough boards and sobbed for Jedan, for herself, for her past, her present and her future. She had lost everything. Her friends, her family, her possessions, her hope. Everything.

Finally, when she was spent, she lay still. If she closed her eyes, all she could hear was the wind in the trees, the birds chirping on the edge of the forest, then a rustle in the bushes that may have been a blackbird, a rabbit, or a squirrel. It seemed impossible that the world could be going on as normal, as if nothing had happened.

After a while, needing to move position, she knelt up and looked over the side of the wagon. Her shoulders hurt, her knees hurt, her head was pounding and the cord was biting into her wrists and ankles. She had to lean forward to wipe her face on her knees and move her hair out of her eyes. Her skirt was filthy. Through swollen eyes she could dimly see Toy sitting on a fallen log a little distance away, with his back to her. He appeared to be sharpening sticks with a knife. She looked for Jedan, but couldn't see him. She laid back down, and closed her eyes. "Jedan," she whispered. "I'm sorry. I'm so, so sorry."

Then in a rush of anger and she sat up. She couldn't give up! She had to get to Jedan! She had to see him one last time. Even if she was caught, at least she might be able to say goodbye first, and explain everything. And maybe they would be able to untie each other's cords, somehow, and get back to Amma and the house...

Checking that Toy still had his back to her, Chella slowly and cautiously tried to stand, but with her legs tied together and the tilt from the broken wheel, she couldn't get a proper grip. She slid back, hitting the floor with a thud. She scrabbled to her knees and fought back a howl of pain as Toy turned and yelled at her.

"What's the matter with you? *I told you not to move.* Women! Nothing but trouble. If you try anything else, I'll break your legs. And arms. With this." He brandished the rusty metal bar that had caught in the spokes of the wheel.

Chella knelt back down. She tried to think of nothing, but it didn't work. The rope chafed her wrists, making them bleed. Birds sang around her, the beauty of creation bloomed, but everything was ruined. If Jedan wasn't dead, he would be soon. Amma would be waiting for them in that beautiful house, making soup, but she would never see her again. Her heart flipped as she thought of Mikiah. *"I did the best I could, Nidala,"* she whispered to the silence.

Her desperate thoughts were disturbed by a scraping under the wagon. She froze, until she heard her name. "Chella," Jedan hissed quietly.

Chella shuffled over to the back of the wagon where the voice was coming from, laid on the floor and put her face to the gap in the boards between the tailgate and the side. Through a crack in the wood she could see a sliver of Jedan's face. A wave of relief flooded her body and soul. "Oh, Jedan," she breathed. "I can't believe you've managed to get here, after all they did to you!"

"My chest hurts; otherwise I'm not too bad," he said, but his voice sounded husky. "They didn't hurt you, did they?"

She swallowed hard. "Not really."

"Good. Tell me if the guard goes away. Maybe we can escape."

"I already tried. . ."

Jedan's voice sounded fierce. "I know, I saw you, but we'll try together if we can. Maybe that man will go for a walk or something. If he doesn't, and they take you back to the Area, I'll come and get you. I promise. I'll find a way."

Chella pressed her face against the crack in the wooden boards. Jedan did the same on his side. She so desperately wanted to feel his arms surrounding her, comforting her, telling her this was all a dream and in a minute they would wake up. But it didn't happen. She could hear him breathing heavily, as if in pain, and anger, and she wept silently as the reality that she might never see him again hit home. Tears dripped down her cheeks and neck and mingled with the dried blood from her nose. She tried to stop herself shaking, and steady her breathing, but her body couldn't do it. "You should go now," she whispered, "in case Solod comes back. I should have told you about him. You heard what he said about. . . him and me?"

"Sweetheart, this isn't your fault. I have to tell you something. Can you watch the guard and still hear me?"

Chella sat up and looked over the side of the wagon. "Yes," she whispered.

"Tell me if he goes away." Jedan's voice sounded thick with emotion. "A few years ago, Solod was part of a gang I belonged to. He used to escape from the Elite Zone sometimes, and come and hang out with us. We thought we were so cool, mixing with an Elite boy. We used to go to the border..."

Chella felt a shiver rise up through her body. "You were Solod's *friend*?"

"Sort of." Chella couldn't see Jedan, but she could hear the misery in his voice. "Remember you wanted to know why my parents didn't like me? It was from those days. I was constantly in trouble, and every time I got caught they were penalised. Solod used to bring alcohol with him, so we'd drink together, then he got us into stealing..."

Chella was so shocked she could barely speak. Even as the question *why didn't you tell me?* formed in Chella's mind, she knew the answer. It was the same reason she hadn't told him about her past. Shame. How do you start a conversation like that? She could feel her world crashing down around her – everything that was left. "That's why you never wanted to talk about the past."

"Yes. And there's worse. One night, we got into a fight with another gang. Most of us were caught and arrested. Only me and Imrew, my best mate escaped. Somehow Solod managed to get away with it – don't ask me how. Me and Imrew decided to go clean after that, but Solod wanted the three of us to keep stealing stuff. We refused, so he organised a beat up for us from a couple of trainee Correctioners.

One of them might have been that man there." Chella assumed he was indicating Toy. She couldn't speak, but Jedan continued after a pause. "I'm so sorry, Chella. This is so hard to say, so hard to have to talk about again. . . we decided to get our own back. We crept into the Elite Zone one night. The hedge wasn't as thick then."

Chella closed her eyes. She had so not expected this.

Jedan continued. "We watched him go into his apartment. I soaked a rag in oil and lit it. When it started to smoke, Imrew threw it into an open window then we watched to see what would happen."

"Oh no." Chella's face crumpled. She already knew how this story ended.

"It was just smoke, we wanted to frighten him. We thought he would smell it and put it out. We didn't realise his grandfather was in that room. They got him out, but he died from breathing in the smoke. Solod sent a message to tell us one day he'd get even, but he couldn't admit he knew us, so we got away with it. I never saw him again, until today. But I guess all this time he's been waiting to get revenge." Jedan's voice lowered even further. "I'm so sorry I dragged you into it. If I'd have thought. . ." his voice cracked and petered away into silence.

Chella could hardly believe this was happening. This wasn't the Jedan she knew, the Jedan she loved. He was one of the evil people Solod had told her about. "What happened to your friend?" she asked.

"He disappeared soon after. I have no idea what happened to him. I searched everywhere for him – all our old haunts – but I never found him. I can't tell you how awful it was, living with this terrible secret. What I'd done. It got to the point... I couldn't bear the pain any more. I was going to end it all. Then I met Amma in the library. She smiled, you know how she does?"

Chella could barely speak. "Yes," she whispered.

"She asked if I wanted to go for a walk with her to catch up on news. So I did. I told her I'd done a terrible thing. She reminded me of the story of the prodigal son going back to his father, and how his father welcomed him with open arms. I'd forgotten it, but it gave me hope. She suggested I pray with Sheji, you know, from the church in my block, so I went and found him. I told him everything. I told him I deserved to die, and he agreed, but reminded me that Jesus died in my place, for my sin." Jedan paused and took in a deep breath. "You know we were singing *Amazing Grace* just then? No one could be more of a wretch than I was. I can't tell you how good it was to find peace, after that prayer." He sighed deeply, and the wind in the trees seemed to sigh with him. "But I still can't go back and change what I did."

Chella didn't answer straight away. If anyone knew the truth of that last statement, she did. The rhythmic sound of Toy's knife scraping on the sticks hung in the air. Somewhere in the distance a dog howled, then another answered it. "We should have talked before," she whispered.

"We should," agreed Jedan. "After I'd prayed, and it was all forgiven, I never wanted to talk about it ever again, or even think about it. But I should have done. I should have told you. You deserved to know, and I kept it from you." He paused. "And you were his girl?"

235

Chella took in a deep breath. "He came into our Parkland and found me."

She could hear Jedan shifting position. "When?" he asked, in a strangled voice.

"Last year, after my dad died. I was so lonely." There was another silence, but Chella knew what Jedan wanted to know. "We shared a bed," she admitted. She closed her eyes, as she thought back to those terrible days.

"Did he force you?"

"At first he persuaded me. Later he forced me. I thought I was his only girl, I thought it would be forever. He was so charming. We were to be married. He took me to his home – we were living with his parents. He needed a wife because they wanted a grandchild to carry on the family name." Chella heard Jedan sigh, but whatever he thought, she felt a wave of relief at finally coming clean. "He changed once I was trapped in the Elite Zone. After I'd been there a week I found him in bed with the maid, and I realised he'd never really loved me, so I left him."

"He let you go?"

"No, I ran away. His parents were fixing things so we could get married and I could be sworn in with the Elite. I tried to tell them what he was like, but they told me it was just part of life. I hid in the hedge till it was dark, then when someone opened the gate, I slipped through and ran home. If the guard saw me, he didn't follow." Chella paused as a flock of ring-tailed parakeets passed overhead, screeching as they flew in a cloud of shimmering green. "I was going to talk to you," she whispered, "but I was so ashamed. I could never find the right time to tell you."

"Oh, Chella, look at me, I'm not perfect! Far, far from perfect. We need to treat this as a lesson learned. From now on, only honesty, however hard. We'll make a new start."

Chella screwed up her face as dread filled her stomach. "There isn't going to be a new start. They're going to take me back."

Jedan's voice cracked. "Oh, Sweetheart, don't say that. We have to hope. You can't go back there! What's the man doing?"

"He's still there," whispered Chella. "You'd better go back to the house, to Amma. If he finds you here... he's got a metal bar."

"Let me spend one more minute with you," Jedan begged. It sounded as if he was weeping. "Will you forgive me for not telling you what I'm really like?"

Chella could hardly believe what Jedan had done, and that he hadn't told her. But she knew in a rush that she had to forgive him, she needed to forgive him. And she needed his forgiveness, too. "Yes," she said. "Will you forgive me?"

"Of course. You did nothing wrong, anyway. He took advantage of you."

"I made a wrong choice. And I didn't tell you." For a moment there was silence. The smell of honeysuckle hung in the air, and clouds continued to drift overhead as if nothing had happened, but so many things had changed. "Jedan, do you still love me?"

"How could you ask? Never more. Do you still love *me*?"

Chella couldn't see Jedan, but she could feel the ache in her soul echoing his, and the weight of shame begin to fall away. "I do."

"Do you think he came to find us because he knew we were together?"

"Maybe, I don't know. Does it matter?"

Jedan sighed. "I suppose not."

"What about Lavitah?" whispered Chella with a shudder. "Did you hear what Solod said about her?"

"Yes," Jedan replied darkly. "All the time she was waiting to betray us. Pretending to be a believer, being friendly, living in your apartment. We'll have to find a way to warn Old Erimah, somehow."

Chella ignored his last comment. She couldn't even think about that. "At least Amma and Mikiah are safe."

"Solod hasn't mentioned them, has he? Do you think Lavitah didn't tell him they came with us? If so, that's the only point in her favour. Maybe she does have a conscience."

"I don't know. Solod wouldn't care what happens to them. He's got what he wants."

"I don't think he realises there really are Christians living out here, do you?"

Chella felt a sudden wave of panic. "You don't think that house is a trap, do you?"

"No, no, I'm sure there really are believers there. It was too real. Perhaps the Lord has a plan for Mikiah, and we had to take him there, to that house, so he could be safe with the Old Church." Jedan groaned as he moved position. "There has to be a reason for all this."

"Maybe," Chella whispered. She shivered as a cloud passed over the sun.

Jedan sighed again. "Sweetheart, I'd better go, before they find me here. I'll get back to the house somehow, then

I'll come and get you, or die trying. I promise. Perhaps the people from the Old Church will help me."

Chella wanted to reply, but her heart was so full, she couldn't speak.

Jedan pressed his face against the crack in the wood again. "Whatever happens, I will always love you."

Chella lay back down and put her face over his. "I love you too."

"I don't have the words to pray right now, but I will pray for you every day. I promise with all my soul."

"Me too."

"The Lord be with you."

"And also with you." Chella swallowed hard as she heard Jedan begin to move slowly away from the wagon. Fear crept over her like a dark cloak. For the first time in her life she was going to be alone in that huge, empty, heartless world. And soon Solod would be back.

THIRTY-THREE

East

Chella lay in the bottom of the wagon with her eyes shut tight. She couldn't watch Jedan go. She couldn't bear to look up and see if Toy had heard or seen him. She wanted to scream, but held it in until her whole body shook with the effort. Never had she felt so desperately alone.

When Toy shouted, "Hey!" out of the quietness, she jumped out of her skin and let out a cry. "Shut up, cow. I'm going hunting. Don't cause me any bother while I'm gone, or you're dead meat."

Chella scrambled up on to her knees and watched him walk away into the forest, carrying his pile of sticks and the metal bar. Hope rose in her soul, like water seeping over a parched field. Perhaps she could get away with Jedan after all! Maybe they could manage to undo the knots in each others cords... Maybe they really could start again.

She watched Toy with beating heart until he was out of sight, then shuffled quickly over to the other side of the wagon and leaned over, but her heart missed a beat. A tall woman in dark clothing was creeping up to Jedan.

"Do not cry out," the woman warned them both, putting a finger to her lips. She made the sign of a fish on the ground and whispered, "Do not be afraid, I am a believer in the Lord Jesus Christ. I'm sorry I wasn't able to welcome you to our safe house last night." While she was talking she cut Jedan's cords with a pocket knife, then ran to the wagon, climbed nimbly up and over the seat, and cut Chella's bonds.

"Oh, Chella," Jedan whispered, taking her gently in his arms as the woman helped her out of the wagon. "Ouch, sorry I can't hug you tight, my chest hurts."

"Look at me my friends," the woman said as she checked them for signs of concussion. "Are you bleeding; any broken bones?" They shook their heads. "Feel sick, headache? Any dizziness? Can you walk?"

Chella's wrists and ankles were stiff and sore, and her shoulders ached from having her arms tied behind her back, but she felt she could run a hundred miles if she needed to, to get away from her captors. "I'm fine," she whispered. "Thank you, thank you so much."

Jedan gingerly took a few steps. "I'm OK, except my chest hurts a bit. I don't think I can go very fast, but I'll do my best."

The woman nodded. "Your best will be good enough! Tell me if you start to feel sick or dizzy. And try to avoid leaving footprints in muddy puddles, if you can." She began to lead them back down the road they had come in on. Jedan was limping and slow, and his face was screwed up in pain, but he hobbled along as fast as he could.

"Jedan, we're free!" Chella whispered to him in awe and amazement, looking back at the empty, horseless wagon.

How incredible this was – surely the Lord had sent an angel to save them! Jedan nodded in reply. The woman gave him her arm to help him as his breath came in gasps, and Chella gave him hers on the other side after grabbing her cloak from where Toy had thrown it on the road. "Can we get our bags?" Chella asked, pointing out the house they had left them in. "They are just in there."

"Sorry," said the woman, shaking her head. "We can't stop now." Chella tried not to mind, but her eyes smarted at the thought of losing her last few remaining possessions – clothes, her spare shoes, her bag.

"Are we going back to the house?" Jedan asked. "Safe house, did you call it?"

"Safe house, that's right, but no, we're not going back there tonight. We're going to our Base Camp – so is the lady you were travelling with. She and the baby will be well on their way by now, with my brother. We came together, but we decided it would be better if I came to find you, and they made a start."

"Oh!" cried Chella, her lost possessions suddenly paling into insignificance. "Thank you!" That had to be the best news ever – Amma and Mikiah were safe and on their way to the Old Church!

"You're welcome! We should have been here to pick you up long before Solod arrived, but we decided to take the risk and go back and get a horse and cart when we knew four of you were coming instead of two. It's too far for an older lady to walk. If you'd been in the house with them, we could all have gone together, but, hey, never mind, we should be home tonight, and you'll be back together again."

Chella and Jedan looked at each other in astonishment. "You knew we were coming?" Jedan asked the woman. "I don't understand."

"There are some things I will never be able to tell you," she replied with a cheerful grin, "but at least I managed to stop the wagon!"

Chella's mouth dropped open. "It was you who. . ."

"Put the metal rod in the wheel," finished the woman with a low chuckle. "Yes, that was me! It's an old trick."

Jedan raised his eyebrows, and opened his mouth to ask another question, but the woman stopped him. "I'll explain more later."

"But. . ." began Jedan but the woman shook her head.

"For now, let's concentrate on getting away."

Chella suddenly caught the woman's twinkly eyes, and she smiled back in gratitude. The woman was definitely a person, not an angel. She wasn't young, exactly, but hadn't yet reached middle age. She was tall and wiry, with a ready smile and a confident air. Her short dark hair bounced around her shoulders, her boots were the neatest leather, and her clothes blended in with the forest. Her smile was the most serene smile Chella had ever seen. Just to look at her face filled her with reassurance.

The woman led them over the road bridge then on to a narrow track which wound alongside the rushing river. A bubble of gratitude rose through Chella's soul as she thought of their deliverance. Every step meant they were further away from danger! Even when it seemed that all was lost, the Lord had sent this woman and her brother to save them all.

She felt a pang as she thought once again of her beautiful bag lying in that filthy room, but shook the thought away. She was free! She had lost everything she owned apart from the clothes she was wearing, and Jedan's clothes weren't even his own, but they were safe, and they had each other. She looked up at Jedan. His face was streaked with drying blood. His hair was matted, his lip was torn and his eyes were bruised and heavy, but he was alive, they were together, and she had escaped from Solod. Amma and Mikiah were on their way to safety, too. The woman was a mystery, but however she had found out about them, it didn't matter – they were safe.

The track alongside the river was muddy from the previous day's rain, and narrow in places, with rocks and tree roots barring their way. Jedan sometimes groaned in pain as he had to take a longer step to get over a fallen tree, or clamber over rocks. "We'll stop soon," the woman assured them as Jedan stopped for breath after a particularly stony patch. "There are some things we need to sort out, and I have some ointment to ease the pain of your bruises."

The river bubbled its way through the steep valley, guarded by whispering trees. In different circumstances it would have been a glorious walk. The sparkling water rushed over and around rocks of all shapes and sizes. Little birds Chella didn't recognise dipped and fluttered around shallow pools near the river's edge, feasting on insects. Here and there the sun broke through the cover of trees in shafts of light, like rays from heaven.

The woman continued to lead the way until they came to an ancient stone hut covered with moss and ivy. "Come in here and sit down for a minute," she said, finding the way in behind a curtain of creepers. The wooden door was hanging off its hinges and it squeaked and scuffed the floor as they pushed their way in. Fallen leaves covered the ground. The hut was damp and smelled of the wild – of animals and green, living things that didn't have to obey mankind.

Jedan gingerly lowered himself down on to the leafy floor, leaned back against the hard stone and closed his eyes. Chella sat next to him and reached for his hand. "We're free," she whispered, with a smile, still half amazed, and he nodded and squeezed her hand.

Opening her backpack, the woman gave them a leather skin of water to share, then crouched down next to them. "I'm sure you will have many questions, but before anything else, we have some urgent business to attend to," she said. "Do you know how Solod followed you?"

"One of the girls..." began Jedan, but the woman shook her head.

"You were a prisoner, I understand?"

Jedan nodded. "That's right."

"You will have been implanted with a microchip. It's called a tracker, because it tracks you wherever you go. They inject every prisoner with one, so if they escape, they can be found. They will have injected it under your skin."

Jedan and Chella looked at each other, then back at the woman. "A *tracker*?" repeated Jedan with a frown, as the woman's words sank in. "Does that mean they know where I am? Here? Right now?"

"Yes. You've seen the ancient satellites go over on clear nights?"

"Of course!"

"Some of them still give out signals. Anyone with the right equipment can follow the signal."

Jedan sat up straight, then quickly rolled up his left shirt sleeve. "The only injection I had was for vitamins – or so they told me."

The woman grimaced as she felt for the chip in his arm. "No vitamins there, I'm afraid."

"Are you sure?"

The woman gave a wry smile. "Certain."

"How do you know all this?"

"Experience."

Chella took a deep breath. So that was how Solod was so confident he would find her again. As long as she was with Jedan, neither of them would ever be safe. "What are we going to do?" she asked, looking at the woman with wide eyes.

"We have a choice. If we leave the chip, they will always know where you are and can come and get you any time they like. I will have to leave you here; I can't risk taking either of you with me, assuming you want to stay together."

"Can you get the tracker out?" asked Jedan.

"Do you want me to?"

"Yes, yes, of course!"

"I'll have to make a cut in your skin."

"What with?"

The woman showed him her pocket knife.

"Just a minute," Jedan said. "Are you from the Old Church?"

The woman grinned. "Yes, I am."

"Have you done this before?"

"Oh yes. I rescue people all the time. It's my job."

Jedan's eyes opened wide. "Your *job*?"

The woman nodded. "I'm what we call a ranger."

"How can we be sure? I mean, sorry, but, this is all so... strange, and... unexpected."

"It's a fair question, and I understand," the woman replied with a smile. "Maybe we can pray together now. I will close my eyes and give you the knife. Take this," she said, giving the open knife to Jedan, then she knelt to pray. She smiled at them both before she closed her eyes; a beautiful smile, with light in her eyes and a freedom that made Chella's heart thrill. She had lived with fear for so long, it was difficult to remember the feeling of being safe, but there was something about this woman's face that radiated peace, and hope.

After the prayer, Jedan handed the knife back. "You'd better do it."

"Don't worry. The tracker is only just under the skin. It won't be much more than a scratch, and it's safer than not doing it. We need to do it quickly, though. Do not cry out."

"While you press on the wound," the woman said to Chella when the deed was done, "I'll put the chip in the river in this." She showed them a small, hollow wooden ball, which she twisted apart in the middle, then snapped back together with the tracker inside. "The current will carry the ball downstream. We will be going in a different direction – that will confuse them! Make the most of the breather. When I get back we'll need to get away." Before stepping out of the hut she gave them each a sweet, chewy bar, wrapped in a small square of cloth. "Eat these," she said. "They will give you energy for the journey."

Chella and Jedan didn't speak while the woman was gone. There was so much to say, but it was impossible to know where to begin. Chella pressed on Jedan's wound until the bleeding stopped, and they fed each other with the chewy, oaty bars. Chella could feel the warmth of her love for Jedan returned. *Love never fails*, she thought to herself, as Jedan gently stroked her hair and kissed the top of her head. She saw Jedan in a new light now. He wasn't the perfect man she had thought he was. He had fallen from the pedestal she should never have put him on. Nobody was perfect, and she certainly wasn't perfect, either. Surely only God was perfect. But there was forgiveness. For them both.

"My name is East, but do not tell me your names, or anyone else's," the woman from the Old Church said as she crept back into the hut with a bowl of water, to which she added a few drops of something pungent. "You will be given a new name when we get to Base Camp. Everyone does. It's a safety precaution." While she was speaking, she began to clean their wounds and check for other injuries.

"What do you mean: *safety precaution*?" asked Jedan.

East sighed as she dabbed the cuts on his forehead. "Before we knew about the trackers, some people were re-captured before we got back to Base Camp, and... well anyway," she continued, "the law was made on name-changing, so no one can give anyone else away."

"So your name isn't really East?" asked Chella.

The woman grinned. "No."

248

"What is Base Camp, exactly?" asked Jedan. "Is it like your headquarters?"

"It's where everyone goes who has been rescued. Please don't ask me where it is. . . for the same security reason. At Base Camp it's decided which Chapter you'll go to, depending on your gifts and where you're needed most. Chapters are like villages," she explained, seeing Jedan frown. "I understand you're good with horses," she added, taking Jedan's pulse. "That's a much needed skill. Can you ride, or would you be willing to learn? We so badly need good riders."

Jedan smiled properly, for the first time since their rescue. "That's my dream!"

"Excellent!" said East, with a big grin. She made Jedan take some deep breaths. "Nothing broken," she decided, "except possibly a cracked rib or two, and they may just be bruised. Praise the Lord! He has been good to you. It could have been a lot worse."

Chella let out a huge sigh, as East opened a pot of soothing ointment for their cuts and bruises. She could feel the tension beginning to drain away as she rubbed the fresh-smelling salve into her ankles and wrists. Jedan was going to be OK, and finally, this was it: they were on their way to the Old Church, and it all sounded so wonderful, so safe. She touched East's arm as she re-packed her bag. "Thank you so much for saving us."

East smiled back. "You're welcome. Now we need to go."

Jedan grimaced as he stood up. He breathed heavily for a minute and clutched the wall. "Will they know we were here?"

"I'm assuming Solod will have a trackermate with him," East replied, "which will tell him where the chip is right now. They have better equipment in the Area, which will give them a lot more data." She led the way out of the hut. "We don't need to worry about that right now, though. Let's go, my friends."

"Do you have one of those devices?" asked Jedan.

"A trackermate? Sadly not," she replied with a grin. "Not yet, anyway! I was hoping Solod would have left his in the wagon, but unfortunately he took it with him. Didn't want his friend to have it, I suppose."

Jedan groaned in pain as he ducked under the door and stepped back outside into the light of the day and the bird song of the green forest. "All this is a bit overwhelming," he admitted. "There's so much more going on in the world than any of us knew about."

Chella nodded in agreement as she followed. "There really is. How long will it take us to get to your Base Camp, East?"

"We should be there before nightfall, I hope."

Chella smiled to herself. Tonight they would be with the Old Church! "Are all your safe houses like the one we stayed in?" she asked. "I loved it so much! It was so beautiful, so natural and homely."

"Thank you! It's peaceful there, isn't it? But no, they're not all like that. They come in all sorts of shapes and sizes. We could have stayed in that one tonight, except they may have tracked you there."

"Oh yes, of course." Chella's heart sank as she imagined

Solod and the Correctioners trashing that beautiful home. "I'm so sorry we gave it away, where it was."

"We've made so many mistakes," admitted Jedan.

East shrugged as she climbed up and over the trunk of a fallen oak tree, which blocked their path. "They may never bother to follow your footsteps, once they discover they've lost you, and my brother will have hidden everything away. Anyway, one thing I have learned in my job, is that the Lord always has a plan. Everything happens for a reason."

"Thank you," said Jedan, letting out a deep sigh as he followed East over the fallen tree, then gave Chella a hand over. "For everything. Risking your life to save us. Your kindness. When you don't even know us."

East grinned. "It's my pleasure! And anyway, we needed to get to you before you found us, or we'd have been in trouble."

Chella and Jedan stopped in dismay and stared at each other as the truth began to dawn on them. "Keep walking my friends," East urged them.

"Let me get this straight," said Jedan, as they set off again. "Did they arrest me, implant me with the tracker, let me overhear information, then deliberately let me go *so they could find you*?"

"That's about it. Were you not surprised you weren't followed, when you left?"

"We thought the Lord was helping us," said Jedan slowly.

"I'm sure he was, but perhaps not in the way you thought."

Chella couldn't speak, but her thoughts went back to the day they had left. Not only had they not been followed,

251

but Jedan had simply walked out of the Correction Facility. The Correctioners who had detained her hadn't asked if she'd seen Jedan, or looked in her bag. Odina had let her go home from work... Perhaps even Odina was in on it. Odina! Was nothing what it seemed?

Jedan shook his head. "But when I was in prison I had a vision, and a dream in the night. I heard the Old Church singing. I know I did. I'm sure I didn't imagine it!"

East smiled. "Well, that proves God is with you! We know he uses even the wicked to accomplish his will. And the Old Church does sing – you will love it!"

"But I was tricked!"

"You were. But your faith has kept you going, Almighty God has kept you safe, and now here you are, walking towards freedom."

"I can't believe it," said Jedan. "I thought I had to come to warn you that you'd been discovered. I was actually putting you in danger." He shook his head. "I can't believe I could have been so stupid. So ignorant."

"There's no way you could have known what they were planning," East reassured him. "You did what you thought was best. Believe me, it's not just your Area Council; all the Areas in the region have been trying different things. They want to find whoever is responsible for holding up their wagons and taking the people they have despatched."

"Despatched," repeated Chella. "I've heard that word, but I don't know what it means."

"It's a nice word for the slave trade."

"Slave trade?" exclaimed Jedan. "But the World Council is against slavery!"

"Human nature has reared its ugly head, I'm afraid. It's common practice for Areas here to exchange prisoners with Areas abroad. Rangers like me stop them."

"The foreign maids and other servants in the Elite Zone!" exclaimed Chella. "Are they slaves, then?"

"I'm afraid so."

Chella thought of Walt and Sheva's maid, and despite everything, wished she'd tried to get to know her. Perhaps she was a believer. Perhaps Solod had forced her, too, to do things she didn't want to do. She felt the horror of it in the pit of her stomach. "That's terrible."

"Indeed it is."

"Why don't they use their own prisoners as slaves?" asked Jedan.

"Think about it. If you're in a foreign country and don't speak the language, you're powerless. You can't escape — where would you go? Foreign slaves are more compliant. Resigned. It nearly happened to me and my brother."

Chella's eyes opened wide. "Really?"

"We were saved by rangers just before they put us on the ships. That's how we got our names." She turned and grinned at them. "They split you up from family and friends. I was supposed to be going east to India, and my brother was supposed to go west to Dominica, to work on the sugar plantations. One of the rangers jokingly called us East and West, and it stuck!"

Jedan frowned. "This is all still going on, right now?"

"More than ever."

"So you decided to become rangers, too?" asked Chella.

253

"Yes. A wonderful woman heads up the programme. Mostly our job is intercepting the wagon trains of slaves, when we hear that believers are being taken away. We stop as many as we can. We can't let them get away with it."

Jedan nodded vehemently. "I totally agree. But I don't understand why Solod doesn't believe in the Old Church, if he knows what's going on?"

East shrugged. "Maybe he thinks it's random outsiders. It seems he had his own personal agenda for finding you both, and he played on the Council's fears, no doubt, to get his own way. *They* may suspect it's the Church, of course, which is probably why they agreed to send you out. Having said that, though, I doubt if they care who's taking their prisoners – they just want to stop us. Hence arresting you, tracking you, then letting you go."

"But why send us to Anderley?" wondered Chella.

East smiled. "Solod was helped in his choice."

"You know, don't you?" said Chella, picking up on the tone of her voice. "It has to do with you knowing we were going to be here."

"There are things I can't tell you right now for the safety of – well, for certain people, but yes. They have spies and informants, as I'm sure you know, but we have our spies, too – agents, who pass on information. But of course, their identity needs to stay hidden, or our whole operation could come crashing down – not just in your Area, but all the way from here to the coast."

Jedan frowned. "Was it your spies we saw riding the horses yesterday?"

"You saw horses?" asked East. "How many?"

"Two. Two riders on horseback. We hid, so they didn't see us."

"Ah," she replied. "That would have been the Council, I expect, checking on your tracker, making sure of your whereabouts, seeing how far you had got – if you had found us yet."

"They knew we were there, as they passed us?" asked Chella, horrified to think of the trap they had been walking towards in complete ignorance.

East smiled at them kindly. "I know this is all very shocking, but you no longer have to fear. The tracker is now bobbing down the river, and tonight you will be safe at Base Camp, God willing."

Jedan shook his head. "That's great, but as soon as we can we need to go back and warn our church that someone we thought was a friend is actually one of their spies. She's completely infiltrated the church. She..."

"You can never go back now," East interrupted him. "And, well, people are not always... people can... tell one person one thing, and another person something else. Even those who..." her eyes twinkled. "Those who *seem* to have betrayed you."

At first Chella didn't understand, but East turned and winked at her. The look in her smiling eyes made Chella frown. What did she mean? Then suddenly she breathed in sharply and grabbed Jedan's arm. The woman was talking about Lavitah. *Lavitah was a double agent.* If Lavitah was her name. She had known everything all along, *from both sides.* Somehow she must have alerted East and her brother that they were going to Anderley. It all made sense. Her thoughts racing, Chella went back over that last morning in her apartment. Lavitah had had everything under control. She had made sure she had breakfast, and helped her pack. She had made an extra batch of sweet biscuits *the day before*. She had bought extra eggs and an extra loaf of bread, too. *She already knew.* She had walked with her out of the apartment, to make sure she left with Jedan. She had known that Amma wasn't part of the plan. *She had known everything.*

The woman smiled at Chella's shocked face, as if she read her thoughts. "I'm afraid I can't talk to you about. . . the people who help us. They risk their lives to help people get away to safety. That's all I can say. Some of it I don't even know myself. But I *can* tell you that we were alerted of the danger you were in, and we came."

Jedan's eyes opened wide and he looked at Chella in comprehension, then opened his mouth to speak, but East said quickly, "Don't speak anyone's name. Just thank God for them, and for your freedom."

"This is all so incredible," said Jedan, shaking his head. "But why didn't – the person – tell us about you, and warn us about the tracker, before we left?"

"If you were caught, it would put everything we do at risk." East paused. "It was better that you knew nothing. We should have got to you a lot quicker, but then your friend decided to come and bring the baby so as I said, we had to go back and get the horse and cart. That nearly put a spanner in the works! But here we are. You are safe, they are safe, and your friend back in the Area is safe, too."

"We're not safe yet," countered Jedan.

"True," admitted East, grinning at him, "but at least we're on our way."

THIRTY-FOUR

Followed

Chella thought about Lavitah as she and Jedan followed East through the forest. She had heard of secret agents, of course, but had no idea they were still operating in the Areas, and in the church, of all places! She thought of all the risks Lavitah must have taken to save them – and not just them, but others, too. Maybe all the people in Lavitah's block who had disappeared. . . maybe she had helped to save them as well?

Chella racked her brain to think of any clues that Lavitah was anything other than who she said she was, but couldn't think of anything. Their life had seemed so normal. Work, groups, meetings. . . she couldn't think of anything out of the ordinary. Everything East said made sense, though, including the foreign slaves in the Elite Zone. The maids, the handymen, the gardeners. . . when she had been living there she had been so worried about her own problems, she had never thought to wonder why they were all foreign. She prayed for them silently, and felt ashamed that she didn't even know any of their names, or where they came from.

After she had prayed, she allowed her thoughts to drift, and as she did, Nidala and Hamani came to mind. "Are all prisoners despatched?" she asked East suddenly, her heart beginning to thud in her chest.

"No. Some stay to work in the Powerhouse. It's mostly believers they despatch – I guess they make the least trouble. Hardened criminals might fight back."

Chella breathed in sharply. "Oh! Because my best friend and her husband were arrested just after Easter." Her mind was racing so fast she rushed over the words. "Is it possible you may have rescued them, too?"

"I guess. What do they look like?"

"They're our age. The girl is dark, like Amm... like her mum, who was travelling with us. The baby is their son."

"They don't write and illustrate Bible stories for children, do they? There was a couple we picked up, maybe three or four months ago?"

Chella gasped out loud and her hands flew to her mouth. "Yes, yes, oh yes, it has to be them!" She turned to Jedan and wanted to hug him tight, but remembered his bad chest just in time. They laughed together, though, and East laughed with them. Chella jumped up and down and wanted to shout and sing. Nidala and Hamani were alive! "Will they be at your Base Camp?" she asked breathlessly, hardly daring to believe it could be true.

"Probably, unless they've already been assigned a Chapter, but most people stay for six months or so, to get used to being free. It sounds strange, but it takes a bit of getting used to."

"Oh I can't wait to see them again, and Nidala will have

Mikiah back..." Chella's hands flew to her mouth as she realised her mistake. "Oh, sorry, I said their names! Oh but this has to be the best day of my life ever!"

"Best day?" said Jedan with mock horror, pointing out his bruised and cut face, and they all laughed.

Walking became easier as the ground levelled, the trees thinned out and they joined a small road. The next couple of hours passed in a daze of mostly happy thoughts for Chella, punctuated every now and then by a shiver of repulsion as the enormity of what they had escaped from pierced her soul. She barely noticed her aching legs and the mist which began to drift among the trees. She imagined her reunion with Nidala and Hamani, Mikiah and Amma, then imagined them all settling down to live together in a Chapter of the Old Church in beautiful houses, with pretty quilts and cushions and curtains. How wonderful it would be! Away from oppression and fear. Away from restrictions and danger. Away from worrying who would be the next to disappear. A few days ago she wasn't even sure the Old Church existed – now she was going to be part of it!

Jedan's chest and bruises improved with East's ointment, and the pain eased. He gradually returned to his cheerful self, but somehow he was just a little bit quieter and gentler then before, and sighed every so often, and squeezed Chella's hand when there was room for them to walk side by side. Chella knew why, and it wasn't just the pain. There was a new closeness between them now. She could feel it. How amazing, she thought, that being honest about even the terrible things could bring them closer. She could almost be glad Solod had found them, for that.

Jedan was as eager as Chella to get to the Old Church, and asked East all sorts of questions about the farms and horses, and how the Chapters worked. East chatted cheerfully about the elders, the communities, the weekly markets, the food production and the collective worship. Chella listened, enthralled. She loved the idea of the markets, and wondered if she would be able to make bags and clothes to sell.

As the sun began to lower in the sky, East pointed out a long, high bridge in the distance, going over the road they were walking on. "We're going to climb up on to that road," she told them. "It's a big old motorway. It's a steep climb, but we'll stop to rest for a few minutes at the top, so you can enjoy the view – well, what we can see of it in this mist."

East was right – it was a steep climb, up a slippery bank, to the motorway, but there were sturdy rhododendrons to hold on to, which helped. They had to stop several times to get their breath back.

"Wow!" breathed Jedan in awe, grabbing Chella's hand as they reached the top. "Look at that!"

The view was foreshortened by the mist, but what held their attention was the road. Chella stared at it, stretching into the distance as far as they could see in both directions. The little roads they had walked on paled into insignificance compared with this immense structure. The forest was encroaching on either side, and here and there trees and bushes had grown through the tarmac, but for mile upon mile an enormous strip of grey road grazed the countryside like a long wound, with a wall through the middle that looked like dragons' spines. Further on, the road had been built through a cut in the hillside! Chella tried to imagine it covered with noisy traffic, as she knew it once would have been, but it seemed impossible – how could all that space have been covered with vehicles? "It's so much bigger than I imagined!" she exclaimed.

East grinned at their amazement. "This section has eight lanes, plus a hard shoulder on each side, so it's one of the widest ever built in this country."

"How far does it go?" asked Jedan, staring first in one direction, then the other. "I can't believe people made this!"

"You can walk all day on it and not get to the end," East told him. "Awesome, isn't it? It's often misty here, because there are lots of low-lying lakes and rivers in the area, but on a clear day you can see the sea."

She pointed into the distance, where misty hills rolled away to meet the sky. Jedan's mouth dropped open and a smile spread over his face. "The sea?" he repeated. "I've got to see that one day!"

"I never get tired of bringing people here," East said with a laugh. "It's quite something, isn't it?"

"It really is," Chella agreed.

"I don't just bring people here to wow them, though; the motorway is useful to us," East explained as she led them to the centre. "There are junctions all the way along, so we can walk on it without leaving any trace of where we left it. Right, shall we have a break for a few minutes and enjoy the view?"

They sat down and leaned against the central wall for a rest, with their faces to the sun. East provided water, a handful of nuts, and another of the delicious sweet, oaty bars. Chella almost had to pinch herself, that this was real. Used as she had been to living in such a tiny bubble of reality, it made her breathless to think of the scope of how Workers in the Areas were kept in ignorance, and all that was going on in the world without them knowing. Strangely, though, her old life in the Area already felt like it was melting away, like a dream vanishing in the morning. She suddenly thought back to when Jedan had asked her what she really wanted, and wondered if, when they reached Base Camp, she could work in the nursery with the children. She was about to ask if that might be possible, when East's face suddenly changed. "Quiet!" she whispered urgently, holding up her hand. "I need to listen!"

They all stopped still and strained their ears. Sounds were muffled in the mist, and for a while there was nothing but the incessant bird song, moisture dripping from the trees and a bird of prey calling somewhere high above. Then, as East jumped up and packed the water bottles into her bag, they heard it again, behind them, on the road. Far in the distance, wagon wheels were rumbling towards them.

Jedan frowned. "Is that bad?"

"Yes," said East. "It's your captors, following us."

"What?" gasped Chella, scrambling to her feet.

Jedan's stood up quickly, too. "Solod? How do you know it's him?"

"I'm a ranger." East turned to look at them both. "There's another tracker. There's no other way he could possibly know where we are. Any ideas?"

Jedan frowned and shook his head, puzzled, but Chella's

heart began to race and she went hot and cold. "My arm!" she gasped, fumbling with the buttons and ties on her cloak. "The top of my arm! When the Correctioners detained me, they pinched and twisted my arm..." A sudden remembrance made her shake. "There was a box on the table..."

"Show me!" said East. She quickly ran her hand over the top of Chella's arm, near the shoulder. "There's a mark here," she said, pressing on it. "Does this hurt?"

"Ouch! Yes."

"Well there it is," said East. She let out a breath and grimaced. "You didn't know they'd injected you?"

"No! No, they pinched and twisted my arm behind my back just before they let me go. They must have done it then, but I couldn't see."

East pursed her lips as she rummaged in her bag. "So they've upped their game. You'd better sit back down for a minute. You want me to take the tracker out, right? Sorry, I have to ask; it's policy."

Chella nodded. Jedan looked pale. He crouched down next to her and held her hand as East quickly swabbed the area and cleaned her knife. "I can't believe this. Why didn't they follow the other chip?" he groaned.

"It's taken him a while to get here, so he may have checked it out first," East replied. "Actually, more likely, he knows this is the one he wants, and he's been waiting for us. He's taking a big risk coming this far, so late in the day. He must be very sure of himself." Chella closed her eyes and gritted her teeth as East made the cut and removed the chip. "Press here," East told Jedan, giving him a clean cloth to press on the wound. "Any more possibilities of trackers? No more injections?" They both shook their heads. "Are you both absolutely sure?"

They nodded as East re-packed her bag. "Right, listen to me carefully. It's essential you follow my directions *exactly*, so you don't get lost. There's a river – you can't see it yet, but you will soon. I'm going to run and put the tracker in it further back downstream, to make them think you've gone that way. You must run as fast as you can, the same way we have been going. Keep going on the motorway until you come to the next junction. You know what a junction is, right?"

Jedan and Chella both nodded. "It's where two or more roads meet," said Jedan.

"That's right. Take the side road, off the motorway, that goes down towards the river, OK? You *must* stay hidden; I can't stress that enough. They mustn't see you, or they won't turn round when they realise the tracker's going the other way."

Chella's heart was racing. Surely they couldn't have come this far, only to be caught a second time? She should have known Solod would never give up.

"Turn off on to the footpath that runs alongside the river," East continued. "As long as you haven't been spotted, follow the path along the river upstream, until you come to stepping stones going across." She stopped and checked to see if Chella's arm had stopped bleeding. "If you are certain no one can see you, cross the stepping stones, and keep going in the same direction on the other side of the river.

OK? If you cross, put three small stones on the first step, so I know where to find you."

The noise of the wagon wheels and the horse's hooves suddenly sounded a bit louder. "Can't we just run into the forest and hide?" asked Jedan.

"No! Whatever you do, don't do that. Unless you know it well, you can get lost in the forest – you might never find your way out."

"But what if they see us; what if we're followed?" Jedan asked.

East grimaced. "Pray they don't. I'll be praying, too. They should turn round and start following me pretty much straight away. Stay on this side of the river if you think you've been spotted, though, but hide somewhere close to the path so you can be sure of finding it again. Cross the river as soon as you can. And don't forget; three small stones on the first stepping stone if you cross, OK?"

"I'm so sorry," whispered Chella, pulling her cloak back round her. "I didn't think to tell you I'd been detained." Her heart was still thumping in her chest, her arm throbbed, and she looked in horror at the tiny microchip East was placing carefully into a second wooden ball. How could something so small cause so much trouble?

"It's not your fault; it's mine. I should have asked more questions, checked every angle. I'll catch you up. It might take me a while, but don't worry. As I say, they should turn round and follow me soon. Try not to make any noise. This mist carries sound. Now repeat the directions to me."

Chella shivered as Jedan repeated East's instructions. The sound of the horse's hooves and the wagon wheels rumbled nearer. Surely Solod and Toy would be able to see them soon! "What about you?" Chella whispered to East.

"I'll be fine." Another sound rang out, like a whip; then there was a shout, and they all scrambled to their feet. "Go!" East urged them, and they went.

THIRTY-FIVE

The River

The mist drifted and swirled like a living thing along the road and around the trees, as Chella and Jedan ran silently down the motorway. They stayed close to each other, clinging to the shadows of the trees as much as possible. Bumps and cracks in the tarmac made running difficult, but although they both stumbled a couple of times, they managed to stay on their feet. When they could run no further, they walked for a while, gulping the air, but as a shout from Solod echoed round the damp air, they began to run again, hand in hand.

Jedan's face was a picture of pain. Chella felt sick at the thought of how her tracker had so nearly given them away. Why hadn't she thought about what the Correctioners had done to her arm, after East had explained about the injections? Why hadn't she guessed?

The constant, ever-nearing rumble of the wagon wheels and clip-clop of the horse's hooves behind them kept them moving onward as fast as they could. Birds twittered and a crow cawed in a tree, high above. An alarmed fox slunk away from them into the darkness of the forest. The world was vast and beautiful, but it was broken and frightening.

Just as Chella thought her chest would burst from running, Jedan pointed out the river East had mentioned. At the same time a narrow ribbon of road appeared through the mist, leading downwards off the motorway into the fog below.

"That's our turning," Jedan said, breathing heavily.

"Why isn't the wagon turning round?" Chella replied in desperation, as they ran towards the slip road. "It will reach us soon!" She stumbled in a muddy crack as they picked up speed down the hill, but managed not to cry out as she fell. Jedan helped her up, and questioned her with his eyes. The wound in her arm was bleeding again, her legs felt like they had turned to jelly, but she managed to nod. "I'm fine." She wiped her eyes with a shaking hand, and they kept going.

"The wagon could follow us down this road," whispered Chella, wildly looking round for cover. "They mustn't see us. They mustn't know we've come this way."

They couldn't see the river from where they were – all they could see was the flat river plain stretching out before them, before it disappeared into the mist. The road was lined with waving grasses, but there were no trees – just a few straggly bushes here and there that would hardly hide a rabbit.

Jedan grabbed her hand to help her along as they left the cover of the trees. "We have to run to the river, Sweetheart. Can you do it, or would you rather try to hide in the trees? Maybe that would be safer?"

"East said don't run into the trees," panted Chella.

Jedan nodded in return. Chella paused to look back at the forest and the motorway, then forwards towards where the river must be, somewhere in the mist. Her heart thudded. The wagon couldn't be far away now. "I think we should go for the river." Jedan squeezed her hand, and they set off again at a run, hand in hand, side by side.

By the time they reached the river, their breath was coming in heaving gasps. They left the road and dropped down into the long grasses on the river bank, taking deep breaths. Chella lifted her head to look back at the motorway. . . and there was the wagon, slowing down as it approached the junction.

"Why don't they know they're not following the tracker any more?" Jedan groaned, then he answered his own question. "Maybe they've realised we tricked them, like we did with my tracker."

Chella didn't reply. She had already thought of that. She turned her head to look at the river. It looked deep and wide. The water gurgled serenely around bulrushes and irises. It had no idea of the danger they were in. A duck quacked, then another replied, a little further away. Chella followed the sound with her eyes, and saw a path of stepping stones stretching across the water. "I can see the stepping stones," she whispered to Jedan . "Shall we run across now? They'll never see us if we're on the other side, the mist is too thick."

Jedan turned to look. "We can't go unless we're certain they haven't seen us."

Chella sank even further into the marshy ground. "Of course." The cold dampness soaked through her clothes and made her shiver, but she barely noticed. Jedan was right. They couldn't risk giving away the direction to the Old Church. "Oh turn round, please turn round," she whispered to the wagon.

Even as she spoke, the horse stopped at the junction. She and Jedan flattened themselves into the ground as Solod stood up on the seat of the wagon and looked round in every direction.

Chella closed her eyes. She could hear the water lapping behind her, water birds crying out with calls she didn't recognise, then Solod and Toy began to argue. The words were muffled by the fog, but soon Solod sat back down and the wagon slowly began to turn. Even with her eyes closed, Chella could hear Toy whipping the horse. Finally the wagon started back the way it had come.

"At last," said Jedan with a sigh, lifting his head to watch as the wagon picked up speed. "They must have picked up the tracker going the other way."

Chella let out a huge breath. For a few minutes neither of them moved, then as the noise of the wagon gradually became more faint, they sat up, and watched it disappearing down the motorway, into the mist.

As silence fell, they slowly got to their feet. Chella was desperately thirsty, stiff, cold and weary, and she realised she was shaking again. Her clothes were torn and filthy, her cloak had lost two buttons, and blood was trickling down her arm where East had removed the tracker.

Jedan sighed deeply. He put his arms round Chella and held her gently, then noticed her arm bleeding and made her sit down again while he pressed on the wound. For a few minutes they just sat there, on the damp ground, leaning against each other. When the wound had finally stopped bleeding, Jedan sighed. "Oh, Sweetheart, I would never have asked you to come with me if I'd have known it would mean putting you through all this."

Chella smiled at him. "Do you mean you'd rather have left me behind?"

"That's not what I meant and you know it!" Jedan retorted, smiling back. He gently wiped the hair out of her eyes. "Look at us, miles from home, with no idea where we are going. We could be lost forever in this mist! I wonder if Mary and Joseph's journey to Bethlehem was as hard as this?"

"Probably. But God took care of them, and he's taken care of us. And we can't get lost. We just need to go over the stepping stones and follow the river. East said so. What made you think about Mary and Joseph, though?"

Jedan squeezed her hand and grinned. "I don't know really. I suppose I was thinking a donkey would be handy!"

Chella laughed. "Oh yes, a donkey! Not that we've got any bags left to carry!"

"No, we've lost everything, haven't we?"

"Pretty much." Chella pulled his shirt tails. "And your clothes don't even fit you properly!"

Jedan grinned. "Grim colour too, this shirt, isn't it? Mud colour doesn't really suit me!"

Chella laughed out loud. "No, not really, and. . . no, I'd better not say that!"

"Say what? Come on," he said, playfully grabbing her

round the waist, "we've promised to tell the truth to each other, remember?"

She laughed again. "It's old man style," she said. "It's too baggy!"

He hunched himself into his jacket to make her laugh. "We're not exactly going to arrive in style, are we? Just look at us!"

"Us? At least my clothes will look nice when they're washed!" she teased.

Jedan grinned back. "True. Good thing it doesn't matter what we look like, does it?" he said, pulling her into his arms.

Chella let out a big sigh and closed her eyes. "I guess not." She felt Jedan's warmth and love surrounding her. "Is your chest better?" she asked.

"Actually, do you know what, it is," Jedan replied soberly. "I actually thought, at one point, that I was going to die. When they were kicking me into the bushes. But I felt God's protection. Like a blanket surrounding me."

"Wow."

"Yeah."

"There must be a special reason the Lord wanted us to be here. I wonder what it could be?"

Jedan grinned at her. "No doubt we'll find out."

Chella smiled back. Yes, no doubt they would. For now, she just wanted to get to Amma and Mikiah, and hopefully Nidala, too. She looked around that flat, damp, misty land as they started to walk towards the stepping stones in the stillness of the evening. No East, yet.

The river was so wide they could barely see the other side through the mist. Fish swam in the shallows by the bank, in amongst grasses and reeds. Ducks and coots swam and bobbed. The stepping stones stretched out and away from them, like beads strung on a necklace. "You go first," said Chella, checking behind again. Still no East. She bent down and picked up three little stones and laid them carefully on the first step. "Will you wait for me on the other side?"

Jedan made a silly face. "Well," he replied, "I suppose I might as well!"

Chella laughed as Jedan pretended to straighten up his clothes, then he almost leaped over the stones, eager to get to the other side. Chella watched him disappearing into the distance as she stepped carefully on to the first stone, then the second. The sound of rushing water filled her ears. She took a deep breath, looked up and kept going.

In the middle of the river she stopped and turned to look backwards. Everything that had gone before was now in the past. She might never see her old home again. But who knew, perhaps one day some of her church friends might come and join them.

"Thank you," Chella whispered to the gentle silence, and turned to face her new life.

THIRTY-SIX

Going Home

Chella had never been in a boat before. The wooden craft felt like an enchanted thing, carrying them to a new life, new hope. The lake smelled fresh and new, pure and clean.

East rowed with strong, sure strokes; the water rippled and swished softly against the gently rocking boat. The chill in the air crept through Chella's damp clothes and made her shiver. Coots and ducks called their final evening calls and birds fell silent in the bushes along the banks of the river, as darkness fell. Just as the far shore appeared in view, Chella saw the first, bright evening star pierce the darkness through a sudden gap in the rolling mist, and knew in a breath that no power could defeat the purposes of God. No man, no principality or power. It didn't matter if Solod carried on searching for her all his life; her life was in God's hands. The Lord Almighty was with them; the God of Jacob was their defender.

At the other side of the lake, a young lad helped pull the boat up on to a jetty, helped them out one by one, then ran ahead to tell of their arrival.

East smiled at them. "He will tell your friends you're on your way."

Chella and Jedan walked arm in arm down the stony path, towards a circle of buildings. As they approached, they heard the sound of singing; the voices of men and women rising in praise to God, sweet on the air, rising and falling, clear and bright, not silent nor bound, not whispered and in fear, but gloriously free and clear and beautiful and holy.

"Must be the end of evening worship," East informed them with a smile.

The words of the ancient hymn hung in the air:

All I have needed, thy hand has provided
Great is thy faithfulness, Lord unto me.

Tears began to streak down Jedan's face and he clutched Chella's hand. "This is what I dreamed," he said, "that night in prison."

It was so beautiful, Chella couldn't speak. Suddenly a light shone as a door opened, and a small group ran towards them. Nidala reached Chella first, with Mikiah asleep in her arms. She cried out in joy when she saw Chella. "Oh, my sweet, sweet friend, when they told me you were coming, I could hardly believe it, and oh, you brought our son. Thank you, oh thank you — I can never thank you enough! I can't tell you what it means to me to have my son back, and my dear mum. All these months, not knowing, it has seemed so long, such an eternity. You were so brave." They wept on each other's shoulders. Chella couldn't speak. Hamani was hugging Jedan and they were talking as Amma put her arm round her, too. "Oh, Child!" was all she could manage to say.

Chella held her tight. "We're here, Amma! We made it."

"By the grace of God, we did," Amma replied, with tears in her eyes. "Just wait till I show you everything; it's so wonderful! But before I do, there's someone here for you, Child."

A lady around Amma's age, with tears running silently down her cheeks, was standing slightly behind, watching the joyful reunion. She seemed familiar, in a strange way. Chella looked at her and smiled. The woman stepped forward out of the shadows and took both Chella's hands into her own. "My baby girl, all grown up, and so beautiful."

Chella looked into the woman's face and took a deep breath in. "Mum?"

Reading Group Questions

1. In the Areas, religion has been banned, supposedly for the sake of world peace. What do you think of this arrangement? Have you heard of any countries where practising religion is illegal today?

2. What do you think it would be like to have to meet in secret, as the church does in the Areas? Would you be part of a secret religious group, if you lived in a place where it wasn't safe to practise your faith openly?

3. What do you think of the faith of the Christian characters in this book? Do you think their circumstances made them more earnest than people who have freedom of religion? If so, why?

4. One of the themes running through this book is trust in God. Do you think there is a God who cares, and who is in charge, ultimately, of everyone and everything? How do you think that idea fits in with free will? Give reasons for your answer.

5. *"Freedom is a very precious thing"*, said Amma. What do you think of this statement?

6. Who could you compare Walt and Sheva with in real life? Do you think things should have been fairer in the Areas? If you were on the Council, what changes would you make?

7. The Elite in Area IF208 kept their Workers ignorant of many things that were going on. Do you think it is ever reasonable for governments and authorities to do this, to keep order in difficult circumstances, or is it always unacceptable? Give reasons for your answers.

8. Deception and secrets abound in this book. Chella and Jedan both withhold information from each other. Solod uses deception to get what he wants. Lavitah appears to have many secrets, and East deliberately withholds information. When do you think it is OK to have/keep a secret, and when is it not acceptable?

9. Do you know anyone charming like Solod, who tricked Chella for his own selfish purpose? How can you prevent being taken in by people who seem to be caring, but in reality they are using you?

10. The World Council may have been well meaning to begin with, but ideals had clearly begun to slip by Year 0033, in favour of the Elite. What do you think of the idea of "human nature rearing its ugly head" (East's phrase)? Why do you think the ideal of no slavery wasn't adhered to? Do you think human nature can change? If so, how?

11. This is a work of fiction. Are there any elements of this story that you think could not happen? Why not?

12. Can you identify with any of the characters in this book? In what ways? What can you learn from their individual stories?

If you enjoyed this book you may also like:

Rebecca and Jade: Choices
by Eleanor Watkins

Rebecca and Jade have become friends, despite their different backgrounds. When one of them discovers she is pregnant, both are faced with choices that could affect their own lives, and those of others. Rebecca and Jade don't agree on the way forward. Will their friendship be strong enough to survive the difficulties ahead?

"A fantastic book!" – Eleanor

"A really good story. It covers issues including pregnancy, relationships, friendship and support." – Jo

London's Gone
by J.M. Evans

London has been bombed by terrorists. The government has been wiped out, there is widespread power failure and throughout England riots have begun. Maria saw the war planes fly over her home and watched in horror as the smoke rose from the direction of the city. Now she must make a hazardous journey to safety. . . but is anywhere safe now?

"I just couldn't put this book down." – Gilly

"Really well written." – Laura

"Very exciting; full of atmosphere." – Eleanor

The City Kid
by Clive Lewis

John Ouma has had enough of village life in the African bush. He's not interested in religion or knowing God - he wants independence, money, power and success, and dreams of making it big in the city. But life in the city has a darker side. . .

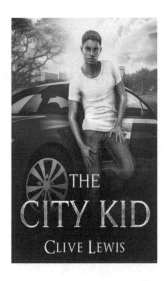

"I really enjoyed reading this book and give it five stars." – Mihalis

"The City Kid is a story of hope. Riveting." – Patrick

"Reading this book has strengthened my faith." – Samuel

If you would like to be a Christian, like Chella, Jedan, East, Amma, and millions of people in real life, the first thing you need to do is to pray. You can start by saying something like this:

Dear Lord God, I realise that my sin has stopped me from knowing you in the past, but I now believe Jesus loves me and died in my place. I'd like to live my life your way from now on. Please forgive and send me your Holy Spirit to be with me for ever. Amen.

After this first prayer, carry on praying every day, reading the Bible and meeting up with other Christians, so you will grow in your new faith!

If you would like to contact the author about anything you have read in this story, please do so through the contact form on the Dernier Publishing website:

www.dernierpublishing.com